Beryl Fletcher is a feminist novelist. In 1992, her book *The Word Burners* was awarded the Commonwealth Writer's Prize for the best first book published in South Asia and the South Pacific. Her first two books, *The Word Burners* and *The Iron Mouth*, were awarded a place in the Top Twenty of the NZ *Listener* Women's Book Festival. She has been the recipient of three Writer's Grants from the New Zealand Arts Council. In 1994, she was chosen as Writer in Residence for New Zealand at the International Writing Program at the University of Iowa, USA.

T0164447

Spinifex Press Pty Ltd
504 Queensberry Street
North Melbourne, Vic. 3051
Australia
spinifex@publishaust.net.au

First published by Spinifex Press, 1996

Edited by Jo Turner
Typeset in Adobe Garamond by Claire Warren
Cover design by Soosie Adshead: The Works
Made and printed in Australia by Australian Print Group

National Library of Australia
Cataloguing-in-Publication data:

Fletcher, Beryl, 1938–
The Silicon Tongue

ISBN 1 875559 49 3

I. Title

NZ823.2

# THE
# SILICON
# TONGUE

## BERYL FLETCHER

*To MG*

. . . The tablet becomes a page becomes a screen becomes a world, a virtual world. Everywhere and nowhere, a place where nothing is forgotten and yet everything changes.

From the introduction to *Cyberspace: First Steps*
Ed by Michael Benedikt. The IT Press: (1991, p. 1)

# 1

## *Alice*

The first problem is the tape recorder. She can't get it to work properly. The girl fiddles with it, asks me to speak slowly into the microphone, then she rewinds the tape and plays it back. Nothing. She tries again. This time, a faint hiss, a whisper.

"I was born Alice Nellie Smallacomb . . ."

My voice sounds strange. I had imagined a deepening with age, a richness. But it squeaks and crackles like a young lad in puberty, and the words come out differently from how they sound in my head. Maybe I have lived too long in this warm island wind. Deep grooves in my skin and now these thin quavers. I never thought my voice would pass away before I did.

I boiled the kettle when she arrived and she drank two cups of tea and ate a buttered pikelet. But I could tell that she was impatient to begin. She's a pretty girl, very smart with her little buckled shoes and fine silver flecks in her black stockings.

This girl tells me that she collects life histories from old women who came to this country from Britain in the 1930s. "Here's your money Alice," she says. "In cash, and each time you speak into the tape recorder, I'll give you another five hundred."

I never dreamt my spoken words would have any value. Ten fifty-dollar notes, each with a glittering thread. I fold them carefully, with reverence. Then I'm scared. I lust after this money. There are so many things that I need. I will try to spin out my life story for as long as possible. But what if I don't give her what she wants? What if she finds my story boring?

The girl gives the tape recorder a thump, then she speaks the date and time into the microphone. Back it comes, clear as a bell.

Her voice is young and fresh. One of those confident educated girls. Not scared of anything.

"Are you going to ask me questions?" I ask.

"As few as possible. I want to hear your story in your own words. Maybe we could start with memories of your childhood."

How can I get my early years across to her? I have been alive for seventy-five years. It is like looking back over a vast and sullen ocean towards a single candle about to flicker out at the edge of the horizon. Dead time, frozen in history. At least, this is how she will see it. I don't know if she will believe that I have total recall of every important conversation and event that has shaped my life. It's too soon to tell her about my system for storing memories. She may think I'm a crazy woman, with my talk of beads and kaleidoscopes and coded colours, red for life, white for death, black for renewal.

"Where shall I start?"

"At the beginning, where you were born, that sort of thing."

"I was born Alice Nellie Smallacomb. My mother was only fifteen when she gave birth to me, but I know who my father was. He was only fifteen too, his name was Nigel Warrington. In later life he became a famous barrister, then a judge. She wasn't married to him, his parents would not allow it. They thought her too low-class. At the age of eleven, she went into service as a scullery maid. My grandparents were her Master and Mistress. My father was their only son, a schoolboy at the time. They allowed her to stay if she promised never to tell anyone whose child I was. They made her sign a paper claiming she had been seduced by a stranger at a May Day dance."

"It must have been hard for you."

"In some ways it was the happiest time. My mother adored me and Mrs Warrington kept me supplied with clothes. She used to put aside dresses and pinafores and the least worn boots from the jumble that she collected for her various charities. Once she gave me a little muff made of real fur, it hung from a leather cord around my neck.

"Mrs Warrington liked to watch me at play without me knowing she was there. The swishing of her long skirts gave her away. I would turn suddenly and try to catch her out. I thought it was some sort of game that ladies played with little girls. When I was older, she would occasionally have me brought to her private sitting room and allow me to play with some of her treasures. I remember a little set of black lacquered boxes that fitted inside each other and a kaleidoscope that spun infinite webs of glass threads and a crystal pendant that shed pinpoints of blinding colour. She would sit bolt upright in her high-backed chair and look at me without speaking. I remember her pale blue eyes very clearly. She had those large trembling sort of eyes that made her look as if she was always on the brink of tears."

"Did she ever acknowledge who you were?"

"Only once. She was very religious and refined. She held great store by good manners. Good morning Alice, she would say. I pray that you are behaving yourself. I had to do a little curtsy to her, hold my petticoats and skirts out like this, and bob down. She must have suffered dreadfully when it became obvious that her only son had got my mother into trouble. Yet I remember feeling that I was quite important to her. Sometimes she used to give me extra treats from the kitchen. Cook didn't approve. She would wait until the Mistress had gone and then make pointed remarks to the kitchen skivvy asking why a certain young lady received favoured treatment. Although I was too young to understand what she meant, I felt dirty and ashamed. I knew that I had done something very wrong but I didn't know what it was.

"My favourite treat was jam turnovers, made from scraps of left-over short pastry. The Mistress would pick them up with silver tongs, crisp and hot and runny with strawberry jam. She would wag her finger at me and whisper, don't tell your mother. Oh the warm sweet taste that would run into my mouth.

"The memory of playing in her sitting room haunted me in later years. The fragile threads of the kaleidoscope became fixed in my mind in one particular pattern. Diagonal forms, each one filled with glass beads shaped like multi-coloured tears. This pattern came to represent those things that would soon be denied me, the objects and emotions associated with her beautiful house; the warmth of her fire, her rustling silk dresses, the security of knowing exactly what I had to do. Everything in its place, a place for everything.

"In the desperate years that followed, whenever I thought I would die of wanting, I would conjure up a picture of the kaleidoscope pattern and chant silently; I did see it, I did see . . .

"It was a good time, in that big house with the Warringtons. There was a marvellous quality to the light, it changed with the time of day. In the morning, it was candlelight. The servants' rooms did not have electric light. I can see my mother now, her long fine hair falling down her plump back as she washed her face in the china bowl, sluicing cold water over her shivering body. The flame flickered on her rosy face. She was so big and healthy. I would lie in the warm bed, watching her dress in her uniform. Everything was black and white, a frilly apron and a starched cap and black lace-up shoes. I thought her very beautiful.

"Then on foggy mornings, the smell of the sulphur matches that my mother struck against the metal grate to light the coalfire in the stove, the green flare of the fire starters, the pool of yellow from the electric light that came down on a long cord over the scrubbed kitchen table. I remember the glistening skin of the apples that the skivvy peeled in long curling spirals, the yellow eggs broken into the creamy butter and sugar in the mixing bowl, the dough kneaded into fat high loaves and the glazed buns thick with raisins and preserved peel.

"At night, after the table had been scrubbed down one last time, and my mother had laid the fires for the morning, she would come into our room and light the candle for us. I was never allowed to light it by myself. My mother said that she had not brought me into the world to be burnt alive. I would lie for hours in the dark, unafraid, thinking of her.

"The only real problem was the Master. I was terrified of him. I made sure I kept out of his sight as much as possible. He was tall and had a booming voice. He was what they used to call a gentleman. He was very wealthy, from inherited money."

"How did they treat your mother?"

"She never complained, she used to say, we're lucky, so lucky. It was only later that I knew how right she was."

"What happened?"

"The Mistress became very sick, we never knew what was wrong with her. She was in terrible pain for months. My poor mother was run ragged caring for her as well as doing all her other duties. One night, the Mistress struggled down the stairs to where my mother and I shared a bed in the basement. My mother was busy upstairs in the kitchen and I was all alone. The old lady appeared at the side of my bed, where I lay shivering under the bedclothes. It was a chilly night in the middle of winter.

"She clutched me with her thin hands and kissed me all over my face. Her breath smelt of violet cachous. She frightened me with her staring eyes and her gaunt face. I said, go back upstairs, please please Madam, I will help you. And then she said, remember your Granny, remember me . . .

"I was shocked. I thought my Granny was the old lady that my mother sometimes took me to visit. She lived in an ancient building, full of old women and damp sour smells. I was a little afraid of her. Sometimes she kissed me and stared into my face and called me her baby girl. Other times she spoke sharply to me, called me a little nuisance. But my mother kept going back. I found out much later that the old lady was actually my great-grandmother and that she was the only relative of my mother's who would speak to her after she got into trouble."

"Where did she live?"

"A hideous place, brick and blackened stone, little rooms on the ground floor, each with one small barred window and a wooden door. Old ladies would sit outside those green doors on kitchen chairs, separated from each other, with chill white faces turned upwards . . ."

I pause. Outside my unit, gentle spring rain is falling. The lawn seed that my daughter Joy sowed last week is already showing a faint green fuzz. I'm scared that I'm going to cry in front of this poised stranger. It is ridiculous that I can still weep for that old lady, dead now for so long. I offer the girl another cup of tea. She says no thanks, and looks at her watch. I take the hint. I am used to having visitors who are in a hurry to get away.

"Do you have to leave?"

"I have another appointment soon."

"I hope you have not been disappointed in my story."

The girl smiles. "It is exactly what I've been looking for."

I hesitate. "Is it worth what you paid me?"

"Yes, and there's a lot more where that came from. Now, before I go, can you finish telling me about that night when Mrs Warrington revealed herself to you?"

"Where was I?"

"She came to your room."

"Oh yes. I was frightened because she kissed me over and over and this had never happened before. Although I was only five years old, I managed to walk her back up the curved wooden staircase, back to her sickbed. A small table beside her bed was covered with bottles of pills and medicines. There was a peculiar smell. She asked me to bathe her forehead with a sponge soaked in vinegar and water. I did so, and she lay on the bed with closed eyes and murmured thank you my dear, thank you.

"Then the Master came in as I was smoothing her coverlet and said cold as ice, get that creature out of here at once. Or I shall have her beaten.

"And my mother appeared at the door and scolded me for daring to come up to this floor which was strictly out-of-bounds.

"I wept over the injustice of it. He refused to listen to me when I tried to explain that the Mistress had asked me to help her upstairs. My mother believed me in the end, I know she did. But we soon had worse things to worry about. My grandmother died that night and within two days, we were given our marching orders. We were put outside, onto the street, literally in the snow. We sat in the gutter with our bundles. My mother threw her cloak over her face and wept for hours, rocking backwards and forwards. I just sat there, paralysed, I couldn't feel anything. I had never heard my mother sob like this before. Then when it was nearly dark, Cook came creeping up the basement steps, and whispered something to my mother and gave her a package, then said loudly, you have to leave or else the Master will call the constable to have you forcibly moved on. This is a house of mourning.

"To my surprise my mother dried her tears and looked almost cheerful. She told me to get moving, it was time to find a room for the night. She gave me a little cloth haversack to carry across my shoulder and placed my frozen hands in my muff.

"It seemed that we trudged for hours before we found a narrow house in a street of identical narrow houses, with a sign stuck behind the lace curtain in the front room. My mother read it aloud, *Room to Let, Working Man Only, Sober Habits*. Oh is that so, she said, we'll soon see about that.

"And she marched to the front door and beat the knocker against the metal plate, rat tat tat. Soon, a diminutive woman came to the door. She had a hump on her back and was not much taller than me. After a brief conversation during which my mother opened the package given to her by Cook and produced a five-pound note, the tiny lady opened the front door and we went inside. The room to let turned out to be the best front bedroom. Oh the relief, the warmth. The high double bed was covered with a brown velvet bedspread. The dark wood of the bed and the wardrobe was polished and shiny. In the corner there was an armchair with side wings and a lace antimacassar. The dressing table, a fancy sort called a duchess, had a pink flounced skirt to keep the drawers hidden.

"Our new landlady Mrs Pickens brought a tray of tea things to our room. My mother said this makes a change, someone waiting on us. And she let me pour the milk into my tea and gave me a sugar lump to suck. But after we had taken off our wet things and gone to bed, I heard her weeping again, softly, so that she would not disturb me."

"Did you stay there long?"

"Until the money ran out."

"From the package?"

"Yes. There were many five-pound notes. And my mother earned small amounts of money from time to time."

"Did you ever find out who helped you?"

"My mother wouldn't tell me but I like to think it was my

father Nigel. He might have still felt something for her."

"Maybe it came from Mr Warrington. Maybe he paid her off to keep her quiet."

I am getting rather annoyed with the turn of the conversation. I want to believe that the money came from Nigel Warrington, not the hated Master. I decide to change the subject. "Do you watch Coronation Street?"

The girl shakes her head.

"Well, if you did you would know the sort of house we went to. Those joined-up ones. They were much meaner in those days. The exact width of one room. One bedroom over the front room, a landing, a smaller room at the back over the kitchen, the attic under the roof with steep narrow stairs, a basement with a dirt floor and a set of stone steps leading down from the kitchen. The back door led to a lean-to containing the scullery and it opened out into a brick courtyard shared by all the other houses in the terrace. They were built around a square. There was one water tap and one privy that we all shared."

"You have a clear memory of it."

"I thought it was a wonderful place. So cosy after the big rooms at the Warrington's. The landlady was strict but kind. I was never allowed to make a noise or run around inside but Mrs Pickens said she enjoyed my company. Being what she called a widow-woman with no chick or child. I would sit with her for hours while she taught me to embroider and do needlework, doilies, dressing-table sets, you know the sort of thing."

"How long did you live there?"

"About two years. At first my mother managed to get work in a cosmetics factory, packing soap and beauty aids, but she got laid off and so she had to go back to domestic work. She tried being a daily cleaner but it was hard on her health and very badly paid. She couldn't get a live-in job anywhere because of me. Then, after we had been there a few months, she started to change."

"In what way?"

"She gave up trying to be respectable. Sometimes she stayed out late and came home drunk. She cut her hair short, and wore bright red lipstick that she'd stolen from the factory the day she was laid off. She had a whole box of bits and pieces, hidden on top of our wardrobe. Rejects she said, things that would have been wasted if she hadn't brought them home. Beige powder and a lamb's-wool puff on a silver stick, and pots of cold cream and bottles of rose-water and talcum powder in floral packets with perforated metal lids. I loved the way she smelt.

"Then one autumn night Mrs Pickens died. She had lit the first fire of the season in the front room and asked me to go down to the basement to fetch some pieces of coal. I struggled up the basement steps with the coal scuttle as quickly as I could. It was a dark spidery place and I was scared of going down there after dark. When I got back into the front room, she had died in her chair. I thought she had gone to sleep. I took the chance of playing with the poker. This was strictly forbidden. She said I ruined fires, spread the coal around too thinly. A wicked wanton waste. And I did, I spread the coal dust and strips of paper and the fire starter apart and it flickered out and I turned around scared stiff that she would scold me or even threaten to tell my mother what I had done.

"She was so still. I couldn't wake her. I ran next door and hammered on the front door and the big red-faced woman that lived there said your mother needs a whipping leaving you to look after that cripple all alone.

"My mother came home shortly after, merry and laughing and flushed, until she saw the neighbourhood women gathered silently around the body in the front room. She sat over the body for hours, tears ran down her face. This was only the second time I had seen my mother cry and I couldn't bear it. I didn't realise that she was weeping more for us than for Mrs Pickens.

"Mrs Pickens had one nephew, who came to take tea once a week with his aunt. He always came alone. He wore a dark navy suit and had oiled hair parted in the middle and false teeth that clicked when he ate. Mrs Pickens called him one of life's unfortunates. But Alice, she said, he is all I have left to remind me of my sister and blood is thicker than water. He is just another cross for me to bear.

"She left her little house to him and he moved in immediately after the funeral. My mother had to wait on him hand and foot. After a week or two she stood up to him, told him to get his own meals. He claimed that she owed his aunt thirty pounds in back rent. He put the police on to her, so we did a moonlight flit. My mother tried to make it into an adventure but I sensed that she was under terrible stress.

"Imagine, a girl in her early twenties, with a child aged seven, nowhere to go, no money, and no welfare in those days, not for the likes of her. I hated her for what she did to me. I understand now that she had no choice, but then, it was a different story. She left me in a terrible place, an orphanage, and my nightmare began."

"So she abandoned you?"

"That's what it felt like at the time."

"Did you ever see her again?"

"Oh yes, much later. Here, in New Zealand."

"So she actually came here! This is great news."

I am surprised at her reaction and I tell her so. She asks me if my mother is still alive and I snap at her. "Of course not."

She says, rather defensively, "It is quite possible. After all, people do live to ninety."

I wonder how she knows how old I am then I remember that she wrote down my age and date of birth before she turned on the tape recorder. And I did say that my mother had me at fifteen. Even so, she worked it out very smartly. I wonder why she is so interested.

I don't want to tell her any more today. I hope that I have done the right thing. What will Joy say when she finds out that I have been telling a stranger our family secrets? "You won't play this back to anyone," I ask nervously.

The girl is packing her tape recorder away. "I promise to show you anything that I write before it gets published. And I will not divulge your real name unless you give me permission."

I am relieved at her answer. I watch from the front window as she gets into her car. She speaks into her cellphone for a few moments then drives away up the hill. The rain has stopped. A rising westerly breeze rustles the spring growth on the one tree in my garden. My pride and joy, my baby oak. Joy had pleaded with me not to plant it in the middle of my front lawn. It will darken your unit Mother (she always calls me this when she is cross with me), and it will cost an arm and a leg to get it chopped down.

Already, like Joy, the oak tree is six feet tall. I wonder when the first acorn will fall. I hope many acorns fall before I die. With the little brown pipes we used to say the garden faeries used. Every tree in the old country has its hobgoblin or Jack-in-the-green just as every pool and river has its undine. I wonder if my oak will lure a spirit down from the north. I wonder if faeries can travel southwards over trembling green seas and the hot winds of the tropics without losing their essential nature.

The tree is planted in line with my front door. The door is made of clouded cut glass so that the light can enter but only shadows are visible from the outside. For privacy and safety they tell me. Especially for someone in your situation, a vulnerable old lady, living on her own.

Living? Some days, when it is raining hard, that drumming sweeping rain that comes across from the western hills, and the grey sky cranks down lower and lower, and I am experiencing the latest episode of bodily treachery from within, I would like to turn the door inside out so that my light flows outwards and the shadows are banished from the interior of the house.

I don't like the glass. I would rather have a door made from wood, but this is a rented house that belongs to the government. And they do not allow tenants to make any changes to the basic structure. Paint and wallpaper can be altered but nothing important, nothing of substance.

I boil the kettle and make another cup of tea. The pikelets look rather forlorn. I have buttered too many and now they'll go soggy before I can eat them. I should take them next door and share them with poor Wilf, but I don't feel up to him at the moment. He repeats the same things over and over. I know he doesn't do it deliberately but it wears me down.

If he sees home cooking, away he'll go again, stories of his dead wife in her spotless kitchen in their farmhouse at Te Awamutu where anyone could have gone down on their hands and knees and eaten from the floor if they had a mind to. All those prizes she won at the agricultural and pastoral shows, year after year, for her breads and jams and pickles. According to Wilf, nobody could hold a candle to her scones and roasts and boiled fruit puddings. For fifty years, night and day, it seems she had stuffed him with food.

Sometimes I look at his frail body and spotted skin and listen to his boring monologues and think what for? For what purpose all that hard labour and all that devouring? Then I feel guilty for thinking like that. Every life has its purpose, even a sad and boring old man who talks incessantly about long-lost feasts.

I feel unsettled. Talking to a stranger brings freshness to old visions. Each time I speak of the past, the memory of it becomes slightly altered. There is a danger that too much talking may change it beyond recognition.

I wonder what the girl will think of me next time she comes? Joy tells me I regress to the dark ages in my orphanage stories, she says they don't belong to this century. She claims that I read too many novels and that I have stolen the reality of my life from fiction. But she is wrong.

I was a victim of the so-called virtuous ones who thought that belief in God could be beaten into a child. It is not my fault that I was plunged temporarily into a version of hell where to be a child of the poor was the ultimate sin.

I am Alice Nellie Winter nee Smallacomb, child, mother, old woman and worthwhile inhabitant of the twentieth century. And I can prove it.

# 2
# *Joy*

There is disorder in everything today. The very wind is confused. The willow trees down by the creek look like headbangers throwing their long green hair first this way then that. One minute it's raining sharp and clean on the iron roof, then the clouds race away and the sun draws up curtains of steam from the tarseal.

That little strip of road outside my house functions like a mood stone. Pale and shimmering with heat on summer days, dark grey, almost black, with brown rivers running in the ditches when it's raining. This happens often on this raging coast where the sheer hills rip the scudding rain clouds apart. Everything is sucked into the vortex of this western harbour; orcas, dolphins, kahawai, driftwood, seaweed, whales and wind-surfers, bodies of drowned fishers.

I feel so tired and lazy today. I can't be bothered doing the dishes from last night. I want to lie here all day, listening to the sea, reading, sleeping. But I know from past experience that this will make me feel worse. I curse my childhood training that makes me feel guilty if I lie around and do nothing. I try to legitimate my desire for inactivity by pretending that I have the beginnings of a headache or a sore throat but it doesn't work.

The trip to Auckland to visit my mother was disturbing. The streets of my childhood got to me this time. Those smug houses with painted weatherboards and tiled roofs thick with lichen. I flipped back to the years I spent walking these same dull footpaths, wearing the badges and costumes of apprentice servitude to a future that had already been mapped out for me by gossiping women in the kitchens and living rooms of my street.

I should have returned to Raglan earlier but I thought that if I stayed a day or two longer, I might find out where Alice is getting her extra money from. I asked her of course, but she pretended she hadn't heard me. She put on that vague elderly-woman act that she knows infuriates me.

We have always been a family that talks openly about money. This does not mean that there are no secrets between us. Far from it. There have been sexual secrets, evasions about time elapsed between births and marriages. But never about money. It goes back to our childhood days in Sandringham when we watched Alice counting out the coins stolen from our father's pockets on pay nights as he lay stinking of booze, snoring on the squab in the kitchen. Alice would hold up the coins and kiss them. How much did you get Mum, we would whisper as she hid her spoils in the money jars in a place where he would never look. In her grocery cupboard, behind innocent canisters of rice and barley and flour, those reassuring jars of brown ten-shilling notes and silver half-crowns.

She always told us exactly how much everything cost and how much she had to spend. Because, she said, when I was your age, nobody ever talked about lack of money and it became a fearful thing to me. I always thought I was on the verge of starvation. I don't want you to go through what I went through.

She made it into a game and she shared the rules of the game with us. Never take too much, he'll suspect. He's so drunk on pay nights he can't remember how much he spent at the pub. Never ask for an advance on your housekeeping. Practice good housewifely skills. This jar is for food, this one for rent, this one for treats. Once the money is saved in one jar, it must never be spent on anything else. Never rob Peter to pay Paul.

Even today, I know what my brother Morry gets on the dole and how much he earns under the table. He showed me his weekly budget. I was impressed with his frugality. Then he showed me his treat jar, packed with twenty-dollar notes. Nothing illegal Sis, he said. Just good hard physical work. Weeding, mowing, trimming the gardens of the lucky ones who still go out to work.

I know exactly how much Alice gets each fortnight for her pension. I go through all her bills and accounts. I advise her on how to cope with the complex bureaucracy that rules our lives. I found out she was not receiving her due so I helped her to fill out a government form to get the living-alone allowance.

What a handicap to admit to, what a failing, living alone. But I have fallen even further from grace. The pittance I get each week is actually called the Woman Alone Benefit. What words! Woman alone. I am defined by a lack, an absence; no child, no man, no friend, no keeper.

Still, it comes into my savings account once a week, on the dot. And I am the only one who can lay my hands on it. I spend it how I please, I am answerable to no one. There have been times in my life when this would have been equivalent to living in paradise. Especially when I was married to Dennis, the compulsive gambler.

I'm worried about Alice. She's acting very strangely. I challenged her about the expense of her new "toys" as she calls them but she closed her lips and refused to answer.

It's not that I begrudge you these things, I said. I'm pleased that you have a new vacuum cleaner and a new electric frying pan and a cordless jug. But don't get into debt again, remember how long it has taken me to get your affairs into order. Please don't put me through that again.

Alice has changed in the last few years. Sometimes she spends money on inappropriate things and then does not have enough cash left to pay her electricity bill or rent. A far cry from the careful housewife of my childhood years who put money aside before a bill was due.

I called into Morry's place on the way home yesterday. I sometimes feel resentful that he leaves all the worrying about Alice to me. He won't take any responsibility. I have decided to force the issue, make him see that he has some sort of obligation to help care for her.

His place is looking even more dishevelled than usual. The paint is peeling from the window frames and the garden is a mess. His excuse used to be that if he wasn't hanging around on chilly railway platforms or driving trains, he was trying to sleep in the middle of the day when the neighbourhood kids were screeching in the back yard. No time then for working around the house or garden. He's been unemployed for nearly two years. I wonder what he uses for an excuse now. Probably that he does garden work for survival money and that makes him too tired to do his own.

He was sitting in front of the TV watching cricket. I came in through the open ranch slider and became briefly entangled in the net curtains that were billowing into the room.

"Gidday Joy, want a beer?"

"No. I want to talk to you about Alice."

His eyes took on that familiar glazed look. "What's she done now?"

"I don't know."

"Yes! Another wicket, keep it up!"

"Morry, listen to me."

He turned off the sound with the remote but kept looking at the TV screen. "Sure you won't have a beer?"

I gave in. "Okay, just the one."

"Bonita!" he yelled. "Come and have a yarn to Sis. And bring some more beers."

I wish he wouldn't call me Sis. And I wish that he wouldn't order Bonita around like that. Not that she seems to mind. She is a big pear-shaped woman with hips that jut out like shelves. She calls them her love handles.

Bonita came into the room with three cans of beer. Morry pinched her plump bottom. She responded by poking him in the arm with the ring top from the beer can. Although Morry likes to think he rules the roost, Bonita makes all the decisions. She insisted that they buy this house at Te Kowhai with his redundancy money. He wanted to buy a fish and chip shop. For once, I took her side. I am fond of my brother but he has his limits and running his own business is definitely one of them.

I was pleased when they bought this place. I drive to Auckland once a week to spend a night with Alice and I pass through Te Kowhai on my way. It means that I can pop in and give them news of her without having to make a special trip. Even though I know Morry for what he is, I do love him. He's five years younger than me. I'll never forget the day I first saw him. His tiny pink face and unfocussed eyes, his milky smell. I thought Alice had fetched him from the nursing home especially for me. I wanted Alice to have more children after Morry but she refused. I've got my pigeon pair, she said, I've done what I set out to do. Besides, it's no picnic, one day you'll understand.

If my father Jack had not been a drinker and if they'd had more money, things might have turned out differently. I might not have become obsessed with getting pregnant and my relationship with my mother might have been more comfortable than it's been. Even though I try to remind myself about the punitive attitudes of the fifties, I find it hard to forgive her for what she did to me. Even after forty years.

I drank beer with my brother and Bonita. She treats him just like Alice treated my father. A working man, a precious jewel, the saviour of the family. He must stay alive and well at all costs. Alice always gave Jack the best piece of meat and the first turn in the bath before we clouded the hot water with our mud and bruises. She gave him protection from the noise and disorder and raw emotion that erupts ceaselessly around daily life with children.

All three of Bonita's children have left long ago. They are scattered around the world; two married daughters in Australia, her only son travelling somewhere in Europe. She and Morry are both fifty. They are on the married person's dole. Half of the money is paid into her bank account, half into his. For the first time in her life she is equal with Morry. Yet she still treats him as if he is a railway man, the sole support of his family, breathing in diesel fumes on those long night shifts, risking his health to keep his dependants snug and fed and warm.

Supervision. That's what Bonita plays at, relentlessly. She tells Morry what to wear, what to eat, when to rest. He is under perpetual surveillance. It would drive me crazy.

But although Bonita waits on him hand and foot, she is never verbally subservient. She laughs at him right to his face, calls him a silly bugger, a dickhead, a wanker. He just laughs right back at her and teases her unmercifully.

There is an undertone of violence in their interaction that makes me uneasy. I tried to discuss it with him once but he just frowned and said, you don't appreciate our sense of humour. And, if you don't mind me saying so, if you had learned to lighten up a little maybe you wouldn't be living all alone in that dump of a place at your time in life.

I finished my beer and tried once again to get Morry to listen to me about Alice. He pricked his ears up when I mentioned that she was throwing money around. He knows that I handle her financial affairs. Maybe Welfare overpaid her? No? A gift?

I told him I had gone through all the possibilities with her. Alice made a vague statement about saving on groceries and petrol. New shops at St Luke's Mall, just opened. She went there every day. So cheap Joy, you wouldn't believe! That was all I could get out of her.

Morry just shrugged. "You worry too much."

I exploded. "And you won't take any bloody responsibility!"

Bonita flew to his defence. "He does what he can."

"Like what?"

"He rings her up."

"Big deal."

"Anyway," said Morry. "She doesn't need as much help as you think."

"What do you mean?"

"Nothing," he mumbled.

"No Morry," I said. "I'm not going to let you get away with saying that."

Bonita burst out, "We think you treat her like a child."

The irony of Bonita saying this to me!

"The thing is," said Morry. "Mum still drives, and does her own housework and shopping. She could look after her own money too."

"What rubbish! Things were in a dreadful mess until I took over."

"She only lets you do her accounts to make you feel needed."

I was angry now. "Why the hell would I want that?"

"Guilt. Over what you put her through when you were young."

I had no idea how long he had held this absurd notion about my guilt. Alice is the one who should burn. She has always been convinced that she did the right thing. And now that she's seventy-five, she's probably too old to change her mind.

I couldn't answer Morry. Bonita did it for me. "You have a loose mouth Morry, you go too far at times."

Within seconds, they were at it hammer and tongs, trading insults, casting aspersions on the other's sexual performance, body parts, too much of this, too little of that . . .

I left them to it and drove furiously towards the coast. It was almost dark when I arrived in Raglan but I didn't go straight to my house. I went down to Wainamu Beach to watch the incoming tide and the tumultuous surges of seawater growling and thumping into the rocky throat of the bar. Beating, beating, the pounding of a deep salt drum. I sat in the sandhills and let my anger seep into the sea.

Later, the moon broke through the high thin cloud and the wind faded and the surface of the water became flat and almost milky with light. The taniwha that lives on the submerged mud floor between the town and the opposing hills, fell asleep.

I calmed down too. I couldn't blame Morry. All his life he has been told what to believe by women. Alice has been whispering words of mischief in his ear from the moment he was born. And Bonita has chained him to her by a constant flow of addictive and insulting words masquerading as love.

Morry phoned me after I got home. "I didn't mean to bring up that stupid stuff from the past. Sorry Sis."

I thanked him for apologising, even though I was sure that Bonita was beside him twisting his arm, literally.

Sometime during the night, the wind rose again, from the south this time, a cold cheerless wind, and the tide went on the turn again, and the rain came beating on my iron roof. Then the morning light, washed and weakened, and the willows blowing this way and that, and the rain stopping and starting every five minutes.

I make a pot of tea and stare out of my upstairs window. I can see my neighbour Rangi fossicking for pipi at the low tide mark. She is wearing a long black dress and is carrying a red plastic bucket. There is no sign of anyone else on the beach. The narrow strip of sand at the bottom of the bank is dark with rain. The forlorn tents and caravans across the estuary are battened down. A group of oystercatchers stand in a ruffled formation with their backs to the wind.

I feel an irrational anger at the weather. It's not that I care about rain. I would never have bought this cottage and moved to the west coast if I could not tolerate wet weather. But today it can't make up its mind. Sun one minute, rain and wind the next. Indecision. I catch the mood. I can't decide what to do with my day. I am menaced by balloons of expanding time, waiting for me to fill them with some meaningful activity. The more I think about the empty hours stretching ahead, the longer and flatter they become.

The weather doesn't seem to bother Rangi. She carries on regardless, taking her food from the sea. Like me, she looks decidedly middle-aged. There the similarity ends. I've tried hard to be friendly, but she won't come into my house. I have asked her to share a coffee with me but she says, maybe another day. When I'm not so busy. She smiles and waves at me, she leaves garden produce on my back verandah but except for brief greetings, she won't stop to talk to me. Always busy, cleaning, weeding, fishing, caring for her animals. I know little about her except that she cares for a very old person. Sometimes she carries this person, wrapped up like a baby, and lies it down on the verandah sofa. I can't tell if the bundle contains a man or a woman.

She has many relatives and friends who come and go in bewildering configurations and at odd times of the day and the night. Laughter, noise, ancient station wagons and expensive cars full of children and dogs and old people, boxes of food, celebrations. Then they disappear and it is quiet again except for the gentle bleating of her goats and the constant noise of the wind and the tides.

I dread the sounds of cars pulling up. It wouldn't matter so much if they went home at a decent hour. I hear guitars playing all hours of the night. And the children immediately head for the video games she's had installed on her back porch. Over and over, whines and bleeps and the sound of electronic gun shots. Mindless mechanical noise. I hate it.

The rain is beating down, thick and heavy. Rangi is walking back towards our street, head down, almost lost to sight in a curtain of water.

My house sits in a strange relationship with the sea. The street runs right down into the water. Just a white post with a reflector, then a low bank, then the high tide mark. I am right next to the sea but the family who built this cottage over sixty years ago decided for some strange reason to ignore it. My house faces the cottages on the opposite side of the street. To see the Oputere River and the ocean beyond, I have to climb upstairs and peer through the small high bedroom window. This is the only window on this side of the house. If I had the money I would demolish the peeling timber and replace it with a wall of tinted glass, clear and thick and strong. Then I could lie in my bed and watch the pull of the water and the pipi gatherers and the people having picnics under the phoenix palms and the children daring each other to leap off the bridge into the swift green current.

The house itself is very unusual even for Raglan, a village famous for its eccentric dwellings. It's very basic, two small rooms downstairs divided by a hall with a kitchen and bathroom on a lean-to at the back. The front door opens directly onto the steep narrow wooden staircase that leads to my bedroom. From outside, this room looks like a small box stuck into the side of the roof as an afterthought.

Morry snorted the first time he saw it. "You're never going to buy this dump. It needs too much doing to it."

I told him with glee that I had already signed the contract. "It's exactly what I'm looking for. I'm going to fix it up, and seeing that the condition of the house upsets you so much, you can come over and give me a hand anytime you feel like it. Besides, it's dirt cheap, I can pay cash for it and still have enough left over for a new car."

I've been here for two years now. I was fifty-three when I was made redundant from my firm. I had become complacent, I must have been asleep during the tumult of the eighties. I thought that being sacked happened to incompetent workers, those who had slacked off. Never to someone like me, the indispensable Ms Joy Knight, office manager and personal assistant to the director of one of the oldest engineering firms in Hamilton. I was an accountant, an organiser, an interviewer. I chose every member of the office staff and I never made a mistake. My firm! How ironic that sounds to me now. They gave me two hours to clear my desk, two hours!

The anger still burns. I plot revenge, bizarre acts like spraying weedkiller over the bald head of my boss Trevor, who I once thought of as a true friend. And acts of industrial sabotage. I like to imagine that I could invent a process that would cause their fibreglass power poles to dissolve like sugar in the rain or cause their electric fences to blast hunters instead of animals.

Trevor insisted that he had nothing to do with my dismissal. Nobody would give me any information. People I had worked with for over twenty years. There was a wall of silence as if I had become contaminated with some unpleasant disease and that if they spoke to me, they may well become the next victim of this terrible plague.

So I still don't know who pulled the plug. One day I will find out. Then they will learn that I am no longer that faithful woman who groomed herself to be the perfect office manager; sexually attractive but not common, confident but not aggressive, bright but not too clever. I walked a fine line over those years and for what? To be thrown out at the whim of an anonymous business consultant?

I was labelled as a Surplus Labour Unit by the government employment bureau. I crawled there, broken but still hoping, the day after I was sacked. I was still half asleep it seemed, the penny hadn't dropped yet as my mother would say. Date of birth? 1940 . . . mmm. Well, things are tough out there. And of course the new technology doesn't help people like you. People like me? Surplus Labour Unit, too old to retrain, and unfortunately, your skills have been superseded by computers. And there are so many young ones unemployed . . .

I finish my second cup of tea and decide that I will clean the kitchen cupboards, write some letters and go for a drive along the road to Whale Bay. The heavy shower has blown over, the clouds are racing over my roof towards the northeast. I feel more cheerful now that I have a plan for my activities. November is always a difficult month for me. The smell and look of the season reminds me of my pregnancy at the age of fifteen. Sixth months gone, ill and frightened, binding myself into a corset to hide my swollen abdomen. It was at this time of the year, early summer, that I was taken to a home for unmarried mothers to await the birth of my Joy, the baby who was later stolen from me.

Alice named me from the poem by Blake, *i have no name, i am but two days old, what shall i call thee? i happy am, joy is my name, sweet joy befall thee . . .*

I named my Joy after myself, my last act of defiance when they came for me. The child welfare officer came through the door of the barn where we were hiding. He said we do not want to harm you. If you care about your baby, please give it to me. Or the police will be called and it might get hurt.

It? Before he snatched her from my arms, I whispered into her tiny ear, *Joy is your name, sweet joy . . .*

My fall from grace has led to a life-long search for her. I want to know if she is still alive, I want to find out if she hates me for giving her away to strangers. Most of all I want to feast my eyes on her physical presence, her body, her face, her hair, her teeth. I crave solid proof of her existence, nothing else can quench my terrible need. To find her is my quest, my motivation for continuing to write the narrative of my existence when almost everything else that has given my life meaning has been taken from me.

I know that I gave birth to a child when I was fifteen, I know that my body bears unmistakable scars and signs, I know that my medical chart details all the events of a girlhood pregnancy and a difficult birth. But I can't give physical substance to this knowledge.

I can't grasp the truth of Joy.

I drive along the winding road that leads to Whale Bay. The bush is teeming with water. A newly sprung ford bursts across the road at the foot of a hill. I hurtle into it and curving waves of storm water slap the sides of my car. I drive to Manu Bay and sit in the car watching young people in wet suits frolicking like seals in the surf. My Joy could be the mother of that golden boy, leaping and twisting like a dancer. Or maybe she gave birth to that long-haired girl, sleek and muscular, riding the waves on her boogie board.

I indulge myself with this fantasy until the rain sweeps in from the sea again. I drive back along the narrow road, carefully this time. I must keep living until I see her face once more.

The year is almost over. I am not looking forward to another Christmas dinner at Morry's, with Bonita half-drunk and crying into the dishes over the loss of her children, and Alice saying smugly, at least I have my own around me, and all of them alternatively pitying me or cursing me because I am divorced and childless.

But I am about to make a move. I am going to try one last time to find my child. I have had my name and address with the authorities for years, ever since the law of secret adoptions was altered. She could have found me by now if she had wanted to. Either she hates the thought of meeting me or she is dead.

I have decided to take the last of my savings from the bank and hire a private detective. Whatever her status, above or below the earth, hostile or friendly, I swear that I will find her.

# 3

# *Alice*

Here she comes, knocking at my door, the golden girl with the money. Today she wants me to tell her the story of the orphanage and how I came to this country. I am feeling very nervous. I haven't talked about it for years. I always get the feeling that nobody here believes me. Joy once accused me of reading too much Dickens and pretending that I was Oliver Twist or David Copperfield. I have always found comfort in books but it's not true that I have borrowed fictional experience and claimed it as my own. Morry says that my obsession with reading fiction is escapism. Why is this wrong? When I was young, novels gave me a sense that other lives were being lived, far beyond the brute reality of my own. Now that I am tied to the limitations of my failing body, my mind is still free to fly. Imagination is the only mystic journey left for me to make.

There were few books in the orphanage. We had religious tracts and classics like *Aesop's Fables* and stories that were meant to refine our crude working-class souls like the *Children's Book of Moral Lessons*. There was a glass-fronted cupboard in the sitting room where a dozen or so recreational books were kept under lock and key. On Saturday afternoons, for one hour only, we were allowed to choose a book to read. Most of them were from last century, old books, with blue and red covers and embossed titles of black and gold. School stories for girls, adventure books for boys. I found the girls' books boring, but I loved the stories about sailing ships and wars and strange new lands. I particularly loved the books about the wild South Seas, a place of sun and adventure and colourful natives and hidden treasure.

Imagine my disappointment on that chilly spring day in 1935

when I came ashore to a ramshackle wharf in Auckland. Nothing exotic. Just corrugated iron sheds, a howling wind, and shabby people bundled in coats. I said goodbye to the other young orphan girls who had shared my voyage locked beneath the heaving waves in a twelve-berth cabin. It seemed almost like a slave ship, endless illness, frugal food, relentless surveillance. The stern chaperone Mrs Bates, who read the bible to us every day and lectured us constantly about the importance of purity in all its forms. Cleanliness, both inside and out, in heart and thought and deed. I was so innocent, I didn't know what she was talking about. All I knew was that she watched us day and night in case we spoke to the sailors or passengers. We were taught that men were dangerous, but were not told why, which of course made them very interesting to us. My friend Emily did everything she could to get near them. It was whispered that she managed to hide in a lifeboat with one of the passengers, a rather elderly man with a toupee and glasses and that she "did something" with him. We thought she was daring and clever, she was our queen, our leader. But she would never tell us what she did in that boat, even when we tried to bribe her by offering to do her chores for her. I think she invented her tale as an act of defiance against our situation. Which, as I discovered later, was nothing less than that of ignorant lambs being led to every imaginable kind of slaughter.

We were sailing to New Zealand under a scheme that provided domestic servants for selected religious families. Mrs Bates told us we were going to a life of good honest work, and perhaps a chance of marriage in a new place where our lack of background and money would not count so heavily against us. We had been chosen for our diligence and good character. Mrs Bates hoped that we would not let her down. She was determined to deliver her flock in pristine condition and as far as I know, in spite of Emily's tall tales to the contrary, she did.

The girl is knocking at my door again. Today is her third visit and I'm growing used to her. The first visit was rather awkward because I had never spoken into a tape recorder before. The second visit she didn't do any recording. She wanted to get some background information. I told her all about Joy and Morry and my three grand-children and my dead husband Jack.

The girl is warm and kind and pretty. Her name is Wendy McDonald.

Joy rang me last night and interrogated me again about the extra money and the new things that I have bought. I have quite enjoyed stringing her along but I shouldn't give her this worry, tempting though it is. Things are getting out of hand. I know that she suspects me of stealing. I'll have to tell her soon.

I open the door. The tarred road shimmers with heat and the cicadas are humming. Wendy comes in, looking lovely. She's wearing a long black dress and her arms are bare and she has coloured sandals on her smooth white feet. I ask her about the amber beads she is wearing. "They are old, really old," she tells me. "They belong to my partner's mother."

I make her tea and apologise for serving bought biscuits instead of the usual home cooking. The weather is too hot for me to turn the oven on. She laughs and says not to worry, I come here for your stories not your pikelets or scones. I must have looked crest-fallen, because she added quickly, not that I don't adore them, but please don't feel you have to cook for me.

I know what she's up to now. After her last visit, I went to the public library and got out some books on oral histories and I found out that there is a huge industry building up around the spoken memories of old people. They want to take down our stories before we die and put them in books and make a lot of money out of us. Even someone ordinary like me. I'm glad I have found this out. Makes me sound official and important. It will help me to explain to Joy what I am doing.

"Now Mrs Winter . . ."

"Please call me Alice."

"Thanks, I'd like to. Today I want to continue recording your story. Can we link it back to where you ended last time?"

I am nervous and I tell her so. She quickly puts me at my ease and I begin.

"Did I tell you about Mrs Pickens dying and her nephew

putting the police on to us?"

Wendy nods.

"Well, that night we did a moonlight flit and we ended up staying with one of my mother's friends. It was late autumn, a windy night with driving rain. I kept pleading with my mother to knock on one of the closed doors that we passed, any door, so that we could get away from the rain and my terrible fear of being out on the streets in the middle of the night. I could hear Mrs Pickens' voice, warning me against ever going outside after dark. There are things that happen to little girls, she said, a bad man will snatch you away and your poor mother will never see you again in this life . . ."

"Just let me get my dates right," says Wendy. "This would be about 1927?"

"Let me think, yes, I was just over seven so that would be right. September or October, 1927."

"Sorry for breaking your flow, but I want to make sure that I get the timing correct."

"My mother told me not to be afraid, I was quite safe with her. But everywhere I looked, I saw shadowy figures sheltering in doorways and crouching against alley walls. My mother laughed at me. You silly goose, look closer Alice, they're ladies, they won't hurt you."

"Were they prostitutes?"

"They must have been. Why else would they have been there? Of course I didn't realise this until I was much older. Anyway, by the time we arrived at Mrs O'Neill's house, we were soaked through and freezing."

"Who was Mrs O'Neill?"

"Mother's friend, Colleen. She was an Irish woman who used to work in the cosmetics factory with my mother until she too was sacked. She had six children and her husband had died or run off I forget which but anyway she was left to fend for herself and all those children. Mother hammered on Mrs O'Neill's door but it was ages before she came down to open it. That closed door, and my mother's raw fist pounding against it, that terrible feeling of loss and homelessness, it has never left me.

"At last the door opened. The two women clung to each other and Colleen said, you done the right thing, coming to me in your troubles. I have never heard sweeter words. She heated up soup on the gas burner in the communal kitchen in the basement and brought us dry clothes. It was a terrible place. There were old newspapers on the floor and a stinking toilet on the first floor that everybody in the house had to use. Colleen and her six children lived in two rooms on the top floor. For the few hours remaining of that first night, my mother and I slept on the floor of the landing outside their bedroom, bundled up in our coats. The house was suffused with that peculiar kind of mould and stale air that comes from years of poverty and neglect. Never a window opened, never a fire lit. The cold seemed to penetrate my very bones. I cried myself to sleep.

"After that, Colleen made us a little nest under the wooden table in the living room. It was the only floor space available. In the bedroom, there were two double beds with a canvas army cot between them. There were three children to each bed and Colleen slept in the cot. She offered to squeeze me into one of the beds but I refused. I was a little afraid of her children, especially the older ones. They were tough, skinny and wild and ran around the streets of Islington without fear. The eldest, a girl called Deirdre, was particularly mean to me. Her mother would carry on about my long fair hair and my good manners, she called me a little angel come down to earth. I could see Deirdre's face grow sharp and mean. And I knew that as soon as we were alone, she would pinch my arm or give me Chinese burns and chant horrible rhymes at me. I spent most of my time lying beneath the table trying to hide myself away.

"My mother had found a feather eiderdown in a pawn shop. One of those beautiful ones covered with pink satin, all whorled and stitched into wonderful patterns that formed hills and valleys and islands. That eiderdown became my make-believe world, my haven. The place where I felt safe."

"Did you go to school?"

"Sometimes. I wanted to very much, for the books, but my mother disliked the local school. It was a violent place, the teachers beat us at the slightest provocation. I stayed home quite a bit. Each morning, my mother would decide whether or not I should go. Your shoes won't keep out the wet Alice she would say, let me feel your forehead, you're burning up with fever, better stay indoors. Then she would blow sulphur powder down my throat with a straw or dose me up with castor oil. I didn't care as long as I had something to read and could lie snug and warm beneath the table. From time to time I would see various sets of skinny scabby O'Neill legs appearing in front of me. Deirdre would try to kick me but the other kids ignored the fact that I was lying underneath the table."

"I need to get your story about the orphanage on the tape today. Can we move ahead a bit more quickly?"

I am surprised at the urgency in her voice. "Why the hurry?"

She looks flustered. "Ah, I'm on a time limit, my research money, you understand."

I am beginning to enjoy myself in the same way that I do when Joy tries to fob me off. I know that Wendy is hiding something. I put on my innocent but befuddled old lady act. "I'm so sorry dear, you must forgive me. I get tired very quickly these days, be patient with me."

It works. She apologises profusely and offers to pour me another cup of tea. I let her fuss around me for a bit before she turns on the tape recorder once again.

"The orphanage, let's see . . . we stayed with Colleen for about six or seven months. My mother went out a lot, looking for work, doing the odd cleaning job, drinking with her friends. Colleen by this time had found work selling fruit and vegetables from a van that went around the streets selling door to door. This job was a godsend, because she brought home the outside leaves of cabbages and potatoes that had started to sprout and apples with brown spots that were not good enough to sell. Once she gave me an orange. I loved the sweetness of the juice and the bright colour of the skin. I scraped off the white pith with my teeth and kept the skin until it had shrivelled into brown strips."

"She seems to have been a kind woman. Why did you leave?"

"I'm getting to that." I stand up and walk slowly to the window. Outside, the sun is high and hot overhead and the painted tin roofs of the houses are fluid with shimmering heat. For a moment I see flashes of liquid metal leaping like red lightning from roof to roof. What is happening? I can see letters forming in the light, I can hear laughter and voices calling from the left, from the right. Who speaks? Dazzled, I put my hands over my eyes.

Wendy is at my side. She asks if I am okay. I nod my head. She looks concerned. "I hope my questions haven't upset you."

"No, I'm all right, really I am."

"I can always come back tomorrow."

"No, I've found out what you're up to, and I want the truth about the past to be told, once and for all."

She gasps. "What do you know about me?"

I tell her about the books on oral history I've been reading. The fashion for recording the lives of old people and publishing books about them. Making money and getting famous through the memories of others.

She looks surprised. "That was a good thing to do, go to the library I mean. Very assertive of you."

I feel sad that she has patronised me. I may as well be talking to Joy or Morry. Well done dear, you went to the library all by yourself! I decide to say nothing at the moment. When I get to know her better, I will explain to her that careless words can wound. These fresh young tongues speak to old women as if we had never lived, never loved, never given birth to anything. Most of them treat us like defective children.

But I do not want to risk her anger at the moment. I want my story told. Maybe if it comes out in a book, in hard cold black words, people will believe me. I know that Joy thinks that my past is imaginary, taken from books. I can't resist the irony of returning what she sees as fiction to the authority of a published history. I have no desire for sympathy, it's justice I crave. I wonder if any of those sadists who prayed over us at the orphanage are still alive? If so, they would be very old. I almost wish that there was an afterlife, so I could meet up with them there and exact my revenge.

I decide to tell this pretty pampered girl everything about the orphanage, this clean, educated girl, sitting here in this hot still room, so far away in time and place from that terrible institution where I learned that Christians are liars and cheats and bullies.

I am past caring. Does my experience count for nothing? Did I go into a long sleep during those years, did I dream it up? You would think so, given the denials and disbelief that have been dished out to me by my own children. But I was there, I had to live through it, moment by moment, day by day, there was nothing else that I could do. I had no choice.

"The nightmare started early one morning when I was fast asleep beneath my table. The pale pink light of dawn was struggling through the uncurtained window. I was awoken by the sound of quarrelling voices. Colleen and my mother were arguing in the kitchen, and although they were keeping their voices low, I understood immediately that something terrible was happening. Colleen was accusing my mother Elva of keeping bad company, staying out at night and never paying her board. Look at you, she said. You used to be so quiet and honest, and pretty too, but look at you. Painted up like a tart, smoking, drinking and God knows what else. I have my own kids to think of, you're a bad example to them. I can't keep you any longer, I want you to go.

"At first my mother got on her high horse and denied everything but I knew that Colleen was speaking the truth. It was so hard for me to admit this. But night after night I had awoken under the pink eiderdown and reached out for my mother's comforting body only to discover that I was alone. She would sneak into the house before first light, with a smeared face and slurred speech. She would cuddle me fiercely and stroke my face and breathe gin all over me and tell me that she only lived for me. I would go back to sleep wrapped in a warm cocoon of love.

"We were put out on the street again, but not before my mother had fought back. Call me a bad example, she yelled. I'm a bloody amateur compared with your precious Deirdre, everyone in the street knows what she gets up to with the boys.

"Hush your dirty mouth woman, said Colleen, crossing herself. I'll not put up with your vicious slander against a decent hard-working family.

"I was amazed at my mother. I had never heard her use a swear word before. And I hoped that Deirdre was lying awake in her bed listening to what my mother had said about her.

"My mother walked away from that house in Islington full of anger. I could barely keep up with her. It was awkward carrying the rolled-up eiderdown which she had insisted on removing from the house. I carried it because it was lighter than the suitcase that weighed her down but it obstructed my view and I remember calling out to her wait for me, wait for me!

"We slept on the street that night, curled up together in a doorway with an overhanging roof. It was a dry mild night and my poor mother tried to make it into an adventure. Just think Alice, not many little girls have a picnic on the streets of London and are allowed to stay out all night. But I heard her weeping quietly and she stiffened with fear when a policeman walked past and looked down at us. He just shook his head and walked away without speaking.

"The next morning we lined up for breakfast at a city mission. Tin mugs of sweet tea and thick slices of bread and butter. They made us stand up and sing a hymn before we had tasted a mouthful. A well-spoken lady in a brown dress came over to us and told my mother that if she had good character references she could get her a domestic position somewhere up north, but only if I was put into care. Nobody would take her with a child.

"My mother reacted strongly to this suggestion. Oh I couldn't ever leave London, she said. Not for anything.

"Do you have any family that could help you?

"I could see that my mother was getting very nervous at these questions. Oh yes, she lied. I'm on my way to my mother's house right this minute. Come along Alice, your Granny will be waiting for us.

"Granny? For a moment I thought she meant my poor dead Granny, the one who lived outside the green door, sitting on a chair with her face turned up to the sun. But I knew she was gone. I had a clear memory of going to visit her and finding a strange old lady in Granny's chair. And my mother upset because nobody at the workhouse would tell her where Granny was buried and she couldn't go to her old house and ask her parents. She would only have got the door slammed in her face for her trouble.

"We left the mission and my mother was too afraid to go back. This was the beginning of the end for us. We slept rough, and we were hungry. My mother would leave me outside public houses and go inside and beg from the men. She didn't get much, a few pennies here and there. The weather grew cooler and on rainy nights we slept under bridges with old drunks who coughed and wheezed and spat. One morning, she led me back to the doorway of the city mission. Her face was hard and cold. You are to go in there Alice and wait for me to return. Go inside and get warm and ask for some food. If another lady with children comes, sit beside them.

"I pleaded with her not to leave me. But she wouldn't listen. You must do exactly what I've told you. I have to go, there are things I must do.

"I made her promise to return quickly. She swore that she would. She left me there on the roadway without a backward glance. I cried my eyes out. I didn't know what to do. Then a lady came up to me. She took me inside and gave me toast and marmalade and cocoa. I was ravenous. She went away and came back with a man in a clerical collar. They asked me to give them my name and age. I refused to tell them. He said they were going to take me for a nice ride in his car to the police station. I told them I had to wait here for my mother but they wouldn't listen. I fought them, I kicked and screamed, all the while hanging on for dear life to the pink eiderdown.

"They took me away but not to the police station. We drove through the countryside for hours. I was distraught. I remembered Mrs Pickens warning me about men who steal little girls away. I pictured my mother coming to fetch me and panicking when she couldn't find me.

"I folded myself into the eiderdown and fell asleep. I awoke when the car stopped. I had been brought to a strange place with a few mean-looking houses and a muddy roadway. And everywhere empty spaces. Horses standing still as ghosts in the chill mist of the late afternoon. Rolling hillsides and hedges and stone walls and trees looming through the thickening fog. I had never been out of London before. My world had been a noisy crowded place, full of people and tall buildings and activity. I may as well have been taken to the moon.

"The lady got out of the car. I fastened myself onto her. I was terrified that she would leave me alone with the man. She seemed to understand my fear and allowed me to hold her hand as we walked towards a stone house at the end of the long muddy road. I remember her complaining to the man about the state of the roadway and referring to me as a poor little soul. Then they took me inside the big house and she told me she had to leave immediately and go back to London with the man. She kissed me on the forehead and told me to be a good girl and say my prayers. I clung to her. All sorts of fancies were going through my head. I thought I was going to be eaten alive or murdered or locked away in a dungeon.

"Then I heard the sound of children singing and I felt instantly relieved.

"A woman in a white uniform came into the foyer and took some papers from the lady. She took my hand and led me down a long dark hallway towards the sound of the singing. I twisted around and screamed out to the lady. Tell my mother where I am! Tell my mother!

"Then I was pushed into a big room, and I saw rows of odd-looking children standing around long white tables, singing a hymn. They all looked exactly the same. I couldn't tell if they were boys or girls. They had shaved heads and were dressed in identical unbleached-calico pinafores and knitted black stockings and black boots.

"The woman in the uniform took me to the top table where an old woman was busily spooning food from an iron pot into plain white bowls. The singing stopped and the children sat down at the table. She clapped her hands to gain their attention and said, Good evening children. They answered her in a sing-song tone, Good evening Matron.

"A new girl has arrived. Unfortunately I can't tell you her name. It appears that she has forgotten who she is or maybe the cat has got her tongue. Until she remembers, we shall call her Miss Nobody.

"The children obediently chanted, Good evening Miss Nobody.

"I was so humiliated I wanted to die. Although I was hungry, I could not eat the bowl of stew and potatoes that was placed in front of me. The girl sitting next to me whispered, Better clean it up, otherwise they'll bring it back to you in the morning. In the end, she ate it for me. I couldn't believe how deftly she stole tiny portions from my plate. I hardly saw her spoon move in her hand. She whisked away a bit here, a bit there, until the plate was clean and empty. I'm Emily, she whispered. I'm Alice, I whispered back. Ohhh, so you do have a name! But don't be scared, I never tell that old cow nothing.

"Emily became my friend, even though she was four years older than me. That first night, I was comforted when I saw that her bed was in the same dormitory as mine. I was pleased to have my own bed and my own small bedside cabinet and some clean clothes to wear. It was good to be inside again, especially when I saw the windows streak with rain and heard the wind howling around the corner of the stone building.

"After tea, Matron took me to the bathroom and scrubbed me down with carbolic soap. I had long curly hair that my mother always brushed out and plaited for the night so that it wouldn't tangle. I waited for the matron to do it. Nothing happened. I was too nervous to ask her and so I went to bed with my hair hanging down my back. I was scared that my mother would be annoyed with me when she saw the tangles and knots in the morning.

"Emily came creeping along the floor after Matron had turned out the light. She told me bluntly that I was dreaming. Your mother won't come Alice, none of them ever do. Don't you know where you are?

"A hospital of some kind, to help sick children who don't have anywhere to live?

"This is a home for unwanted kids. Your mother don't want you no more.

"I was shocked. I let out a terrible shriek of denial. Emily pressed her hand over my mouth so hard I couldn't breath. Shut up! she hissed. You'll get us thrashed.

"She kept her hand over my mouth while she told me some home truths about the place where I had landed up. You have to do exactly what they tell you otherwise you will be punished. Pray, wash, eat, right on cue. When the bell rings, jump! Always agree with them, and never look into their eyes. Be humble and grateful, make them think you're a proper Miss Goody-Two-Shoes. Watch out for some of the bigger kids too. They can be just as bad. Stay close by me and you'll be all right. They won't dare to touch you when they know that you're one of my girls.

"I had no idea that first night of how lucky I was that she had taken a liking to me. She taught me how to keep a poker face when I was humiliated, how to make pictures in my head of things like rich plum cakes or parcels wrapped in silver paper, so that I had something wonderful to look at while terrible things were happening to my body. Like the second day, when they shaved my head for hygienic reasons. My long hair was swept from the wooden floor and wrapped up in dirty newspaper. Matron instructed me to throw the package into the fire. Emily said, Don't look, don't listen to the sizzle, think of easter eggs made of pink icing. And I did, and it helped me.

"She taught me everything about survival. Above all, she taught me how to tell lies. She was a glorious liar. She had the staff fooled with her fake sincerity. Matron said how pleased she was that I had taken up with Emily. She described her as a god-fearing little girl, hard-working, respectful of her elders. Model yourself on her my dear, and you will reap great rewards. If only she knew!

"Emily had learned how to play the system. Tell them your name Alice, they'll find out sooner or later. Get in first. Say that you're sorry and that you're grateful for being here. But cross your fingers behind your back. This untells the lie so you're not really doing anything bad.

"Six years I lived in Moncreiff House. The first five years I was one of Emily's girls. Then she was sent away into service with her metal trunk full of hand-made clothes and lace and a bible with her name in it. Only the good girls were given a bible. I didn't get one because try as hard as I did, I was not as clever as Emily. I was caught stealing food and this went down against my name in the punishment book. They had all our names and numbers in it. I can still see it, a leather-bound book with neatly lined pages and copperplate writing. They actually read this out when you left, times, dates, sins, in front of everyone. The shame of it.

"Humiliation and physical punishment were used as measures of control. They told us that they were the agents of God, that they were doing his work, and then we were beaten and humiliated for the most minor offences. We were never allowed to be an individual or have ideas of our own. We never had our own clothes, we chose from the pile once a week on bath nights. But they didn't win with me. I knew that they told lies about the goodness of God. Sometimes I imagined that they were actually afraid of us, the children of the poor. We must be locked away and trained to take our humble place in the grand scheme of things. Emily told me not to believe a word they said. They see us as savages, she said, as wild creatures that have to be tamed. But they are the dangerous ones, not us.

"I learned to lead a double life, one in public, one in private. I read as many books as I could although these were strictly censored. We were hardly ever allowed out, we did our lessons inside the house. There was even a small church attached to the house for the use of the staff and the inmates. We had to go twice on Sundays, for morning and evening service. The whole place was run by the Church of England but I didn't know this until much later. We were kept in ignorance of everything, no letters came or went, no visitors except for the doctor and officials from the society who raised money for the orphanage and the elderly clergyman who came on Sundays to deliver his incomprehensible sermons and to feed the body and blood of Christ to those older children who had been through the ritual of confirmation.

"For years I didn't know where I was. I may as well have been in a foreign country. I can remember my sense of relief when a teacher pinned a map of Britain up on the wall and showed us London and traced the road from there to Moncreiff House with her stick. I saw the black web of roads leading out of London, I saw her point to Derbyshire, the name of the county we were in and the names of the villages near Moncreiff House.

"This teacher was called Miss Catley. She was the only staff member who treated us kindly. The very first time she walked into the classroom, I knew that she was different. I was learning how to write with pen and nib and ink and finding it very difficult. The points of my nib kept crossing, catching the paper and making blots. Miss Catley looked down at my work and I braced myself for the expected slap around the ears. But she showed me how to hold the pen gently so that the nib would not tear the paper, and it worked. And she smiled at me and touched me on the shoulder and I fell instantly in love with her.

"Emily warned me to be careful. She thought Miss Catley was good-hearted enough, but she's still one of them Alice, don't ever forget that. Don't tell her anything that would get us into trouble.

"I thought about Miss Catley night and day, I wove a fantasy around her. Miss Catley was my real mother. Elva Smallacomb, the woman who had abandoned me, had stolen me away from Miss Catley when I was a new-born. For years Miss Catley had searched for me and eventually she found me here at Moncreiff House. She came here pretending to be a teacher so that she could be close to me. At night, I would picture Miss Catley searching the streets of London in all weathers, looking into the faces of children sleeping rough, knocking at the doors of police stations, going to soup kitchens and night shelters, asking everyone she met, have you seen my little girl, her name is Alice, she's got long yellow hair, at night I brush it out and make a plait of gold.

"I dreamed this story so often it became the truth to me.

"After about six months, Miss Catley was dismissed. Emily

soon found out why. Nothing happened in that place without her eventually finding out. Matron claimed that Miss Catley had failed in her duty, she didn't set a good example. Emily walked up and down the dormitory with one hand on her breast, making a perfect imitation of Matron's voice. Too familiar with the children, too soft . . . these children will take advantage . . . they have no background, they are weak willed and morally destitute. We have a god-given duty to make sure they are educated to their proper place in life. Do you realise these girls are going to live with families Miss Catley, fam-il-ies, some with (hushed voice) a position in life? These girls will be an in-flu-ence Miss Catley, they will be living in close domestic proximity to their betters, they will become privy to the most intimate aspects of important lives. We must make sure that they will not do anything to bring Moncreiff House into disrepute.

"I was inconsolable. I grieved for Miss Catley, it was like losing my mother all over again. I wanted to die. If Emily hadn't been there, trying to make me laugh with her tricks and jokes, shielding me from the hunger and horror of that place, I know that I would have become very ill.

"When I was thirteen Emily was sent away into service. I withdrew into myself and tried very hard to follow her last words of advice. Play their game Alice, you will only hurt yourself if you go against them. You will not be a child forever. Then you can get your own back, some day, somehow . . .

"A year passed, the worst year of my life. I never heard from Emily and nobody would tell me where she had been sent. Then a miracle happened, the event that indirectly led to me coming to New Zealand. Matron summoned me into the Director's office. I was very frightened. I thought I was about to be punished for something. I was overcome with joy to find Miss Catley there. It transpired that she had opened a private school for girls in the near-by Peak District and she required a domestic servant. She wanted me! I knew instinctively that I must appear to be very composed and show no emotion whatever. Emily's training stood me in good stead. I was very careful not to catch Miss Catley's eye.

I stood there, stony faced, while inside I was raging with a mixture of joy and fear. I was ecstatic at the possibility of leaving this place and terrified that they would not let me go with my rescuer.

"Matron was explaining to the Director that I was ready to be sent out to work but that in light of what had happened here at the orphanage, she had misgivings about Miss Catley as a suitable employer of a Moncreiff House girl. The Director huffed and puffed and said that Miss Catley was of excellent character, and that there had never been any evidence to the contrary. It was her liberal teaching methods that had caused complaints and Alice is no longer a pupil, she is a domestic servant. We cannot keep these big girls forever Matron and times are hard. There are so many younger children who need our care. Alice should be earning her keep and giving thanks to God for the privilege of her time with us.

"I stayed absolutely still and tried to keep my eyes unfocussed and empty. I heard him explain to Miss Catley that half of my wages must be paid to Moncreiff House. She has a debt to us, he said. Nothing has ever been paid towards her care.

"Miss Catley signed some papers without removing her leather gloves. I was instructed to give her a curtsy and a mention in my prayers that night. Curtsy! I would have leaped from the second-storey window if she had asked me to.

"Next day, she came for me. She drove her Austin right up to the front door and sounded the horn. None of us had seen a woman driving a car before. She caused a sensation. Children hung from the windows. A group of boys working in the garden whistled and catcalled at her. Matron came to the front door and her jaw dropped with astonishment. I'm sure that, at that moment, all her worst fears about Miss Catley were confirmed. But it was too late. The papers were signed. I was free!

"Miss Catley allowed me to sit beside her in the front seat. She hardly spoke a word to me but stared straight ahead turning the wheel carefully and wrestling with the gears. We climbed slowly through high twisting roads. It was late autumn. Seas of pink and purple heather, fallen rock walls covered in grèy lichen, brown sheep with twisted horns, and once a ruined village. I wanted so badly to stop and look into the old stone walls and the fallen roofs. I wanted to lie still and quiet within this site of ancient habitation to get a sense of lives long past, of children's voices, of pain and love that might linger with enough force to penetrate my hungry body.

"It was a mild still afternoon with just a hint of autumn mist gathering at the peaks of the hills. Miss Catley pointed out the strange hillocks of white fluor spa, made from tailings from old lead mines that littered this district like vast rabbit warrens. I'm telling you this dear Alice, for your own protection. When you go out walking, be careful of the mine shafts. They are hidden in the most unexpected places.

"Since I had been taken to the orphanage no one except Emily had shown any concern for me. Miss Catley's term of endearment struck me with the force of a blow. Dear Alice! My fantasy about her being my long-lost mother took on a deeper significance than before.

"We drove around the side of a bare hill and descended into a valley. Here the trees were taller, the grass greener and the stone walls were less tumble-down. She stopped the car outside a stone cottage that was partly hidden in trees. I could see a smoking chimney and windows with those tiny diamond shapes of glass divided by strips of lead and two dormer windows set in the roof. The name of the cottage was carved into the wooden pediment above the doorway, *Emain*.

"Miss Catley had not told the whole truth to the Director of the orphanage. She did intend to open a school but it was still at the planning stage. She and her companion Miss Muriel Forester were looking for suitable premises. Miss Forester was a teacher too. Their dream was to open a school for working-class girls, and to give them the best education that they could provide. Miss Forester had money of her own, she did not need to work. She was a perfectionist. She didn't want to make a decision about the school until they had found the perfect place. She had the money and Miss Catley had the passion and the drive. Or that's how it seemed to me at the time. Maybe that's why in the year that I spent with them, in spite of many excursions into the countryside to view possible sites, they never did agree on a suitable place to buy.

"Miss Forester was waiting inside the house for us. She was a big woman with a beautiful voice and long black hair coiled into a knot at the back of her head. She made me feel very welcome. There was a roaring fire and good things to eat. She told me I was an important person, that they really needed me. My job was to keep the house clean and tidy and attend to their personal needs. I had to prepare breakfast but a cook came from the village to do luncheon and dinner and there was a daily woman to do the heavy cleaning and the washing.

"It may seem strange to you that two women had three servants but remember this was 1934 and women like Miss Catley and Miss Forester had not been trained to look after themselves. They could not cook, they could not clean. They had never been allowed to learn. Although they were educated and came from upper middle-class families, they were not independent. Their very happiness and well-being depended on the goodwill and labour of their servants. They simply couldn't live without our help. Although I could not articulate this at the time, I took pride in my essential role. It felt good to be needed, especially by someone like Miss Catley.

"During the year that I spent in their house, I learned many new things. I came out into the world. The winter was freezing, but when the snow drifts melted enough for the roads to be passable, we drove out in Miss Catley's Austin. I spent countless hours crouched in the tiny back seat, looking out at the landscapes rolling past me. I was the princess of the wands, the keeper of the sedge, the wizard of the grass and the hedgerows where my tiny subjects sheltered from blizzards and reapers. The stark hill Mam Tor, the wandering rivers Derwent and Wye, ritual stones marked with familiar symbols, ruined shelters: mine all mine. I had banished the light from my body when I entered that religious house of persecution, but now I allowed the comfort of illumination to reach into my interior.

"The nearest village to the cottage was a tiny place called Eyam. Mrs Riley the cook and Mrs Middleton the cleaner both lived there. They rode bicycles to work but on bad days, when the wind or rain or snow threatened to blow them off the side of the steep road, Miss Catley drove them home. Come along Alice, she would say, drop whatever you're doing and come along for the ride. I jumped at the chance because I knew that once she had delivered the two women to their separate homes, she would allow me to take the wheel for the return trip.

"I learned to drive in that tiny car on windswept snowy roads made of crushed stone and frozen mud. I loved every moment of it. Miss Catley never gave me any instruction. She had taught herself to drive and thought that I could do likewise. Nobody bothered with driving licences in those days, not up there in the north anyway.

"When the winter was over, Miss Catley sometimes allowed me to take the car out by myself to collect provisions from the village or to take Mrs Riley home after she had stayed late to cook dinner for guests. Mrs Riley lived in a row of terrace houses that had been converted from an old silk mill. The windows on the top floor had been designed to let in the natural light for the silk weavers but many had been bricked up. The shape of the windows showed through the bricks. It gave the terrace a blind look. She would tell me frightening stories of trapped miners calling out to her from beneath the earth and of the plague graves behind her house where strange things happened during the yearly celebration of Samhaine.

"Eyam was a village of graves and ghosts. Hundreds of years ago, the whole town had almost been wiped out by the Black Plague. I used to loiter along Church Street to read the names engraved on boards outside the cottages where the victims had suffered and died. And the church where the list of the dead is kept, those brave ones who stayed and did not run in panic when the plague arrived in a bolt of linen from London in 1666.

"I had to ask Miss Catley about the Black Plague. She was astonished that I had never heard of it before I came to live with her at *Emain*. Did you not learn history? she asked. Have you read nothing about our past?

"Miss Catley gave me a book to read, to broaden my mind she said. It was *A Journal of the Plague Year* by Daniel Defoe. I read it with horror and fascination. It affected me deeply. Before this, hell had been presented to me as an abstraction, a mythical place, but this book provided me with a graphic description of a hell that had existed in the midst of life. People had actually lived through this devastating experience, right here in Eyam. I had seen their tombstones and read the Plague Register in the church to prove it.

"I felt afraid sometimes. I wondered if the plague still lurked in the dark soil of Furness Wood, in the water troughs of Eyam, in the foggy air, in the silken coat of Grania, their beloved cocker spaniel.

"When I expressed this fear, Miss Forester suggested that Miss Catley had been at fault in giving me the Defoe book to read. Miss Catley gave us both a lecture on keeping an open mind and not shielding oneself from the past, no matter how unpleasant it could be. Facts are facts she said, do not be afraid to look them in the eye.

"I seized her words and turned them back on her so neatly she could do nothing but answer me. Then tell me about my mother, I said, tell me the truth about her.

"The two women looked at each other. I wanted to say, perhaps *you* are my real mother, but fear overcame me. Miss Catley sat me down and held my hand and told me that my mother had died in a TB sanatorium. The Director had showed her a letter of notification when she came to the orphanage to ask if she could take me into service. She apologised for not telling me sooner but she didn't have the heart.

"I was shattered. It was the end of hope for me. Hope that Elva would one day find me and hope that my fantasy about Miss Catley might somehow be true."

Wendy interrupts. "But your mother came here to New Zealand. You told me so on the first tape."

I stand up and move to the window. I close the curtains against the glare of the noonday sun, hanging high and still above the house. I try to compose myself. "The notification of her death was a lie, a disgusting terrible lie."

Wendy asks me if I have had enough for one day. She tells me that there is about ten minutes left on this side of the tape. Can I manage to speak a little longer? Just to tie some loose ends together, why I left Miss Catley's house and so forth.

She has already laid ten fifty-dollar bills on the coffee table. The silver threads on the notes smile at me. I can't wait to get my hands on them. I speak once more into the microphone.

"I was taken away from *Emain* by force. The orphanage still owned me and the fruits of my labour. They took half my wages from me. They had control over where I worked and where I lived. At the time, I believed that they took me away because Miss Catley had lied to the Director. She had told him that she had already opened the school. I knew that lying was considered a great sin. This had been beaten into me. Miss Catley had stretched the truth a little. It was obvious that she must be punished and punishment always involves the withdrawal of love. What better punishment than to take me away from her and forbid her to ever see me again?

"It was a great loss. She had taught me so much. All through spring and summer I had wandered the hillsides and villages of the Peak District with Miss Catley and her spaniel Grania. She was a great walker. She dressed in a tweed jacket and skirt and strong brown ankle-boots. I had my walking clothes too, hand-me-downs from her. We were almost the same size. When I left the orphanage I was thin and pale but the good food and exercise and fresh air that I had enjoyed since I came to *Emain* had filled me out. My body had found its true path, tall and strong and well-defined. And my hair had grown back into a satisfying thick rope.

"We gathered wild fruits, hazel nuts, strawberries, bilberries, and sometimes raspberries from old abandoned gardens. Miss Catley taught me the name of the wild flowers and herbs. I learned how to gather chamomile, tansy, eyebright, yarrow, comfrey. She showed me how to lift sphagnum moss from shallow bogs. She washed the moss in spring water and dried it on the rack above the wood stove before she stored it in her medicine cupboard. She used it to stop bleeding wounds. And when I had my first period she made me pads of linen wrapped around the moss and it was so soft and comfortable.

"She cared for me, I know she did. I only ever saw her weep

once, on the last morning we were together. They sent The Reverend Mr Bates to take me away from *Emain*. He was very officious, very business-like. There has been a change of plan for Miss Smallacomb, he said. She is extremely fortunate. She has been offered the chance of a lifetime. A new life in one of our colonies.

"All I could see was his cold blue eyes and his clerical collar. I went berserk. I punched him, I kicked him in the groin as hard and as fast as I could. Miss Forester came running into the hallway. Miss Catley stood frozen to the spot. Her eyes looked like glittering black holes.

"A strange woman wearing a dead fox around her neck came flying through the front door in full sail. She screamed at me to leave her husband alone.

"I was almost blind with rage and fear but I could do nothing to save myself. Together, the man and the woman bundled me roughly out to the car. Miss Catley came running out after us. Tears were pouring down her face. I thought she would plead with them to let me go but all she did was sob and say over and over, forgive me Alice, forgive me.

"There was someone else in the back seat of the car. Incredibly, it was Emily. She gave me one of her old looks that meant, say nothing, show nothing, I'll explain everything later. The car drove off in a shower of gravel. I turned my head for one last look at *Emain*. Miss Catley and Miss Forester were standing in the middle of the road, weeping, holding each other. I said a silent farewell to them and to my bed behind the dormer window and to the elder tree that tapped at my window and to Grania's soft coat and my wanderings through the bleak landscapes that had seared love and remembrance for wind and wild plants and sweet berries and stone circles forever into my being.

"The Reverend Mr Bates and Mrs Bates held a conversation in indignant whispers. A disastrous placement . . . overheated behaviour . . . questions would be asked.

"Only the fact that Emily was there in the back seat stopped me from stabbing Mrs Bates with her hatpin or strangling her with her dead animal. I was flushed with a new sort of power. I had enjoyed kicking The Reverend Mr Bates, the crunch of my shoe against his flesh, his gasp of pain. And I couldn't wait to do it again.

"But Emily held my hand and put her finger to her lips and I knew that I must pretend to be docile until I discovered why I was being taken away. We drove for a long time. I knew that we were heading south. Everything looked greener and there were more villages and roads and traffic. At *Emain*, autumn had arrived weeks earlier. The oak and elder trees were turning red and gold and the long grass at the back of the cottage was browned and bitten by frost. The landscape that we were moving through provided images of a fruitful late summer; potato pickers moving with their sacks down rows of earth the colour of dark chocolate; wagons of hay; animals browsing in fields of turnips; wheat stubble blackened with fire.

"It was early evening when the car finally stopped on the outskirts of a large town. The car drew up to an iron gate set in a high stone wall. A small figure was sitting outside the gate on a metal trunk. Emily mouthed at me, another lucky one.

"Mrs Bates got out of the car and spoke to the girl. The Reverend Mr Bates got out too and took some papers from the girl, then frowned and strode through the gate. The girl struggled to lift the trunk into the boot of the car. I wanted to get out and help her. I could see that her face was swollen with tears.

"Emily whispered to me, stay where you are. I must speak with you before you do anything else to the Rev. I understand why you kicked him, and good job too, but you must be careful. Otherwise they won't let us go.

"Go? Where to? I panicked. I clutched her arm in fear.

"Emily told me that we had been selected to go to New Zealand as domestic servants for members of the church who had migrated down there. She had talked Mrs Bates into putting my name on the list.

"I was devastated. I couldn't think of anything worse. I would never see Miss Catley again. I would never be able to ask the meaning of some of the puzzles of *Emain*. And it was all Emily's fault!

"Don't look at me like that Alice, she said. Your number was up.

They were going to take you away from those two women anyway. I have a peep hole in the wall and I heard them say that you were going to be taken back to the orphanage. The next morning, the old bitch asked me if I thought there were any girls from Moncreiff House who would be suitable for this colonial servant scheme. So I said Alice Smallacomb, so clever and pretty and well behaved, she should come too. And then you go and kick the old bastard. Lucky for you they blamed Miss Catley.

"But I can't go!"

"This is our big chance Alice. They can't hold me once I turn twenty-one and that's only two years away. I will come for you wherever you are and we'll run away together. I swear I will come for you. We will be free.

"Mrs Bates got back into the car and our conversation ended.

"I spent my last two nights in London at a mission hostel with Emily and the small crying girl with the metal trunk. Jean was only twelve years old, an orphan like me. We were locked into a tiny bedroom with two iron beds and a washstand. I managed to open the heavy sash window and listen to the noise and smell of a London street. A wave of longing for my mother came over me. I remembered everything that had happened when we had been thrown out of the house at Islington by Mrs O'Neill. I was old enough by now to realise that my mother had abandoned me at the city mission in good faith. She thought I would be better off in the hands of Christians, but I burned with resentment that she had never sent a letter to the orphanage or tried to visit me. I believed that if she had seen that place, if she had known about the beatings and the humiliations, she would have rescued me. Now it was too late. She was dead.

"I wept with grief and rage, and Jean wept with me for her own mother who had abandoned her in similar circumstances. In two days time we would be sailing away from London forever. Emily was right. There was nothing that we could do to change our circumstances but I was frightened of losing my past. I felt that if this happened I too would disappear.

"I leaned on the window sill and I swore never to forget anything that ever happened to me. I would remember everything; weather, colours, words, faces, the feel of cloth, the shape of particular clouds, the taste of particular foods. I would remember every journey I ever made, every person I ever met. I would become both witness and chronicler of my own experience.

"And I began that very night to train my memory. This how I do it. I rehearse the happenings, the feelings of the day, and I put it into the context of the past. I visualise the pattern of the kaleidoscope that I saw long ago at the Warrington's. Diagonal forms, each one filled with glass beads shaped like multi-coloured tears. I colour code the memories and place them into the appropriate bead, red for life, white for death, black for renewal.

"My interest lies in the relationship between yesterday and the day before not today and tomorrow. I let the future lie, I see it as a building that is just out of my peripheral vision. I don't want to know whether it is constructed out of brick or stone or wood, I centre my attention onto the building I have just left and how it lies in relation to the multiple rooms that stretch back to my first memories of the special quality and movement of light. The flame of candles flickering on the rosy wet face of my mother, the pool of electric light over the kitchen table, the glistening spirals of apple skins, the yellow eggs and sugar, the glazed fruit buns.

"Every night of my life, no matter how tired I am, I re-experience my stories. Not as anecdotes but as feelings. I transfer the work of the mind into the storehouse of the body. I retell the stories my mother told me about my birth. I relive her pain, her ignorance, her misguided love. Did you know that smells have colours too? My mother's smell is in the gold bead, cigarette smoke, gin, beige powder. For the first year in the orphanage I was allowed to keep the pink eiderdown and every night I sniffed her presence in the cloth.

"One day Matron forced me to wash the eiderdown with carbolic soap. I never used it again. I gave it away to one of the younger children.

"Gold for warmth, blue for cold. The smell of the orphanage is in the blue bead, unsmiling faces, broken skin, the tears of sad children. Fear is a blue smell, burnt porridge, cold corridors, weeping for lost mothers.

"I re-remember everything. Our life at the Warrington's, the expulsion from my first home after the death of my grandmother, the mysterious gift of money, the death of Mrs Pickens, the taunts of Deirdre O'Neill, the nights on the streets under the pink eiderdown, my abduction to the orphanage, my miraculous time at *Emain*. They are alive and fresh and I can replay them at will in technicolour."

I sigh and tell Wendy that I'm tired. I have had enough for today. The truth is that I am feeling a little shocked at my revelations. I wonder if I could ask her to wipe this section from the tape. I suggest that she deletes the last ten minutes. "I don't particularly want anyone to know about the kaleidoscope."

Wendy is busily packing away her tape recorder. "Why not? It explains your amazing recall of events. You've worked out a good system." She hands me the money from the table and opens her diary to make another appointment for next week. I decide not to make an issue of it.

Once again, I watch her leave from behind my net curtain in the front room. She gets into her smart red car, speaks into her cellphone, then drives away up the hill. I sit in my front room, silent and alone, until the afternoon shadows move across the back window. I raise my aching body and struggle towards the kitchen to prepare a meal of potatoes and fish.

My mind is burning. I am being moved forward to a point in my narrative that I have up to now kept successfully hidden in the white bead of denial.

Joy's father is about to enter my story. The time for my grand confession is drawing closer. Maybe I can use the tapes to tell her. Maybe she can hear everything after I am dead. Then I won't be there to hear her accuse me of telling tall tales that owe more to literature than to life. But in spite of everything that she has thrown at me, I owe her something. I must be present in the flesh to diffuse her anger towards me. She will explode with outrage but I will try to calm her. I must make her understand how it was for us, the poverty, the shame, the hatred. I will force her to acknowledge that I had no choice.

My joints are burning. I close my eyes and concentrate on the colours of the lights, the blue bead melts into gold. She is tugging at my hair with a small black brush, I can smell her breath, I can feel the soft skin of her fingers on my neck.

I did see it, I did see . . .

# 4

## *Joy*

The private detective didn't want to take my case at first. I had dressed with care and made sure that my hair was tidy but I must have still looked poor because he shook his head and told me that these cases were very time consuming and very expensive.

I had already spoken to him on the telephone and he had told me to come into Hamilton and meet him and we could talk turkey. I had expected an older man, a tough-talking man, untidily dressed, a chain smoker. But of course, I had never met a private investigator before and I quickly realised that I was using the stereotype I had taken out of detective books.

The embargo placed by my daughter was the stumbling block. She had instructed the authorities that she did not want to be contacted by her birth mother. The clerk at Social Welfare had let it slip that my child had been adopted into a family who lived in Auckland. This was all I could find out. No name, no address, no other information.

I had discovered this last week. I was greatly excited because it meant that she was still alive and possibly still living in New Zealand. I had even rung Morry to tell him but he was out fishing. Bonita said it was good news but she couldn't resist smugly adding that of course, she could never have given one of her babies away. She knows damn well that my Joy was taken from me by force, but I let it ride.

Wayne Marsh is in his late twenties and quite good-looking in a fleshy sort of way. Dark grey suit, white shirt, plain red tie, smells of shaving lotion. A small and rather bleak office with one dusty palm in a brass tub and a painting of a white bird in a silver frame and a pink venetian closed against the glare. A cellphone, a fax, a computer that beeps and spins coloured triangles across the screen.

The engineering firm that I worked for often hired look-alike versions of Wayne Marsh. These well-educated young men seem to be born with an instinctive knowledge of computers. They seem to delight in using a language that I cannot understand. I never progressed beyond the most basic word-processing program. All this talk of rams and modems and sysops and superhighways builds barriers around ephemeral cities that would never welcome me as a citizen.

I realise now that I have been afraid of men all my life. Not so much of *them* but of what they represent. I fear their talk, the ambience of their self-assurance, their technical cleverness, their authority.

These past two years I have experienced a shift in my perceptions. Not just in my attitudes towards love and men and work. The whole nature of time has changed for me. For the first time in my life I have no structure, no timetable, no obligations. Until I was made redundant, I had always worked. Through both my marriages, through all the pain, the minutes and hours were arranged in neat boxes with ruled headings, fixed and immutable. I fitted myself and my personal life around a timetable that was owned and manipulated by someone else. And the strange thing is that until it melted away I was unconscious of the safety net that it provided. The truth is that my schedule and the work that I performed within its confines had invaded me to such an extent that when it was suddenly wrenched from me, I felt as if I had become disembodied. I became invisible to myself.

I had experienced my home life through the lens of work. At home, I rested, ready for the next hectic day. I washed and ironed my clothes, for work, I had early nights, for work, I arranged my social life, my holidays, for work. I didn't know how to be at home without the expectation that I was continually poised to leave it. For weeks after my last day at work, I arose at six and took my shower and drank my coffee and chose my clothes carefully for the day ahead. For weeks, I took clothes to the drycleaners, kept my weekly appointment at the hairdresser, paid for someone to clean my house and mow my lawn. It took months for me to undo these habits and to realise that nobody cared if I got out of bed or dressed or washed or attended to my grooming. Time could exist perfectly well without form, without reason, without purpose. Why bother to eat, to wash, why bother to keep myself going? I had never asked myself these questions before. There had been no need.

I still have no answers. I am beginning to think that the problem lies in the nature of the question itself. And in the way that I was trained to fit into the world of work as if it was the only world that mattered.

Looking back to the lives of my mother and the women on my childhood street, one word comes over and over into my mind: sacrifice. I saw their lives as domestic slavery and economic dependence on inadequate husbands. They endured a life that I was determined never to enter. Now I wonder who it was that really won the race. My capacity for self-delusion never ceases to amaze me. I had merely replaced one hopeless trap for another. And at least they had been able to keep their babies. With all my so-called success in the world of work, I never achieved this most basic right.

Alice will never admit to the truth of her experience. She lies about her childhood, she lies about her marriage. She will not utter one word of criticism against my father Jack. She calls him a lovable rogue, a good man, a man who liked his beer but who always acted as one of nature's gentlemen.

What a ridiculous phrase! A hang-over from her childhood in England. Even though she pretends to rage against the class system, deep in her bones she still believes in dividing the world into commoners and aristocrats. My father never rose above the class that he was born into. So to elevate him, she calls him a gentleman! Not a real one of course, but one of nature, from the world of woods and trees and pixies that she has never been able to leave.

I was afraid of him. He was the final authority in our house, his word was law. He never hit us but he shouted. Suddenly, unexpectedly, that huge roar of rage. Threatening what he would do to us, break our necks, throw us on the rubbish tip. Then he would roll a fag and smile at us as if nothing had happened. I could never understand his sudden shifts of voice. He was a huge influence on Morry. Sometimes when I hear him quarrelling with Bonita, I hear my father's words erupting like a volcano and I feel the same fear that I felt as a child.

I haven't told Alice about my search for my adopted baby. I intend to, when I get closer to the resolution of my quest. I don't want Alice to get too much of a shock when she sees her lost grand-daughter. I will persuade Alice to agree to my version of events. I don't want my Joy to get conflicting stories. She will have enough to cope with when she finally meets up with us.

Wayne hints that his services will cost a lot of money but he won't give me a firm quote. "To tell you the truth Mrs ah, Miss Knight, and this is dead confidential, it might require a little operation just outside of the law. Just how keen are you to find this ah, missing person?"

"Very keen," I answer. I couldn't care less about breaking the law.

At least I feel as if I am getting somewhere now. Wayne Marsh is reassured by my Visa card and my determination to spare no expense in my search. He is preparing our agreement. Questions fly thick and fast. Your house is paid for? Good, good. No dependants? Great. Yes yes I think we can work together. The information you seek is written down somewhere. Dates, names, judgements of the prospective parents, psychological profiles, the moral and financial facts of all the parties involved. All we need is to open a window and look inside.

"Do you handle many adoption cases?" I ask nervously.

"I could name names that would blow your mind. Adoption was enormously popular for decades, it affected everyone, including Lord and Lady Muck." He peers into the screen of his computer. "This is where the expense comes in," he says. "And the discretion. Do you know anything about hacking?"

"Not much."

"Good, the less the better."

I am getting excited. "Are you saying that you can access the computer at Welfare?"

He snaps at me, "Don't ever say that! Besides, they've got the latest state-of-the-art encryption software, not to mention a fire wall system installed between their mainframes and the Internet."

I don't know what he's talking about but I ask no questions. I decide to flatter him. "Surely someone with your technical knowledge could find a way."

He smiles. "Information is a highly marketable commodity. If somebody wants to find something out badly enough, a trapdoor can be found. Of course it takes time and lots of money."

I feel a sudden resentment towards him. Why have I been forced into this situation? Why do I have to spend the last of my savings on getting information that rightfully belongs to me? I gave birth to my Joy, I suffered the hell of her entry into the world and the pain of her forced removal from me when she was six months old. I have a right to know everything about her, the story of her life belongs to me, no one else. I wrote the first chapter. Why should I have to pay to find her and write the heading "Chapter Two"?

I remember her feet encased in stained woollen bootees sticking out from under the arm of the child welfare officer when he came for us in the hayshed. I remember how hard it was to pull those bootees on, her toenails always caught in the knitted pattern. I felt ashamed at the dirt when he took her. We had been on the run for over a week, and it was winter, no warm water, no spare clothes. Every moment is crystal clear in my mind. The frost and smoke and fog, the emerald green of those paddocks where I saw jersey cows walking slowly in lines, the sun falling like a stone behind the hills, the rotten malt smell of silage. The last refuge of the hayshed when I knew that we could travel no further, the warmth of the dry straw smelling of late autumn harvests, the white frosts spread out in clean sheets across the trampled grass.

"That's as far as we can go today Miss, ah, Joy." He swivels around from the computer screen. "I'll be in touch."

I feel both elated and terrified. I can't wait to get outside into the fresh air. Mr Wayne Marsh is obviously a very tricky character. But he is my last hope. Things will begin to move now, I know it.

I sit on a bench in Garden Place. The sun burns overhead in a sky the colour of faded blue linen. There are no rain clouds but the air smells moist and humid. There is a gang of leather-clad hoons skylarking around the sundial. How can they stand to wear their jackets in this heat?

A little boy walks into the fountain. I watch him anxiously in case he falls beneath the water. Who is minding him?

There are two young women with elaborate pushchairs loaded up with babies and bottles and clothes. The toddler must be with them. They are lighting up cigarettes and eating potato chips and calling out friendly insults to the leather hoons. I hurry over to them to warn them about the child. One of them snaps, "As if we'd let one of our kids do that!" The other one points to a middle-aged woman sitting on the seat next to the fountain. "He's with her, I think."

Then I see the little boy fall beneath the water. I run straight into the waist-high water and seize his trembling body and hold him up high. Water runs from the bottom of his shorts. I walk carefully from the pool, the tiles are slimy and slippery and my sandals are loose on my feet.

The middle-aged woman runs to the edge of the pool and calls anxiously, "Jarrod, Jarrod!" It is my neighbour Rangi. She takes him from my wet arms. Both of them are sobbing. I take off my sandals and try to wring out my wet skirt.

"Thank you Mrs Knight, thank you. If anything had happened . . ."

I feel awkward. "It was nothing, nothing . . ."

She takes a towel from her bag and dries down the little boy. He is smiling now and asking for an ice cream. "I was miles away," she says. "Thank you again." She takes a new tracksuit still wrapped in plastic from her bag. "Good thing I just bought this, I must have known the little rascal would get wet."

I ask her if she's going back to Raglan. I know that she doesn't have a car. She frowns. "I'm meant to be meeting my daughter here hours ago, something must have happened." She tells me that her daughter Moana sometimes leaves Jarrod with her. Moana has five kids, and her husband ran off with a young girl. Sometimes things get too much for her.

We walk to my car. Jarrod is eating an ice cream and it is melting all down the arm of his new red tracksuit. I worry that he is too small to fit into the seat belt in the back of my car but Rangi sits him on her lap and puts the belt around them both. We drive through the winding roads and scarred hills down into the Te Uku valley. Rangi and I hardly exchange a word. She dozes. Then Jarrod announces that he wants to mimi. We stop at the Te Uku store and Rangi takes him behind the building.

There are three buildings in this settlement, the store, a purple craft shop that was once the local post office and a small country school with cream weatherboards, a tile roof covered with grey lichen, black tyres hanging from trees, a metal driveway. Time warp territory. It is exactly like the school I went to in Auckland in the 1940s. I smell sandshoes and greaseproof paper and swimming togs drenched with chlorine, I taste sour milk and soggy tomato sandwiches.

Then a bell rings and a group of children from the school run down to the store, bare footed, revelling in the dust and heat of the roadway. They wear plastic backpacks instead of leather schoolbags and their clothes are casual and ready-made. Otherwise, the time warp holds.

Rangi and Jarrod come out of the store. He is eating a yellow iceblock. My throat is dry and I crave a cool drink. But I feel self-conscious about my wet skirt and bare feet and I don't want to get out of the car.

They settle into the back seat of the car. Then Rangi produces a bottle of spring water from her bag. She smiles. "In this heat you need to drink."

"You read my mind."

We set off for the last part of our journey home. Rangi dozes again and Jarrod has a great time with the iceblock, dropping bits of frozen ice down his front and onto the carpeted floor. I want to say something but I don't want to upset Rangi.

I drop them off at Rangi's gate next to my own. Rangi thanks me for driving them home and offers to take my skirt to the dry-cleaners. "I'm a bit tired today," she says. "Bring it over tomorrow and we'll have a kai. I've got some lettuces you can have, and some beans too."

Obviously she wants to compensate me for jumping into the water to save Jarrod from drowning. I accept the offer to dryclean my skirt, even though I could have easily washed it out myself. I don't want to put her off. This is the first time since I moved here that she has invited me to her home.

I wonder if she knows how shy I am of her? I grew up in a Pakeha working-class suburb, each square wooden box had a white father and a white mother and mobs of little white kids. The forties and the fifties in Auckland were terrifying decades. Closed, deceitful, hostile. Pretending to be a better version of the once glorious old empire, England without the rotten weather or the class system.

This carefully wrought illusion of living in a safe white world fooled me for years. During my childhood, we very rarely moved around other parts of the city and we didn't leave town except for the occasional day trip to Rotorua or Te Kauwhata where my father had relatives. I thought that the new state-house suburbs in West Auckland were a mirror image of the rest of New Zealand. Sandringham and Mt Roskill and Three Kings, row after row of happy families, living in identical houses; working fathers, full time mothers, clotheslines blowing with clean washing, children playing in the middle of the road, no fences, no locked doors; the community glued together with mutual fabrications of consensus and decency.

Talking about anything personal was the biggest sin. Fine to rage against the bosses and the evils of capitalism, fine to run the Tory government down and wear the red ribbon of Labour on election day, fine to criticise the accumulation of money and shares and to point out the evils of invested capital. But never family problems. We were told not to talk about "our business" outside the kitchen door. And we were never allowed to speak ill of other families either. The message was, if you don't talk about it, it can't be real, it can't be true, it can't *exist.*

On our rare visits to the country, we saw what my father referred to as the stamping ground of the *Mowries.* There were beaten-up cars full of children and old people moving along gravel roads and groups of women gathering seafood and children riding shaggy ponies bareback along the edge of the surf. And men driving tractors or draught horses, ploughing or making hay, and sitting on the verandahs of country pubs in the late afternoons, drinking beer and rolling up smokes. Jack, my father, would comment on the leisurely driving of the *Mowries*, their casual nature, their lack of malice. They've got the right idea living out here, he'd say. They'd be no good in the city. They never worry about nothing, we are the stupid ones, we worry about money, the weather, the government, every bloody thing.

Now I have ended up in this coastal place, living cheek by jowl with the original inhabitants, on probation, uneasy. Not through guilt for what my ancestors stole, or the thoughtless racism of my father, but a strange sort of shyness. For me, Maori have always remained a secret people, living lives of mystery in the mists of the mountains or on the edge of rivers and beaches. I don't know how to be with them, I don't know what to say, I don't know what to do.

Like everyone else in the eighties, my firm made a lip-service commitment to living in a bicultural world. They organised a brief bicultural training session on the job. Compulsory, during work hours, two sessions, two hours each time. A young man and an older woman came to teach us stick games and haka and waiata and the meaning of spiritual attachment to the earth. I thought it a superficial waste of time except for the last item. Whenua, the same name in Maori for the afterbirth and for the land. It changed me, this notion. It brought the issue of my lost Joy to the forefront of my mind. This talk of whenua as simultaneous attachment both to the mother and to the land, set me off once again on the search for her that has become an obsession.

I like the word obsession, I enjoy saying it, I enjoy living it. I have been taught all my life to be moderate, reasoned, quiet in word and deed. Now, after everything that has happened to me, I want to rage and scream and cry. I want revenge for all those silent years, when I could never mention the fact that I became pregnant at fifteen and had my baby girl stolen from me. I endured in silence

61

the moral outrage of the teachers at my school and the neighbours, I never complained at the tight binders I was forced to wrap around my swollen belly, I didn't answer back when the matron at the home lectured me endlessly about my fall from grace. I had done the worst thing a girl could ever do. And when I said that I wanted to keep my baby with me forever, they added *unrealistic* and *stupid* to their list of my crimes. This baby is not a doll, they said, not a pretty toy for you to dress in frilly clothes and then throw away when you tire of it.

I make myself a cup of coffee and dial Morry's number. He is asleep, Bonita tells me. Tired out, he's been out mowing lawns all morning. In this heat. He'll do himself an injury but of course he won't listen to me.

I have to talk to someone about my fears but I have no one except my brother to share the things that are most important to me. My friends who worked with me in Hamilton have melted away since I came to live out here on the coast.

"I'll get him to ring you later. Is it urgent?"

"No, it's nothing." I don't know whether to laugh or cry.

"You sound upset, are you okay?"

She sounds genuinely concerned, so I tell her about my meeting with Wayne.

"You never went to a private detective!" she squeaks.

"I've tried everything else, I don't know what else to do."

"Good on you," she says at last.

I'm surprised and tell her so. "I didn't think you'd approve."

"It's exciting, like reading a murder mystery."

"Hardly, he's not that sort of detective."

A short silence at the end of the phone. "Well I hope that you find her, I really do. Kids should be with their mothers." She sounds quite emotional.

Maybe I have misjudged her. She has always been Morry's wife to me rather than a person in her own right. Over the years she has been jealous of my relationship with my brother, or so Morry told me. I am beginning to wonder if he was trying to make trouble between us. He has always sought the attention of women.

"Have you told your mother?" asks Bonita.

"You mustn't say anything to her. Much better if it comes from me."

"Can I tell Morry?"

"Ask him to ring me when he wakes up."

She agrees to do this but before she hangs up she invites me over for a roast dinner next Saturday night. Then I can fill her in with what she calls the gruesome details.

Bonita reads too many crime novels. I am already regretting that I have told her about Wayne. She might blab about it all over the place and make trouble for me. I almost redial the number to warn her to keep her mouth shut but I can't face it. I'm glad that I didn't mention hacking or anything else about computers. I decide to leave well alone until Saturday night, then, over my tussle with her overcooked mutton and stringy parsnips and baked potatoes, I will warn her about the dangers of idle gossip. Tradition has its uses. I will reinvoke the old rule of keeping family secrets within four walls.

Outside my bedroom window I see waves of heat radiating from tin roofs of houses and shops. The tide is nearly full and the tiny beach at the end of my street has almost disappeared. I feel a sudden urge to dive into the sea and drown my head in the calm glittering water.

I walk briskly to the edge of the sea and stride into the full tide. I can never work out the reason for the colour of the sea in this harbour. The sky can be unchanging day after day but the water can move dramatically from an intense blue to a deep green, then to a slatey grey, the colour of wet iron sands.

I am pleased that today the sea has decided to dress herself in green, the colour of bush canopies and summer paddocks and spring ferns. I bury myself in the cooling flow, and open my eyes under water to feel the sting of the salt. The water is warm on the surface, so I float and ripple and blow air like a whale. The sea cradles my body so that once again I hover between sky and land in that water-numbed state of suspension that renders my flesh weightless so that I cut free, to soar above the cliff tops with the gulls riding the warm thermals, feather to feather, eye to eye, tongue to tongue, *i am but two days old, i have no name, i happy am, joy is my name, sweet joy befall thee* . . .

# 5

# *Alice*

I get a surprise when Wendy comes today. She is wearing a long tight white dress. Usually she wears clothes that fall in uneven layers, sometimes a skirt and long loose jacket, sometimes a dress, but always black. And heavy makeup; white skin, red lips and cheeks, black eyebrows. Beautiful indigo eyes with long black curly lashes. I once asked her if she was Irish. She laughed and said that she wished she was because then she might have better luck. I'm glad she's not. I have hated the Irish since my experience with the dreadful O'Neill children and their mother Colleen. Joy tells me that I am prejudiced and that I shouldn't judge a whole group of people on my experience of a few. I know she's right but I can't help it. Besides, it's not just the Irish, it's any sort of sanctimonious religious person who prays to God and then treats other people cruelly.

White clothes unnerve me. In my scheme of things, it signifies the colour of false holiness and purity leading to death of the soul. I am more comfortable with black. I ask Wendy why she has made the change.

She looks surprised. "The heat mostly. Does it suit me?"

I compliment her on the dress in spite of the colour. I don't want to hurt her feelings. I have grown fond of her and in spite of my initial uncertainty, I have begun to enjoy making the tapes. I have relished the chance to express my anger through the retelling of my stories. My anger towards others has kept me alive, and I refuse to give it up, but I must learn to forgive myself for not telling Joy the truth about her father. Today will be the test, the watershed in some ways, because today, I am going to tell Wendy about

Emily and the Winter brothers. How we met, and the lifelong consequences of my dishonesty.

I will have to tell her too, that I want to play this tape to Joy. I want Wendy to be there when I do, not because I'm afraid, but because she has heard the truth about my background. She understands the roots of my homelessness, my longing for love and security. Wendy will back me up, and she can help Joy to come to terms with the truth.

We make idle conversation while Wendy gets the tape recorder ready. I've opened the windows in my sitting room to let in some air. It's been raining all morning but just before Wendy arrived, the clouds disappeared and the sun burst out and steam is rising like white smoke from the iron roofs and the roadway.

"Let's make a start," says Wendy.

"Where did I finish last time?"

"You were leaving for New Zealand with Emily. What date did you arrive?"

"September 1935, in the middle of the Depression, so things were tough. Auckland was a very different place in those days, ramshackle, down at heel. I couldn't get over the bare hills and the temporary and makeshift look of the wooden buildings. We were so ignorant in those days. No television, no radio, no pictures. Girls like us knew nothing about the world except what we learned first hand. I had expected Auckland to be a tropical paradise like the South Sea towns in the adventure books I had read. We landed on a blustery day and it was cold and grey and the wharf building where we waited for our luggage was open to the weather and the wind made an eerie howling noise and tugged at a loose sheet of iron. Slam! Slam! I wept for the soft trees and the mellow stone of *Emain*.

"Emily told me to cheer up, it's no worse than where we've come from. And later, when we rode in a taxi cab up Queen Street my spirits lifted a little. There were some solid looking buildings, banks, shops, plate-glass windows with mannequins wearing elegant clothes. At least we were in a city and not in some dreary country village.

"We were taken to a church hostel in Ponsonby. There were strange trees lining the street with minuscule leaves and clusters of yellow flowers like bells. The building was three stories high with a wide verandah and wooden fire escapes. The sky looked different, higher, lighter, even though it was a cloudy day. Emily and Jean shared my room for the first week. Jean cried herself to sleep every night. The floor of our room rocked under my feet. I felt more seasick than I had on the boat.

"One by one the girls were taken away by their new employers. Jean was lucky. She was chosen by a friendly old lady from Whangarei who called her a poor wee mite and promised that she could attend the local school. Emily and I were praying that we would both be placed in Auckland. I was taken first, to a large house in Parnell. They came for me in a car, the chauffeur and Mrs Pink the house-keeper. I was thrilled. I had been having nightmares about being sent to a country family far from the city, isolated, lonely, trapped. I was going to a big house, with other servants, like my first home at the Warrington's.

"Emily kissed me goodbye and whispered fiercely, don't forget, I will come for you in two years. And I'll write to you, so you'll know where I am.

"And she did write, two weeks after I went to the house in Stanley Street. But she was miles away, on a muddy Waikato farm, cooking for farmhands, washing, cleaning, slaving. Strangely enough, she seemed quite happy, in spite of not being in the city. I have achieved one sort of freedom, she wrote. No more bible-banging hypocrites lying through their teeth."

Wendy interrupts me. "I thought you were going to be working for members of the church."

"So did we. It turned out to be just another lie. The church paid for our ship berths, that much was true, but we were sent to any family that was willing to pay half our wages into the church coffers. Most of them never saw the inside of a church. The families were supposedly checked out to make sure we would be safe."

"Who did you live with?"

"An English family called Vetorix. He taught Greek History at the University, she stayed at home with the children. Everything in their house was brought out from England; the furniture, the tinned food, the magazines."

"Did they mistreat you?"

"I was never physically abused. They didn't need to. The mental torture was enough. There was a strict hierarchy in that house and I was right at the bottom. The girl they had before me was a Maori girl and they sacked her for being too friendly with the children, and for being too light fingered. That's why they hired me, because I was straight out of England. They believed that I had been trained to be subservient.

"I was afraid of Mrs Pink the housekeeper. She was English too, and she really believed in the class system. She told me it was a privilege to work for the quality, and that I must never forget my place. She had a way of looking at me as if I was scum. Low class. She would never touch anything with her skin. She would lift the table napkins with a pair of silver tongs. As if she was in constant danger of contamination. I could do nothing right. She told me that my cleaning was never good enough, I was a slut, a slattern, a hopeless case. I had been there for about a week when she caught me reading a novel. It was after I had gone to bed in my little room underneath the stairs. She knocked at the door and asked me to come out into the hall. I stood there, in my calico nightgown, and she went into my room. I asked her what she was doing. A room inspection Alice, Mrs Vetorix insists on it. After that last girl, we can't be too careful.

"She found the book, spine up, on my pillow. It had black and yellow lettering burnt into the red cover; *Maori and Settler* by G. A. Henty. Mrs Pink stood there, holding it up. Have you taken this from Dr Vetorix's library? I confessed that I had. The gleam in her eye! She opened it at the first page and read the first paragraph mockingly. *Well mother one thing is certain, something has got to be done. It is no use crying over spilt milk, that I can see. It is a horribly bad business, but grieving over it won't make it any better. What one has got to do is to decide on some plan or other, and then set to work to carry it out.* She laughed at me. This is uncanny Alice, she said.

It describes the present situation perfectly. She opened the book further, and read; *With an exclamation of anger, the native drew a heavy knobbed stick from the girdle round his waist, but before he could raise it to strike, another figure appeared at the door. Marion held a gun in her hand which she raised to her shoulder. "Drop that," she said, in a clear ringing voice. "Or I fire!"*

"So, said Mrs Pink. A girl with a gun. I am taking this book from you, it is most unsuitable. It is my duty to inform Mrs Vetorix of this matter. You will see her in the morning.

"I lay awake all night terrified. I had hardly seen anything of Mrs Vetorix. She rested or attended to her mail in the mornings and spent her afternoons driving around Parnell visiting her friends or taking tea in the pavilion at the Rose Gardens. At night, she turned into a thin shimmering figure in her evening clothes, dripping perfume through the hallway, eating tiny morsels of food in the dining room. I was being taught how to wait on table, instructed by Mrs Pink and Mrs Vetorix's maid, Mattie. Mrs Pink complained to Cook about the sheer unsuitability of this arrangement, Madam should hire a separate waitress. It was wrong for a maid and a skivvy to do this important work.

"Up until the incident with the book, I had only been in close proximity to Mrs Vetorix at dinner. I still can't believe how unnecessarily complicated it was. It took over an hour to serve that meal. And Mrs Vetorix was alone more often than not. Dr Vetorix was often at the University, and they seldom had guests. The two children never dined with their parents. A long table, set with the best china and silver and crystal, a side-board covered with dishes and accompaniments to the meal. A nightmare of protocol and rules. This fork for that dish, this glass for that wine. Candles, long silences, wasted food. She ate tiny portions of each dish. Course after course would be served, tasted, whisked away. I wondered what it would be like to eat under the constant observation of servants. Mrs Pink would discuss each meal with Cook; she seemed to enjoy *that*, she hardly touched *this*, better not serve that again, her nose wrinkled a little when she sniffed it.

"Mrs Vetorix had her own office upstairs. Next morning, Mrs

Pink took me to the door, knocked once and pushed me in, then walked briskly away down the hall. Mrs Vetorix was sitting in her armchair, reading.

"To my horror, she was reading *Maori and Settler*. She closed the book and asked me to sit down. She seemed ill at ease and nervous. Mrs Pink said you were reading this, she said. I admitted that this was true. Well, she said, it is good that you enjoy reading. It will help you to make your way in the world.

"I was excited to hear her say this. But then she said, be careful to choose the correct books. This book is most unsuitable for young girls, it is about war and savages in the raw days of this colony and will overstimulate your imagination.

"She then went to her cabinet and chose a book and handed it to me. I forget the title, something about the Upper Sixth at some school or other. The girls had names like Lettice and Monica and were vicious and stupid. I tried to read it, but I couldn't finish it. I didn't dare tell her so of course. And from that day, she gave me a book every week, and she asked me questions about them, so I had to read them. It became a weekly ritual in her room, the handing over of the book from last week, the giving of the next one. They were all the same. The bad girls, the cheats, the tattle-tales were always fat or had pimples or were scholarship girls. The good girls came from titled families and were beautiful and clever.

"It was like being brainwashed. I had swapped the wonderful books of *Emain* for this sort of puerile nonsense. But I coped by playing my memory bead game. I put my compulsory reading into the blue bead, the fear bead, burnt porridge, cold corridors, weeping for lost mothers. Then it swelled, became too full. So I created a new place, the burnt umber bead, the place where I torture bad books to death.

"Two years passed in this fashion. Endless days of crushed lemon verbena and lavender polish and cold looks from Mrs Pink. Each day I lived for the moment when my work was finished and I could close myself into the windowless room beneath the stairs. It was the only privacy I had. Every moment of the day I was with the other servants, listening to the same boring stories over and over until I thought I would go mad. Mrs Pink was the worst. She was a malicious gossip and delighted in telling tales of other people's misfortunes. She told these stories as cautionary tales, the perilous journey that one embarks upon if one does not tread the path of control and godliness. Pregnancy and sexual activity outside the state of holy matrimony were her favourite topics. She never spoke directly about such things. Instead she used a sort of coded speech spoken in a hushed, almost reverential tone, that took me a while to understand. Women could fall, wicked things happened on the other side of the blanket, there could be a nigger in the woodpile, a viper in the nest, a little stranger on the way. And threaded through her speech, a fear of men and the evil they could do and a hatred of women for allowing them to do it.

"Throughout my daily work as a domestic servant and an unwilling listener to Mrs Pink's tales, I centred my being on my room and all that it held. Those sweet hours alone with my simple possessions. Two calico nightgowns, dried flowers, a hairbrush, Emily's letters.

"Mrs Pink asked Mrs Vetorix for permission to check my mail so that they could make sure that I was not being led astray. Luckily for me, Mrs Vetorix refused to allow this on the grounds that the privacy of personal mail was sacrosanct. So when the letter came from Emily telling me that she was coming for me, I was able to keep this disturbing news to myself. I hated this place but I was afraid of going out into the city without money or a roof over my head. At least I was fed here, at least I had a bed to sleep in. I decided to make the final decision when I saw her. Maybe she had already worked out where to go and what to do.

"Two nights after receiving the letter, she came. Not in secret, but boldly, ringing the front door bell as if she was a guest arriving at the house. She refused to speak to Mrs Pink. She demanded to see Mrs Vetorix.

"I was in the kitchen washing dishes. Mrs Pink swept in and ordered me to go to Mrs Vetorix immediately. A young woman claiming to be my cousin had arrived and was causing a commotion. I already knew that it was Emily because I had heard her voice in the hallway asking for me. I pretended to know nothing, and followed Mrs Pink up the stairs into Mrs Vetorix's room.

"The joy of seeing Emily after two years almost swept me away but I held myself together tightly. I observed her from the corner of my eye. She looked a lot older, thinner, but very attractive. She was wearing makeup and a fashionable camel-hair coat with double lapels and a tie belt. I did not hug her or show my joy. I knew that my behaviour in the next few minutes was critical to Emily's plan. She was in full flight, telling the most incredible lies so convincingly that I almost began to believe in them myself.

"She told Mrs Vetorix that we were long lost cousins, poor orphan girls, and that she brought wonderful news. A relation has been found, yes right here in Auckland, an aunt, most respectable. I have prayed and prayed that she was still alive, yes indeed God does move in mysterious ways. Aunt Beatrice insists on seeing Alice at once, she wants her to stay with her tonight, if she can be spared. I left Auntie in tears, she never thought to see her poor sister Elva's child again. Or me, the only child of her dear young brother.

"In twenty minutes we were in a taxi, speeding away from Parnell. Emily pulled out a mirror and fluffed out her hair and applied more makeup, then lit a cigarette and blew out a jet of smoke through bright red lips. That Mrs Pink is a right cow, she said. If they ever find out where we are, they'll have to crawl over my dead body to get to you.

"I had packed my few possessions as if I was staying away for one night. Emily had found a job as a maid in a boarding house in Freeman's Bay. My first sight of the street was a shock. Unpainted wooden houses and sagging corrugated iron fences and muddy footpaths. The houses were very close together and I could hear people coughing and arguing and drunken voices singing obscene songs.

"That first night we didn't go to sleep. Emily told me everything that had happened to her in the last two years. The farm where she worked was in the Waikato near a coal mining village called Glen Massey. And although the work had been hard, she had been treated quite well. They were decent people, especially the wife,

Mrs Angus. Emily had left with their blessing and a good reference. Hence the job here in the big smoke, she said. Good money and somewhere to live. I promised that I would come and get you Alice and here we are. Fancy free to do what we like.

"I was still a little nervous and I told her so. She put her arms around me and held me and kissed me on the face. She told me that my troubles were over, she would never let anything bad happen to me."

I stop talking into the tape recorder. I can smell the scent of Emily's hair and the brush of her soft lips against my skin. My words have conjured up her physical presence so strongly that I almost believe that my body has entered the place where I hold her memory, the green bead, a place of trees and friendship and a sealed sarcophagus with a door that I have never dared to open until now. Wendy asks me if I want to go on. I tell her that I am travelling to a place that I left over fifty-five years ago and that I am afraid.

I suggest that we take a short break and drink more tea and she agrees.

"Please don't feel obliged to tell me everything," she says. "There is no need. Your life will be just one chapter amongst all the other lives."

"I don't want this part to go into the book but I need to tell my daughter Joy about Emily and I think it might be easier if we sat down with her and listened to the story on the tape."

"We?"

"I want you to be with us. If you can spare the time."

She is reluctant at first but agrees after I promise to tell Joy in advance that Wendy will be there too. "Anyway, I want Joy to meet you, otherwise she won't believe me about the tapes and the book and the fifty-dollar notes. She keeps asking me where I'm getting the extra money from."

We drink our tea and I eat two chocolate biscuits. It is almost lunchtime and my stomach is empty.

"The farm next to the place where Emily worked was owned by a widow with three sons and a daughter. Her husband had been killed in a tractor accident some years before. Emily and the daughter

Sally became friends. I am telling you this because Emily's friendship with Sally led directly to my marriage. Here is what happened. Sally got married very young to a man called Denby Winter and after honeymooning in Auckland, they moved to Te Kauwhata. By this time, we had left the Freeman's Bay boarding house under a cloud. The woman who ran the house had a drunken husband and he wouldn't leave Emily alone. Whenever his wife was out of the house, he would grab Emily's breasts or pinch her bottom or try to plant a slobbery kiss on her mouth. At night, he would push suggestive notes under the door of our room. When she rejected him, he accused her of being a pervert. He told lies about us to his wife and she believed him. She turned us out on the street. Emily was furious. She went back and knocked on the front door because she had left her cake of soap in the bathroom. She said that she was buggered if she was going to leave that old cow anything that she'd paid out good money for. She was greeted by a bucket of cold water thrown into her face. I was appalled. But Emily shook herself like a wet dog and calmly lit a cigarette. Then she tossed it through the billowing lace curtains hanging at the sash window and yelled out to me, run for it Alice run for it!

"And we ran along the street clutching our few possessions, Emily shrieking and laughing like a hyena, and me calling out wait for me wait for me.

"By nightfall, the resourceful Emily had found us a new place to live, a beautiful big house in Market Road, white with a grey slate roof, pillars carved like Greek columns and a garden full of flowers. Summer was just beginning and there were rows and rows of old-fashioned pink and red roses standing in beds of forget-me-nots and alyssum. The air was flooded with the sweet perfume of flowers. We walked up the pathway that lead to the imposing verandah at the front of the house. Emily had already phoned to say that we were coming. Mrs James, the housekeeper, came to the door and gave us both a job on the spot. This time, Emily passed us off as sisters which meant that she changed her name to mine. Miss Emily and Miss Alice Smallacomb, just arrived from Home, yes of course we have character references. She pulled a large brown envelope from her valise and handed Mrs James a roll of letters written on heavy yellow paper and tied up with pink ribbon.

"Mrs James was very impressed, especially with the character reference from Sir Nigel Warrington, a famous London barrister. Emily's cheek took my breath away. She had taken the name of my father and given him a knighthood. It took all my control not to burst out laughing.

"Mrs James led us to our rooms on the top floor and asked us to be ready for work at seven o'clock the next morning. This time, my room was on the top of the house and it reminded me a little of *Emain,* with the slanted roof and tiny dormer window. Emily couldn't believe that we had a room each. She danced around her tiny space saying thank you Sir Nigel, you're a brick, a pal, a scholar and a gentleman, until I laughed so much that the tears poured down my face.

"It was a wonderful job and I stayed there until I married Jack Winter. The boarders were respectable working men unlike that terrible place in Freeman's Bay. Mr Gilbraith, the owner, was a widower and Mrs James the housekeeper was his de facto wife. Not that she ever admitted it of course. They pretended to have separate bedrooms but we knew better. Emily liked them both, they were kind and generous and treated us well. And we gave them value for money, we worked hard for them and took pride in our work. At last, at last, said Emily. I have brought you to a place where you can be safe.

"After we had been there for about three months, Emily unexpectedly met up with her friend Sally again. One day in late January, a newly-wed couple arrived to stay for a week in one of the bed and breakfast rooms that were set aside for casual clients. They were standing in the entry hall, shy and young, clutching a worn leather suitcase. Emily let out a shriek and dropped her feather duster over the banister. So you did it! she yelled. You got away, oh you little beauty! Alice, Alice, come quick, it's Sally from Glen Massey.

"Sally and Emily hugged each other and cried. Denby, the husband just stood there looking embarrassed. Sally said oh Emily I wanted you to be a bridesmaid at my wedding but I couldn't find you. I swear I tried everything, Mrs Angus tried, we all did. You just vanished into thin air. And here you are, in this place, it's a miracle.

"Emily finally paid some attention to Denby and shook his hand and said congratulations, how wonderful, you are both so lucky. Later she told me the story of Sally's life and how her three brothers had used her as a slave on the farm. She had to do all the cooking and cleaning and washing and ironing, an enormous job for a young girl especially in those days when there were no washing machines or fridges or electric stoves. Apparently, the mother always sided with the brothers and Sally hated her. They had forced her to leave school when she was fourteen.

"Stanley, the eldest brother was very cruel. Once he shot a dog that Sally loved. For no reason other than it was pining for Sally's dead father. Or so he claimed. He tied the dog to the tank stand and shot it in the heart. Where Sally could hear the whimpers. Stanley tried to break Sally and Denby apart but Sally tricked him and her mother into agreeing to the marriage even though they were both only eighteen. There was a suggestion of a possible pregnancy and the papers were signed in haste. The joke is that it took Sally and Denby seventeen years to have their first baby, my niece Isobel."

Thump! Wendy has dropped the microphone. She looks upset. I ask her what the matter is. She doesn't answer. I try again, "Are you unwell?" She shakes her head but I am not convinced. She is very pale and her eyes are watering. Is she about to weep? Perhaps I moved her with these glimpses of how it was to be a woman in the 1930s. Perhaps she is shocked at the dishonesty. I must make it clear to her that subterfuge was our only refuge in a world that made life and death judgements over the fate of a woman according to the current status of her chastity. I don't want people who read her book to get the wrong impression.

"Shall I continue?" I ask.

She nods. "Please excuse me, I must be coming down with something."

"Emily told me that Denby was quite put out when he found her working at the Gilbraith Boarding House. He thought that

Sally would pay more attention to Emily than to him. This did happen a little but Sally was clever. She would stop talking to Emily when Denby came into the sitting room and turn her attention exclusively to her husband. The truth is that even though she had used him to get away from her horrible life on the farm, she really loved him. Denby was a decent man. She fell on her feet by marrying him, we all agreed on that. Even though Denby's family were initially against the marriage on the grounds that he was too young, they grew to appreciate her. And when I became her sister-in-law, we liked each other well enough, at least in the beginning.

"I didn't meet Denby's brother Jack until a few months later. By this time, Sally and Denby had set up house at Te Kauwhata. They had come to Auckland to visit Denby's parents. Emily and I were invited to Sunday dinner at Mr and Mrs Winter's house in Mt Eden. It was unusual for us to go to a private house as invited guests. Remember that we were English girls, servants, working-class, and say what you will, equality between the classes did not exist then any more than it does today. It was made loud and clear to us by the locals that we were not quite as good as those who had been born here. We were not real New Zealanders. And we had only to open our mouths for the English expatriates to put us firmly in our place at the bottom of the heap. We were not accepted by either group. I've always thought it clever that upper and lower classes had different words and sounds coming from their throats. Instant recognition. No need to ask your address or how much you earn or your occupation. Just listen to the voices and decide, are they high or low?"

Wendy interrupts me. "Sorry for breaking your flow but I am intrigued to hear you say this. You have no trace of an English accent. Did you deliberately cultivate your voice?"

"Yes, both Emily and I practised a new way of speaking. We wanted to fit into New Zealand, we became sick and tired of being called names. People said they were only joking but it hurt all the same."

"I can imagine."

"Anyway, off we went to the house of Denby's parents. We were both nervous but Emily covered up her uncertainty in her usual fashion, cracking jokes, saying funny things. The life and soul of the party, that's how she liked to be. I was relieved to find the Winters to be ordinary people and their house modest. Mrs Winter was very friendly but Mr Winter hardly uttered a word. Emily spoke more and more loudly, almost to the point of desperation, trying to make him smile. She failed.

"He was a tram driver and had to go off to work even though it was a Sunday. Once he had left, wearing his uniform and carrying a beer bag, Mrs Winter visibly relaxed. Don't mind Father, she said. He's a good man but embittered, the Depression you know. Those terrible work camps. Something got took from him. He was never the same when he came back, the pine seedlings and the bitter frosts and the holes that he dug and filled, dug and filled. He can't get to grips with having a job again, he keeps thinking some bugger will take it off him.

"I liked Mrs Winter right from the first day. She was a plain speaker and I always knew exactly where I was with her. She asked me to help her wash up the dishes in the kitchen, leaving Sally and Emily gossiping in the sitting room. Mrs Winter got straight to the point. I can see her now, one red hand clutching the soap-shaker, moving it vigorously from side to side beneath the hot water, tiny bubbles of Sunlight rising around her face while she virtually offered her son Jack to me. Looking for a wife she said, oh make no mistake, a good man, just very shy. But busting to get married. I admit that I asked both you girls here for Jack to have a sticky beak but the silly bugger ran off at the last minute. Not a chronic melancholic like poor Father, just shyness, you have my word. Of course, now that I have met you, I can see that Emily wouldn't be right for Jack. Don't get me wrong, she is very lovely with her pretty hair and dainty shoes, but too much spirit. She would terrify him, he would run a mile, I know it. Now tell me dear, are you thinking of getting married?

"I was struck dumb. Of course I had thought of falling in love and maybe getting married. Emily and I spent hours talking about love and marriage. And sex. This was unusual in the thirties. There was a conspiracy of silence that operated at all levels, even between girls who were best friends. Ignorance was meant to keep us safe. Girls must not talk or even think about sex. But the hateful innuendoes of Mrs Pink had left me with horrible feelings of shame and disgust. So until Emily rescued me, I was terrified at the thought of a man entering my body and I swore that I would never allow anyone to touch me.

"I was very lucky to have Emily as my friend. She told me everything about it. Incredible though it may seem, she'd done it with four different men, gone the whole way, and she said it was incred-ible, abso-lut-ely-su-per, heaven-ly. I asked her many questions but she never tired of talking about it. Think of a sunburst Alice, the hottest day of summer, a bolt of white-hot gold. In you, right up inside. She said I should practise on myself to warm my body up for the big moment. I had to ask her what she meant. She laughed at me, went into hysterics. Oh Alice, she shrieked, you don't know nothing, just as well I am here to take you in hand.

"And she did, she showed me, she did it to herself right in front of me. She lay on my bed and put her hand underneath her floral dress. I could see her hand moving up and down on the top of her white bloomers. I became scared towards the end, I thought she was dying. Her face went bright pink and she shouted out, now! now! She laughed at the look on my face, see how easy it is? You don't have to wait for a fella to come along, you have a little magic button there, you can make it work all by yourself, anywhere, anytime.

"That night, in the darkness, I did it to myself. And although I had been brainwashed about carnal sin at the orphanage, I was so ignorant about the meaning of it that I had never learned to associate sin with pleasure. Sin was always evil, it was a dark thing, death and blood and burning. What I experienced was far removed from these descriptions. So I felt no guilt, no shame. Just absolute wonder that the abandoned body of Alice Smallacomb could perform this small miracle. I entered into my body, I inhabited myself, I walked through a gateway of delight into my first home.

"So when Mrs Winter said these surprising things to me about marriage, I had already lost my fears about what used to be coyly referred to as the physical side of marriage. I already knew what it felt like to have sex with a man or so I thought. I smiled at her and said of course I wanted to marry and have a home and children. But I was too young to make these decisions and besides, I was enjoying my life with Emily at the Gilbraith Boarding House. I wasn't looking for a change.

"Just then Jack came into the kitchen. He mumbled something or other and took a glass of water from the tap. I gave him a good looking over. I thought him quite handsome by the rules of the day. Shiny black hair slicked back from his forehead, good skin, not too short. He wore a Fair Isle pullover and baggy grey pants with brown braces. Mrs Winter introduced us. He didn't meet my eyes, he grasped at my right hand, seized it, desperately tried to shake it, then rushed from the kitchen spilling drops of water from his agitated glass.

"No I didn't fall in love then and there. I felt neutral, disinterested almost. So I was surprised when he telephoned me the following week and asked me to a dance. I could hear Mrs Winter in the background egging him on. And I remembered Emily's words, go out with him if he calls, you have to start somewhere. So I went with Jack Winter to a dance. It was a social organised by the place where he worked. Jack was in the printing trades all his life, he was a compositor and a linotype operator. At the time that we first started going out together, he was working for a firm in Dominion Road who did printing jobs for small newspapers and other organisations. Political pamphlets, advertising sheets, that sort of thing.

"For the next two years we went out once a week. It became a fixed routine every Saturday night. Dances, socials, films, dinners at his parents' house, or just walking around the leafy streets of Mt Eden on warm summer nights. He said he loved me, he wanted us to marry, but I didn't feel the same. I enjoyed kissing him but that's all I let him do. He was a good man, he never pressured me to give him more but I could see that he was suffering.

"Emily had a steady boyfriend too. His name was Harry. I never liked him much, I thought him rather bossy. He used to order her around, get me a cup of tea woman, that sort of thing. The funny thing was that she seemed to enjoy it. She changed a lot in those two years. She became more subdued, sombre almost. At the beginning we went out in a group. Jack and I sometimes met up with her crowd at a hotel or at Harry's house in Grey's Avenue. Harry ran with a fast crowd, drinking, smoking, gambling at the races. Jack thought some of the people there were shady, petty criminals, and after a time, we didn't visit that house together again.

"One night, a cold wet Saturday in the middle of winter, I went to the house in Grey's Avenue with Emily. Jack had a bad cold and was in bed at home being tended by his mother. She had phoned to let me know that Jack couldn't come to get me from Market Road and take me to the pictures as arranged. She took the opportunity to ask me directly if Jack had popped the question yet. I confessed that he had asked me to marry him but I had not yet made up my mind. Soon, soon, I would do so. She seemed satisfied with this and told me not to hurry into a decision, I was still very young and should enjoy my freedom while it lasted. She told me that Jack is a new boy since he met me, a laughing whistling boy, a pleasure to have around the house. You have given him a reason for living Alice, and I am eternally grateful to you.

"I felt disturbed by her words. It was not the first time that she had spoken to me in this fashion, and each time that she did, I felt the cage door beginning to close. She had been caring and thoughtful to me, she asked me about my feelings and my ideas, she told me that she had always wanted a daughter. She sewed me lovely cotton dresses and cooked wonderful meals when I went to their house. But I was made anxious by her love for me, I felt as if I had been taken hostage by her goodness.

"When I imagined spending the rest of my life with Jack in some mean little wooden house, and him coming and going from work with his black apron and his lunch box prepared by me, day in, day out, and me walking around rooms staring at myself in mirrors and peeling potatoes and frying chops, night in, night out, waiting for him to come home for his tea at six o'clock, I felt a sense of despair. But try as I might, I couldn't think of any other way to live. I had the most basic education, I couldn't type or do book-keeping, I hated the idea of going into a factory, all I knew was domestic work. Sometimes I was swept with a deep longing for my own house, my own possessions, dishes, curtains, teapots, a garden with beds of marigolds and snapdragons and a guava tree laden with small sharp fruits. But in my fantasy, I lived alone. I could never place Jack in this imaginary home. Sometimes Emily would drift through the smoked-glass door, or Miss Catley carrying a basket of herbs and sweet scones would call from the front gate, Al-ice, Al-ice, are you there?

"I'm telling you this because I want you and Joy to know that if nothing had happened to me that night when Emily and I went to Harry's house, I would probably still have married Jack in spite of my imaginary life of independence. I could never have hurt him or his mother after all their kindness to me.

"We got to the house in Grey's Avenue after dark. Harry was sitting at a table covered with green baize playing poker with some of his friends. There was a radio in the corner playing the popular music of the day. I felt quite adventurous and smoked my first cigarette and sipped a glass of gin that Emily got for me from the kitchen. I enjoyed myself for a while until I noticed that Emily was getting drunk. She knocked back glass after glass of gin and lit one cigarette after another.

"The men ignored us except for Harry ordering Emily to bring some more beer in from the washhouse. I went outside with her. It was raining heavily by now and the pepper tree beside the wash-house dropped wet black seeds on our heads. Emily was staggering in her high-heeled shoes and almost slipped on the broken concrete path that led to the washhouse door. She sat for a while on an up-turned beer box beside the copper and lit another cigarette. I suggested that she had had enough gin for the night. She smiled at me and patted my face. Don't worry little sister, I know what I'm doing.

"An hour later she passed out cold on the sitting room floor. Harry got up from the table and carried her to the sofa and put a filthy grey blanket over her. It stank of beer and vomit. I wanted to call a taxi and take her back to Market Road but Harry wouldn't hear of it. She stays put for the night. You too. I will bring the stretcher through for you to sleep on.

"But I felt afraid. The mood of the card players had changed. They were quarrelling over money that Harry owed one of them. A small man with glittering eyes began to shout at Harry, calling him a tricky bastard, a bludger and a piker. Harry suddenly lost his temper and hit the small man right in the mouth. Blood spurted over the card table and he fell backwards onto the floor. Then everybody started hitting everyone else. Windows shattered, chairs were smashed, the radio was pulled from the wall in a shower of sparks. I was terrified. I cowered behind the sofa where Emily lay unconscious. I wanted to run out into the night but I was reluctant to leave her there. Suddenly the little man that Harry had hit in the mouth was at my side pulling at my arms and shouting, quick quick, someone's called the police, we must get out. Come with me if you don't want to get arrested.

"I panicked and ran out into the back yard with this stranger. He held my arm and led me to a car parked in a narrow lane that ran parallel to Grey's Avenue. I got into the car and he drove off at great speed. Almost at once I knew that I had made a hideous mistake. He started saying suggestive things to me and I knew that he had no intention of driving me back to Market Road. I sat very still, looking straight ahead, determined not to speak one word to him. He asked me what my bra size was and the colour of my panties. He knew that I had a boyfriend, Harry had told him. Did I know what Harry calls me behind my back? Cock teaser, and after tonight, I can see that's exactly what you are. Cock teasing, in that tight yellow dress, and once when you bent over that drunken slut on the sofa I saw the tops of your legs. You wanted me to see right up to your pussy, I know that you did, this is what a teaser bitch does.

"I tried to keep calm. I planned to wait until he stopped the car and then open the door and run for my life. I quietly slipped off my high-heeled shoes. I kept telling myself, he is smaller than I am, I can run from him or fight him, I can do it.

"He drove to a secluded reserve next to a beach somewhere. I could hear the rain pounding into the sea and the noise of someone in a boat trying to start an outboard motor. Whirr! Whirr! I could hear the noise of the starter cord being pulled over and over again. I tried to scream but the man put his hand over my mouth and pinned me to the seat. Too late, I heard the motor splutter and catch and fade away into the distance.

"Although he was small he was very strong. I didn't have a chance. He pulled my panties down and raped me. I was terrified and in agony. Forgive me, but I must repeat the words that he said. I have a reason for this. I have never spoken them to anyone before and they have lived on within my head for over fifty years, searing me, corrupting me, each letter stabbing me again and again with dirty needles of sound. I want to place them outside myself, I want to lift them from my body and seal them into this tape where they will become defused and harmless.

"Oh you cunt he said you cock teasing cunt you whore you slut you devil cunt you stinking cunt you slime you giver of blue balls you juicy cunt you juicy slime cunt . . . admit you like it he said admit you like cock you whore say it say it say give me cock . . .

"He said these words directly into my ear in a low hateful voice. I feared for my life but I clamped my lips together and refused to say what he wanted. This drove him into a frenzy and after he had raped me, he began to punch me around the head and on my face. Say it, say it say it . . . he hissed.

"I transported myself somewhere else, I conjured up Emily's voice, laughing, telling tall stories. I heard her singing to me, calling to me, hold on Alice, hold on . . .

"At last he gave up and lay back exhausted. I took my chance and opened the car door and ran away as fast as I could. I crouched behind some thick flax bushes at the edge of the grass verge. The car did not drive away. I could see the lighted tip of his cigarette glowing through the curtain of rain. Then I heard him calling out for me through the open window, come back dear, I'll take you home, you'll catch your death out there, don't be a silly girl, no harm meant . . .

"Then he came out of the car and thrashed around in the shrubbery, hitting the trees and bushes with a stick as if he was trying to flush out a wild animal. After a few minutes, he gave up and drove away.

"I had no coat, I had no shoes. I was scared to walk out on the road in case he was waiting for me. I lay there until the dawn broke, not making a sound. The rainwater soaked right through my dress and cardigan into my deep flesh and provided an illusion of cleanliness. I opened myself to the rain, I wanted the water to run into the centre of my body, I was desperate to be clean again. But the words that he had spoken within my ear had burned themselves into my brain, round and round they spun, alive, menacing, so that I began to blame myself for what had happened, yes that dress was tight, yes I did bend over, yes I did get into the car of my own free will.

"When the sky lightened, I realised that I was at Judge's Bay near Parnell where I used to live. I walked all the way back to Market Road, praying that no one would see me. I knew that I could never tell anyone what had happened to me, not even Emily. The shame and guilt that I felt was indescribable. In those days, we were taught that anything sexual that happened between a man and a woman was always the woman's fault. Rape was thought to be impossible, you can't thread a moving needle, there's no no on your lips but yes yes in your eyes... and if violence occurred, then the woman must have displeased the man, turned him against her, slighted his manhood, or was just too unbearably sexual for him to be able to restrain himself.

"I crept into the house. The sense of relief when I reached my little room under the eaves was overpowering. Sanctuary. I started to take stock of my situation. I cannot go out with Jack again. He would hate me if he knew the truth. I could not bear to see the look of revulsion in his eyes. And I will never marry, so no one will ever find out that I am no longer pure.

"Meanwhile, I had to try to cover up my physical injuries. My face was the problem. I had a black eye and a swollen mouth. I was too scared to go down to the kitchen to get some ice to reduce the swelling so I used some of the cold water from my washbowl. I did not have to work as it was my Sunday off. Emily was meant to start work at ten o'clock and I prayed that she would be back in time so that Mrs James would not come looking for her in my room.

"Just before ten Emily knocked at my door. I called out to her, I'm resting but she said I must speak with you. I opened the door and hustled her inside. Jesus! she cried. Your face! Who did this to you?

"I got mixed up in the fight, I said. It looks worse than it is, don't panic.

"I should never have taken you there, those pigs, to hit a woman!

"Say nothing, I beg you, just forget it ever happened.

"I got drunk and left you unprotected. It's my fault, my fault!

"I calmed her down as best I could. She brought some arnica to heal my bruises and some pancake makeup to cover my black eye. By the next day, I looked almost normal. Mrs James must have noticed but she said nothing. After I had finished the dishes that night, I crept into the deserted hallway and rang Jack and told him bluntly that our friendship was over. There was a long silence at the other end of the phone. You've met another bloke, he said at last. No, no, nothing like that. Well then, he answered, there's still hope for us, otherwise I'm a dead man.

"I told him I wanted to be alone for a few weeks to sort my feelings out. He agreed. I hung up and walked away. Before I reached the bottom of the stairs the phone rang. It was Mrs Winter speaking in a whisper, asking what the hell was going on. Jack was lying on the kitchen floor weeping his guts out. Had he done something bad to me? If so, he would have to answer to his mother.

"I reassured her by telling her that I had to have time to think about my future. I promised to contact her in a few weeks.

"The next two months passed slowly. I felt completely changed by what had happened to me. I distanced myself from Emily. I hardly spoke to the boarders or to Mrs James. I performed my work more efficiently than before and I cleaned my room compulsively every night. I burned the clothes that I had been wearing when I was raped. The cardigan was wool and made a terrible smell. I parcelled up the ashes in a brown paper bag and went to Judge's Bay and walked along the sewer pipe that straddled the estuary. It was a windy moonless night, the seawater swelled black and oily beneath the pipe. I was not afraid to walk out alone. I thought, so what if it happens to me again, so what. I have nothing left to lose. The chant of bad words in my head hammered at me every waking hour. I almost wanted to bring them into physical reality, to prove once and for all that I was nothing but a teaser bitch on the prowl.

"I stood there for hours until the tide was out then threw the parcel of destroyed clothes over the side of the pipe. It sank out of sight beneath the surface of the quicksand, invading the pock-marked habitat of mud crabs. Ashes to ashes, filth to filth. I did not wait to see the tide sweep in and take it away.

"A few days after this event I had to face the fact that I was pregnant. I had known for weeks of course, but each time the thought had come into my mind, I had banished it hastily into the white bead of death. Displacement, denial, back to the realm of the impossible. But in spite of the mind games I played, my body clamoured for recognition. I showed almost at once, swollen breasts, brown marks on my face, a thin dark line running downwards from my navel. Burning the clothes was one of several cleansing rituals that I performed as I prepared myself for death.

"I am not being overly melodramatic. There was no possibility of an abortion. The very word conjured up images of criminals and under life and dirty knives wielded on kitchen tables and the humiliation of being caught and thrown into prison. Death was a kinder alternative. So I made my plans and waited for the right moment. Drowning was my chosen method. I had studied the news-papers so I knew that jumping from Grafton Bridge or swallowing poison or dying from a perforated womb were the traditional deaths that pregnant girls chose. But why suffer the fear of falling or the interior burns of poison or the plunge of the knitting needle? I wanted to float away gently, head down, eyes open, and flood my tainted body with that luminous green light that glimmers just beneath the surface of the sea.

"I bought a ticket for the Sunday night ferry to Waiheke Island. I planned to watch the lights of Auckland fade from view then slip quietly overboard from the lower deck. But on the last Saturday night, Emily changed everything. She insisted that we go to the pictures together, just us two, a girls' night out. I told her I couldn't go, I had to catch up with my mail. I had planned to write a letter to her that night to tell her how much I loved her and to ask her to write to Miss Catley at *Emain*.

"But Emily would not listen to me, and I did not want to make her suspicious. So off we went, walking down Market Road towards the railway station. When we got there it was deserted. Oh bum, said Emily, we've just missed a train. We'll have to wait for half an hour. It was a cold night and as we sat on the wooden seat on the platform, a thin bitter rain began to fall. Emily pulled her coat collar up around her neck. She smoked a cigarette without speaking then said, well there's no other way of saying this and it may as well be here as anywhere but I know that you are in trouble. We have to work out a plan, tonight, before we return.

"I burst into tears. I confessed that I had a plan, a final solution to my problem. I told her of the ferry ride, the green water, the fading lights. Emily was horrified; are you trying to kill me too? If you jump, I swear, I will jump with you. I will force you to watch me drown, I will fill my lungs with water before you do, I will hold your face in my hands, I will make you watch me die.

"Then she said, you are being ridiculous Alice, why should we die because of what Jack has done to you? We are going there right now, to confront, to make him marry you.

"I told her the truth, all of it; the car, the beach, the fight, the rain, the burning of the yellow dress and cardigan. Everything, except the identity of the rapist and the words that he had spoken.

"She went very quiet. Then she said, can you ever forgive me? I have been so stupid, I should have known. Listen, this is very important, you must tell me who it was, now, at once . . .

"I refused. Then she said, we must tell Jack, he has a right to know. He is watching the house, did you know that? Standing outside waiting for you to come out. Night after night, over by the cricket ground on the other side of Market Road. Mrs Winter is very worried. She feels that he is losing his mind.

"I pleaded with her not to tell Jack but she wouldn't listen. You have done nothing wrong Alice. Get that into your head once and for all. She insisted that we get into the next train and go as quickly as possible to the house at Mt Eden. By this stage I was numb, I had lost all sense of will. The sense of relief that she was taking charge of the situation was overwhelming. I would have gone with her to Timbuktu if she had suggested it.

"Jack was very pleased to see us. Mrs Winter went into a frenzy of welcome with fancy cups and saucers and slices of buttered tea-cake. After polite conversation and words of praise for Mrs Winter's baking, Emily announced that I had something important to say to Jack. For his ears only. Mrs Winter, looking distinctly nervous, ushered us outside to his sleep-out. From the window of his little shed, I could see her hovering anxiously inside the screen door.

"I told Jack everything. He held my hand and listened in silence. I had expected rage, disgust, anger, rejection. To my surprise, he said almost exactly what Emily had said. It was not your fault, you did everything you could. We will marry at once he said, there is nothing else to be done.

"I couldn't believe what I had just heard. I asked him about the baby. That is up to you, he said. If you want to give it away, then do so. If you want to keep it, I insist that you never tell anyone that I am not the father.

"I gave him my word. And except for one moment of weakness, I have kept the bargain that we made. He saved my life, and Joy's, not from a sense of heroic duty or because he wanted to possess me but because he loved me. And in that instant, I loved him too.

"We went inside and Jack gathered his mother and father and Emily together and announced our engagement. Mrs Winter was over the moon, she cried and hugged me. Emily grinned all over her face and Mr Winter shook his son's hand and poured sweet sherry into crystal glasses from the china cabinet to make a toast.

"The happy ending? Well here we are, Joy is fifty-five and I am seventy-five. Two women alone. A wonderful couple we make, me and Joy. She has never completely trusted me, she accuses me of inventing my life. I must make her see that my suffering is not imaginary or arbitrary and that there is meaning and reason in everything that I do. To be fair, I am probably to blame for her suspicious attitude because sometimes I change my stories. From necessity you understand. For survival.

"There was no happy ending for Emily. Remember, I told you that I had taken off my high-heeled shoes in the car so that I could run from my attacker. Somehow, they ended up back at Harry's house. Emily immediately recognised the shoes as the ones I had lost. She went over the line, pushed by a lethal mixture of grief and gin and white hot rage. She must have got it into her head that Harry was the man who raped me, because she attacked him, she beat him about the face with the heel of my shoe and it had a metal tip at the end and it entered his left eye and burst it open and he broke her neck. Self-defence they said, in his agony he struck out, and he was full of remorse, he had punishment enough they said, he must live with his pain and his partial loss of sight.

*"Emily Smallacomb, a drunken domestic, went berserk with a shoe and tried to batter an innocent man to death.* This was in the papers. I cut it out and hid it away where I could not see it. I did not want to constantly remind myself of my participation in her murder. Oh yes, I killed her too. I should have told her about the little man, I should have told her that he was the rapist, not Harry."

I stop speaking. To my surprise, Wendy puts her arms around me and tells me that I am a courageous woman. There are tears in her eyes. I submit to her embrace for a moment then walk over to the window and stare out at the heatwaves rising from the hot tarseal. I do not want her sympathy.

I enter the green bead, the place of trees and birdsong where I keep the memory of every word that Emily ever spoke, her tall stories, her fibs and fabulations. I break open the sealed sarcophagus and look inside. She is laughing at me . . . tell them your name Alice . . . say that you're sorry and very grateful for being here . . . cross your fingers behind your back, untell the lie . . .

I am not courageous, I am a coward. Emily was the brave one, she tried to exact revenge against the wrong person and died for her trouble. We both made a mistake and she paid for it with her life. If I had named the rapist, we could have put the lights out in both those glittering eyes, Emily the left, me the right, a kindly act done for his own good. So that he could never again be tempted by the sight of the bare flesh of a teaser bitch.

# 6

## *Isobel*

For weeks now, I've become increasingly uneasy at the mysterious work Wendy is doing. I have decided to talk to her over dinner tonight. She won't discuss it with me, except to say that it is strictly confidential, big time, dangerous. She knows that we are meant to share everything and that no topic of conversation is supposed to be forbidden, but this is different. Soon, she promised me, soon they will let me speak about it. Things are coming to a head.

They? I hope that Wendy hasn't let our urgent need for money persuade her to do something illegal. They made her sign an agreement to promise she would not tell anybody. She swore to me that it was all above board in terms of the law but a little dodgy on the ethical front. "Trust me Bel, trust me. Big money, good outcome. What could be better?" But it hurts me to think that Wendy doesn't have enough confidence in me to share information about her work. Since she set herself up as an independent social researcher two years ago, she has always talked to me about her various projects.

Stray unwanted thoughts are beginning to trickle sideways into my mind. Is she seeing someone else behind my back? A wealthy woman, who is showering her with money? I have never had these suspicions before. I can't bear it any longer. I have decided that whatever the consequences for our relationship, I will demand that she tells me what is going on.

Since we first met and fell in love, we have shared everything; the death of my father Denby, the drowning of my sister Julia, the breakdown of her mother. These events had happened within the time frame of eight months, soon after we met. I became afraid to answer the phone, I would not pick up the receiver until I knew that I was safe from another savage piece of news that I did not want to hear. So I bought an answer machine. My friends soon learned the rules. Ghostly voices would call from the machine, Isobel, Isobel, we know you're there, speak to me . . . and I would answer and listen to the latest gossip from the lesbian community and it was not always sweetness and light, but sometimes sad stories of jealousy and betrayal, poverty, bailiffs, family feuds.

But these are transient states, and therefore bearable. They can be resolved at any minute. A friend can be devastated by sexual jealousy one week, madly in love the next. Or unemployed, then suddenly flying to Wellington for a job interview.

But the fate of my sister can never be retrieved. I did not pick up the warning signs that she was losing her mind, I did not understand her retreat into silence. I performed a mourning cry when she died in my arms on that darkening beach, a small high noise in the back of my throat that built into a solid wall of sound that went on and on until the pulse of the sea faltered. There was a brief silence; the breakers stood still, birds froze on the cliff top, a grey gull fell from the sky.

In that terrible time, old certainties were carried away in a flood of grief. Rock solid ideas, carved in bone, written on white paper, burned in a red candle, thrown into the Waikato River. That day when the river seemed to be sulking, slow moving, reluctant to accept my burnt offerings, reluctant to offer the written proof of my guilt to the inquisitive eels and the pull of the distant coast.

On that foggy winter's day, Wendy stopped the car down by the rowing club and we walked gingerly across the soaked grass to the water's edge. "Tide's out," said Wendy. "Those bastards controlling the dams up river have sold us short."

I said under my breath, "I banish my guilt, leave me, leave me," and tossed the ashes into the water but they washed back onto the gravel in front of my feet almost immediately. Wendy said, "Pick them up and throw harder, and yell louder." I saw a group of speed walkers approaching us along the river path, hips thrusting awkwardly from side to side, breath heaving in and out, arms pumping. I waited until they had passed and then did what Wendy had suggested.

I shouted, I raged, and this time, the ashes were taken out into the centre by a series of small eddies and they rode away on the swift current.

Wendy said it was time to leave, too much had happened in this town, and although I loved living in the old farmhouse at Eureka, I agreed with her.

I know that the essay that Wendy and I had written for Julia's course was not the cause of her death but my fears of written language and the violence that words can do, live with me still. I have tried to confront my fears. Wendy suggested that I join a writing group and this has helped. I have discovered that many other women suffer from logophobia, the fear of words. It seems that we have collectively internalised a tradition that women do not have logical minds. This tradition claims that we find it hard to speak from clear evidence, that we shroud even the most banal fact in a fog of obfuscation and emotion, that we speak from the body rather than the mind.

I have learned from the women in my group that the body is a valid source of inspiration and that the barriers between abstract ideas and emotions must be broken down if we are not to go collectively insane.

I have surprised myself by beginning to write short stories. Somehow, with fiction, I am not so worried about the problem of multiple versions that stopped me from writing my doctoral thesis. Every sentence has the potential to be written in a hundred different ways. I acknowledged this intellectually but fell into the trap of always seeking the one truth, the one right way of speaking. Fiction has liberated me from this trap to some extent. And Wendy loves what I write. Now she is insisting that I try to get some of my work published. But I still fear making my work public. I don't want strangers looking within my head. Wendy is certain that I will get over this eventually. I hope she's right.

I wonder what I'll cook for tea. Nothing special, otherwise Wendy will think I'm trying to butter her up. She's very sensitive to what she calls head games between couples. Not that I can blame her after what she's been through with her family. I didn't meet her mother until after her father had run off with a young woman, his secretary. How Wendy raged! "The bastard is a walking cliché," she said. "He could have tried to be a bit more original." Her mother blamed the woman, called her "that little bitch". This, according to Wendy, is also a raging cliché in her mother's circles. The abandoned ones. So many of them have been left by their middle-aged husbands for younger women, who are all "bitches".

Wendy was not close to her mother before the marriage breakup. They fought over everything. Wendy's clothes, her relationship with me, swear words, food, friends, smoking dope, work, everything. Especially her wealthy father who had provided them with material comfort. Alas, no longer. He had cut Wendy's allowance completely and left her mother in relative poverty.

Wendy had always despised her father and had taken him for as much as she could. He had paid for her university education and bought her a red sports car. Through guilt, she claimed. "He doesn't give a shit about me, he's just trying to silence his conscience for neglecting me as a child." But her mother had always defended her husband. "He really loves you," she said. "I know he is difficult at times but he is your father, everything he does, he does for you."

This would drive Wendy crazy. I heard her scream over the phone more than once, "He does it for himself Mother, not for you, not for me!"

But after her mother was abandoned, the arguments ceased. It frightened Wendy to see Elizabeth descend into a nervous collapse. "She won't argue with me any more, she just asks me not to speak to her like that. She begs me! I can't bear it. Her whole identity is fucked, she's lost all her fight."

I tried to tell her that Elizabeth would get over it in time. But she didn't. Five years later, she is still thin and weepy and bitter. She lost her big house in Remuera, she lost her friends, her looks, her reason for living.

I find it difficult to feel sorry for Elizabeth. She lives in a town house in Ponsonby and has a small but adequate income. Compared with other married women who have been abandoned, she is quite well off. Besides, she is extremely judgemental of other women.

She claims that women who have never had children don't know the meaning of stress. Once I mentioned in her hearing that I was worried about my niece Kezia, the daughter of my dead sister. She turned on me. "You have no right to give your opinion. You can never understand what it's like."

I was speechless. She went on, "I loved Wendy so much when she was tiny, and she loved me. She was so beautiful and so good. Why did she ever have to grow up?"

This made me angry. It is obvious that she blames me for Wendy turning out to be a dyke. I have asked Wendy to speak to her about it, to tell her the truth. Wendy was always a dyke, from her first love affair at sixteen. She was twenty-four when we met and I was thirty-five. Hardly the immature girls of Elizabeth's fantasy. It's peculiar. She expounds her absurd theories about lesbians to our face, as if we were not lovers. She is either incredibly ignorant or incredibly rude. Once Wendy would have fought fiercely with her. Now she just changes the subject, talks to her about art and films, while I seethe in silence.

I always welcome Elizabeth to our house for Wendy's sake, but her misery rubs off on me. Whenever she appears unexpectedly at the front door, smelling of cigarette smoke and perfume, my heart sinks. She has formed the habit of turning up on foot just before meal times. Wendy thinks it's great that her mother gets a good vegetarian dinner at our house. "She's got so thin Bel, it's the least we can do for her." I hope she doesn't turn up tonight, when I have my talk with Wendy.

I hear someone coming up the verandah steps. I should stop thinking about Elizabeth, I might conjure her up in the flesh. But it's not her, it's Wendy. I hear her key turn in the lock and the thump of her briefcase on the hall table. She's early. Six o'clock she'd told me, a long busy day, collating all the information she has gathered for her research so far.

She walks into the kitchen and stares at me without speaking. I can see that she is very upset. I say nothing until she has taken off her sandals and her long white dress and changed into a loose t-shirt and shorts. I make a jug of fruit juice with oranges and ice and fresh hyssop leaves. The air is hot and stale in the kitchen so I suggest we sit on the back verandah. Once we are settled, I open my mouth to ask her why she looks so upset but she gets in first. "Don't hassle me Bel . . . give me a minute, let me think."

I drink a glass of orange juice and wait.

Then she says, "Promise you'll forgive me, promise . . . "

So there is someone else! I don't want to hear this.

"Let me tell you from the beginning to the end," she continues. "Don't interrupt, I already know what your reaction will be."

"How can you say that!" My fear turns to anger. "You can't read my mind!"

She looks into my eyes, "Oh Bel, you weren't thinking that about me."

"What?"

"You think I've been fucking around! Say sorry, for doubting me."

Although I am relieved that she is not seeing anyone else, I still feel annoyed. How come it's me having to apologise? "For god's sake Wendy, stop messing me about and tell me what the hell is going on."

"I swear I didn't know until today who she was, I swear it."

"Who?"

"Your father's relation, Alice. I knew her surname was the same as yours but I didn't think anything of it."

"What the hell has she got to do with it?"

Wendy bursts into tears. "Please don't be angry with me Bel, I feel bad enough as it is."

I hold her in my arms and listen in silence as she tells me about the oral histories she has been taking from Alice Winter, the widow of my uncle Jack. He was my father's only brother and had died many years ago. Apart from the odd comment from my mother Sally, I had heard little news since then of Alice or my cousins Maurice and Joy.

It seems that Wendy is being paid big money from a woman called Marlene Hunter to conduct a series of oral histories from elderly women who had migrated here from Britain in the twenties and thirties. Wendy had had her doubts right from the start. The money being paid to Alice was far too much to recoup from publishing a book of this nature. And Marlene Hunter had said a few things to Wendy that had made her suspicious of the enterprise. Something about Alice being the most important woman to record. For more reasons than one. Wendy was surprised too at the insistence on absolute confidentiality. She was not allowed to discuss any aspect of the research with anyone, not even the participants. The name of the publisher did not appear on any letter and she was forbidden to reveal the source of the cash that Alice received. Marlene Hunter had quoted commercial sensitivity but Wendy had thought this a weak excuse.

Wendy has stopped crying now. I am still holding her, but my arms are getting cramped. The sofa on the back verandah has a short back and saggy cushions and I am almost six feet tall. Christobel, our cat, has jumped onto my lap and I know that if I make a sudden move, she will scratch my bare knees with her sharp claws.

Wendy is in full flight now, raving against her employer, threatening to go into debt to return everything she had earned over the last few weeks. "Imagine how I felt today, when to cap it all, Marlene Hunter drops it on me that the tapes I have made with Alice are probably not going to be used for the book after all. Publication is very much up in the air. But she wants me to continue doing the interviews with Alice. She wants me to find out everything I can about Alice's descendants. All the work I've done to find old women who are prepared to tell their life stories has been a bloody waste of fucking time. It was only Alice she was after, Alice and her daughter Joy."

I am mystified. "What the hell for?"

"I don't know yet but I feel like telling her straight that unless she tells me the truth, I'm going to resign. It will ruin me as a researcher if it gets out that I have tricked an old woman. Imagine how I felt this morning when Alice started to tell me about her husband and where she met him and all about his family and I realised that this Jack Winter was your father's brother. I nearly died."

"Just calm down," I tell her. "Is there any real harm done?"

"I should have realised that the economics were up the shit. I was instructed to pay Alice five hundred dollars every time she did a tape for me. It would make the book impossibly expensive if all the story tellers were paid like this. God, I'm so naive, I should have questioned why Marlene Hunter was hiring me for this expensive work when I am still a beginner."

Five hundred dollars! I can't believe this amount of money.

"The money persuaded Alice to tell me her life history. I don't think she would have agreed otherwise. Of course I promised her that nothing would be published without her permission. Now I'm wondering if there is going to be a book at all."

I am intrigued. I persuade Wendy to stay in the project so that we can find out what this woman Marlene Hunter is up to. She looks relieved. "I thought you'd be angry with me."

"You should have told me everything from the beginning. I let my imagination run away with me."

"So you think I should keep making the tapes?"

"Why not? If you back out now, we'll never know what is going on."

Wendy sits up and pours herself another fruit juice. "When Marlene told me that she didn't want me to interview any of the other elderly women that I had selected, I thought it was her way of giving me the boot. But then she said that the tapes I had made with Alice were exactly what she wanted."

I smile at her. "Well at least you did something right. Are you hungry?"

"Starved. What's for dinner?"

"Aubergine and couscous."

"Yum."

"I think you should tell Alice that you live with me. If she finds out later, she might feel embarrassed or tricked."

"You mean come out to her?"

I tell her to make her own decisions about what she says. She knows the situation with Alice better than I do. The truth is that I would love to hear the tapes, especially the bits about my parents, but I know that Wendy would never agree.

"I'd like to come clean, tell her everything," says Wendy. "Especially about Marlene Hunter and the elusive book but I think she'll be quite disappointed if she finds out that her life story isn't going to be published. She told me that she wants to put the record straight."

I can hear someone banging the iron door-knocker on the front door. Wendy looks at me. "Elizabeth?"

"Go and see," I answer.

Wendy grins at me, "Don't look at me in that tone of voice!"

She goes back into the house and sure enough, I soon hear Elizabeth's high heels clacking along the polished wooden floor of the hall and her pseudo BBC accent penetrating through the kitchen walls. "Darling, I know I'm being a frightful nuisance, but I've had a terrible day."

Wendy appears again. Her face is a picture. I don't know whether she's about to cry or laugh. She hisses at me, "Keep quiet about this or I'll murder you."

"What's going on?"

"Ssshhh, keep your voice down." She pulls my head down so that she can whisper into my ear. "She's bloody well gone and fallen in love."

"You're fucking joking!"

"I wish I was."

"Who with?"

"Some jerk that sounds just like my father."

I can hear Elizabeth flushing the toilet. "So why did she have a terrible day?"

"He didn't bloody ring her or something."

The absurdity of the situation strikes us both simultaneously. Wendy says, "I sound as if I'm talking about a teenage daughter!"

Then Elizabeth appears at the back door looking more raddled and miserable than ever, and I am surprised by the wave of compassion that engulfs me for her and all the other abandoned women who played the marriage game. Elizabeth cooked and cleaned, primped and preened, she did it all. And still her husband left her for another woman. She is trying again, to have a lover, someone to love her. And now, right at the beginning of the affair, she turns up here, bewildered and hurt at her failure to hold a man to a promise of a phone call.

"I'm glad you've come Elizabeth," I say. "I'm cooking a special recipe for dinner, aubergines with manuka honey and balsamic vinegar. Have you ever tried it?"

I prepare the meal. The glazed aubergine, dark purple, glistening, lies in a bed of yellow couscous, and it tastes wonderful. I light candles and pour white wine and talk to Elizabeth about the alterations we plan to make to the house. For the first time, I am making an effort to be pleasant to her.

And she responds. She eats a big meal and refrains from lighting a cigarette until coffee is served. She seems almost cheerful. I make a resolution that I will be more friendly to her in future. I ask her to come for dinner tomorrow night, if she's free. She accepts. But only if she's free. That phone call may come later tonight.

# 7

## *Joy*

It is raining heavily and the drive over the deviation is slow and dangerous. A man driving a rusty ute has been riding close to my back bumper for miles. I can see his scowling face in my rear-vision mirror. He tries to overtake me at the top of the passing lane and for a few frightening seconds, I am sure that he is going to hit me and push me through the barbed-wire fence and over the steep cliff. At the last moment he pulls back and I manage to brake without throwing the car into a skid. At the top of the deviation, I pull over to let him pass. I am already shaken enough without the fear that an impatient driver is about to take me out on a wet mountain road.

Wayne Marsh the private detective had phoned me from Hamilton an hour ago. "You'd better come in," he said. "Things are beginning to move along. I have news."

I pleaded with him to tell me what he had discovered but he said too complex, see you at ten, and hung up.

I threw myself into frenzied activity. I washed up the dishes and showered and changed my clothes. I had been lying in bed for the last two days listening to the rain and the wind, immobile, depressed, unable to motivate myself to do anything except crawl downstairs to make coffee and cut slices from a loaf of stale bread.

It is almost as damp inside my house as it is outside. In the bathroom a strange fungus is imitating a paper rose, blooming out of a cracked yellow tile. Mould is moving like a trail of ants across the ceiling of my bedroom and down the corners of the walls. If I had lain on my bed much longer, it could have reached me and marked my skin with indelible blue spores.

# Joy

I arrive at Wayne's office and park the car. He is on the telephone but waves me towards the chair in front of his desk. The office looks the same as it did two weeks ago except that the leaves of the dusty palm have been oiled and the pink venetian blinds have been opened to let in the light.

The person at the other end of the line is arguing with Wayne. I cannot hear the words but the tone is low and angry. Wayne doesn't say much in reply, an odd grunt here and there, oh well that's the breaks, yes yes, I'll be more careful in future but I have to have the relevant data, no info no output.

At last he puts down the receiver. "Sorry about that Ms ah Knight. How are you today, wet enough for you?" He swivels around in his chair and looks at his computer screen. "Now where have I hidden your file, mmm, here we go." He clicks away at the keyboard. I can't see the screen. The printer hums into action and produces a single sheet of paper. He holds it up. "Here is the name and address."

"You mean you've found her?"

"Of course. But there are complications."

I want to seize the paper from him and run from the office. I am terrified that he is going to tell me that she is crazy or subnormal or dying of cancer.

"I can't give you this information unless you agree to certain conditions."

"Anything."

"If you ever tell anyone where you got this information, I will deny it. And call you a bloody liar."

I am disturbed by the menacing tone of his voice. He must have caught the look on my face; because he smiles a little. "I risked my reputation to get you this, so you must promise never to tell."

"I promise, I promise."

He relaxes. "There's something else. She is not alone, she has a child herself, a daughter."

I cry out, "Wonderful, wonderful."

"Calm down Ms Knight, please. There is more." He stares down at the paper. "It appears that Marlene is very rich and successful but there may be a problem with the daughter."

Marlene. Her name, her bestowed name. I barely listen to Wayne talking about Pixel the daughter. Eighteen, never leaves the house. Writes weird stuff. Looks like something out of a vampire movie.

I come out of my dream. "How do you know all this? Have you seen them?"

He looks a little uncomfortable. "Not in the flesh, no."

"I don't understand."

"Look Ms Knight, ah Joy, I may as well come clean. A friend of mine has been doing a little judicious hacking. Not quite legal but all in a good cause as I'm sure you'll agree. I can give you all the data if you swear that you will never show it to anyone else. And you will have to pay me extra, for the risk you understand."

I am desperate, I have to know everything. "I will pay you whatever you ask."

"Okay, I am going to trust you, but I beg you, be very very careful. This Marlene Hunter is a rich and powerful woman, she has a reputation for being one tough lady."

I am excited to think that my Joy has evolved into a woman who can frighten a man like Wayne.

"I tried the legal way first," he continues. "But there was an embargo against your name at Social Welfare."

I knew this. I had already tried to get her name and address from Welfare. All they would tell me is that she is living somewhere in Auckland. I am sad that Marlene does not want me to contact her.

"This makes it difficult," says Wayne. "You can't just turn up, or ring her, she will demand to know how you found her. And the trail might lead back to me."

"I understand."

"There are other concerns. Do you know a woman called Wendy McDonald?"

"No, why."

He pulls a file from beneath his desk and wets his finger and flicks through a pile of papers. "Her name appears on Marlene's accounts in conjunction with your mother Alice. Marlene is giving large amounts of money to this Wendy person. Something to do with a book about the life of Alice Winter."

I am stunned. "I know nothing about a book."

"Marlene owns a company called Hunter International Publications. Are you sure that your mother has never mentioned this?"

"Positive. But it explains something that has been puzzling me for weeks."

"The wads of fifty-dollar notes that your mother has been receiving from persons unknown?"

I am immediately wary. This man seems to know more than I do about Alice. I choose my words carefully. "I do not pry into my mother's financial affairs. It is of no concern of mine if she is earning money under the counter."

"But I thought you did all her accounts and her tax returns."

Now I am really frightened. I try to keep my voice light. "Oh sometimes I help her out, not so much these days."

He laughs. "Sorry to tease, but if you could see the look on your face!"

I do not like this note of intimacy. "Mr Marsh, I wish to keep our conversation strictly business."

He stops laughing at once. "Now you listen to me, I have taken big risks to dig up this information. I don't appreciate your holier than thou act, you knew damn well that I would have to hire a hacker."

"But why investigate me? And where from? I don't even have a computer."

"You have no idea how easy it is. Especially in this case. The hacker said it was like taking candy from a baby. The Social Welfare was simple in spite of the fact that they have a firewall between their data and the Internet but my hacker came in through a trapdoor they don't even know exists. And if they do find it, my hacker will be one jump ahead, he always is. You have nothing to be afraid of. The hacker will keep the information about you and Marlene totally confidential. The thrill of the hunt motivates him, he doesn't give a stuff about the nature of the information he finds for me. It's the process that excites him. Who needs crack or shit, he says, why bugger your body with stuff when the ultimate high is achieved by lurking around the Net."

Now I'm really sweating. "Who is this person?"

"I've never met him and I never want to. All my business is done over the Net. I only know him by his electronic signature, a severed head and the initials TIM."

I am determined to find out as much as I can about this sinister character. Wayne smiles when I tell him that I would like to meet the hacker. "He is very ordinary, there are thousands like him and the joke is that nobody can stop them, nobody. Not the police or the government."

I have mixed feelings. I want to know as much as I can about Marlene and Pixel but I hate the thought of an unknown computer hacker prying into my family business.

"We gained access into the Hunter Corporation computers but there was little there that would interest you," says Wayne. "The big bonus came from the computers at Marlene's home address. Pixel is one of those arrogant young netheads who think they know everything about computer security but then create doorways wide enough to drive a tractor through."

He hands me a pile of printouts. "I took the liberty of downloading some of her files. And Marlene's. For you to read at your leisure."

I am reluctant to take the papers. I want to meet my daughter and my grand-daughter face to face and form my own opinion of them. I mumble something to that effect.

"Take them, you have a right to read everything we have discovered," says Wayne. "Besides, information is power. How can you make decisions if you don't know what is going on?"

I dislike him more than ever. I try not to show it on my face. I need his advice on how to arrange a meeting between Marlene and Pixel and myself. I know that he doesn't want me to go to the house but there may be another way. Before I bring this up, I ask him if he can give me any more information about Alice and the proposed book about her life.

"I've given this matter a lot of thought," says Wayne. "And I've come to the conclusion that we are not the only ones who are using unconventional methods to discover important information. I think that Marlene is investigating Alice through the pretence of writing an oral history recorded by this Wendy McDonald."

"Oral history?"

"Your mother is telling the story of her life into a tape recorder and she is paid five hundred dollars per session. The tapes have been transcribed into files that Pixel keeps on her hard disk."

I am more confused than ever. And angry. I'm sure that Alice has no idea that her words are being read by Marlene and Pixel and hackers and private investigators. She would never have consented to speak if she had known this. Even with the lure of the money.

"I believe that Marlene is recording your mother's life because she wants to know all about your family background," says Wayne. "She is preparing herself to make contact with you. This is good news surely."

I laugh bitterly. "If you knew Alice you wouldn't say that. Her account of what happened to me is slippery to say the least."

"Do you mean she tells lies?"

"Not exactly. But sometimes her memory plays tricks with her."

I am worried that Marlene will believe Alice's version of events surrounding her birth and adoption. Marlene will hate me for giving her up to the welfare officer. I must provide another story, a counterbalance to prove to her that I did not voluntarily abandon her. She was kidnapped, stolen away, taken by force. I ran, I hid, I begged. I was only fifteen years old. What more could I do?

I do not want to say this to Wayne. Instead, I ask him if there's any way that we can get my side of the story across to Marlene before we meet in person.

He gets up and pours two cups of coffee from his machine. I shake my head when he offers me milk or sugar. He sips his coffee. "Yes there is a way, bit dodgy, but it could work. I'll contact TIM, see what he thinks."

He taps rapidly on the keyboard of his computer. He swivels the screen around so that I can read the text flashing across the screen. He writes:

From: Mar@eye.det.org.nz hello TIM, can you go surfing to find a way to plant data in pixel@hunt.pub.org.nz

The answer comes almost instantaneously.

> From: TIM@adhoc.org.nz this nethead is megashrewd so will have
> to be tight
> she is fanatical mudder, could you break in there
> no Mar, others will read. Must be through email
> does she hack
> is the pope a catholic
> any ideas
> okay Mar, think on this. I could break into pixel@hunt.pub.org.nz
> and leave a footprint not too obvious in case we frighten the horses
> then she backhacks and gets exactly what we want her to see no
> more no less
> will have to be your footprint, no hackback into my system mate too
> <fucking> risky
> <get knotted> why should I be the fall guy
> because I pay you megabucks
> pax Mar, we can set up a purpose-built system, no need to sacrifice
> our safe space
> fine, get back to me asap
> okay Mar, will do it just for you goodbye :-)

The screen goes blank except for a pattern of flying triangles twisting and turning. Wayne looks slightly embarrassed. "Sorry ah, Joy, we get carried away at times. No offence meant."

He waits for me to say "none taken" but I remain silent.

Wayne says, "Did you get the drift?"

I tell a lie. "No problems."

"Write down what you want Pixel to know and fax it to me."

"Marlene, not Pixel."

"We have to go through Pixel to get to Marlene."

"How can we be sure that this will happen?"

"Read those papers I gave you, it's all in there."

He looks at his watch. "Shit, must rush. Keep in touch. And remember, don't contact your daughter yet. Be patient, I feel sure that she will lift the embargo soon. Then you can do everything above board, to the letter. Better for all of us in the long run."

I thank him and leave the office clutching the pile of papers. I am out of my depth. My hunger to know them overwhelms me. I know that I will read every word avidly. I forget my guilt about reading papers that were not intended for my eyes. Besides, if Wayne is correct about Marlene investigating me through Alice, then it is a case of tit for tat.

I buy a sandwich and a bottle of water and walk down to the river bank. My feet are hot in my running shoes so I slip them off and sit on a seat close to the edge. The water slides cool and green past my bare feet. I read the files in the order that Wayne has marked.

**1Pixel.doc** On tape one Alice claims her mother came to this country years after she herself arrived. Alice thought she was an orphan but she was lied to as a child . . . *imagine a girl in her twenties, with a child aged seven, nowhere to go, no money, and no welfare for the likes of her . . . so she abandoned you? . . . that's what it felt like at the time . . . did you ever see your mother again? . . . oh yes, much later here in New Zealand . . . so she actually came here! great news . . .*

Wendy nearly blew it by showing too much interest. Yet later, on tape two, Alice says . . . *I wondered if the plague still lurked in the dark soil of Furness Wood, in the water troughs of Eyam, in the foggy air . . . Miss Catley gave me a lecture on not shielding oneself from the past, no matter how unpleasant, facts are facts . . . then tell me about my mother I said, tell me the truth . . . Miss Catley sat me down and held my hand and told me that my mother had died in a TB sanatorium . . .*

Wendy spotted the contradiction and reminded Alice that she had told her on tape one that her mother had come to New Zealand. Alice told her that the notification of her mother's death was a disgusting lie. Wendy did not question her further. I will tell M to remind Wendy to follow this up next time. Important for my quest to find out if Elva came to these shores. Did she really come here or is this another wishful fantasy from the lips of Alice?

At least I know these names now, Joy, Alice, Elva. Three generations back on the nurture line. A start, for the resolution of my data base. The only ones who are together are Alice and Joy, me and M. The rest are lost. There are breaks, silences, secrets. But at least these women are able to recite the names of their mothers and fathers and know that behind each name is real lived experience, a womb, a fuck, a birth.

I know little about my origins except that I was an orphan before I was born. I have a double line to trace, the nurture line and the mystery of my biological past . . .

**1Marlene.doc** Alice lives alone in a pensioner flat, very poor, difficult relationship with her daughter. Why? Joy seems devoted, she comes to the flat once a week, does the books and sometimes helps her with housework. Alice looks ordinary, average size, old-lady hair style, print frock, cardigan, drives a car like a maniac, reads books from the library on social history and about the movements of planets. She takes biscuits to the old man in the flat next door and listens to him mourn his dead wife's cooking.

Joy lives alone in a broken-down bach at Raglan, redundant office manager, no one seems to visit her. She is childless and has divorced two husbands, Samuel Robertson in 1964 and Dennis Knight in 1985. She swims in the sea at all hours of the day and night, gazes from her window at Rangi her neighbour, drives to Whale Bay and walks alone along the beach. Sometimes drives into Hamilton or to her brother Maurice's house in Te Kowhai. Another dilapidated hovel. I am suddenly surrounded with poor relations. Joy is very tall, lined face, thin. Black hair. Lonely or self-sufficent or both.

**2Pixel.doc** That sicko nethead Joachim is annoying me again. When I throw him into the refuse file he bloody goes and changes his words. He gets through my defences. Have I ever eaten human flesh he wants to know urgently, tonight. I ban him again, I block roast, taste, meat.

Why would I want to add the sin of cannibalism to my persona?

I was an orphan before I was born. I was half egg, half sperm, separate yet together. Joachim has a theory that origins and beginnings are the true meaning of fate and that flawed creation necessarily creates a flawed being. Ergo, I must be the ultimate phreak.

It was probably stupid of me to be so true to my own life when I first went mudding. I should never have put that Petrie dish into my character Coblynau as the physical site of my conception. I might have known some cleverdick would take it literally and see it as the truth.

I am growing tired of Coblynau, I think I will leave the city soon. I could force them to expel me by breaking the code. Maybe I could kill off Joshua of the Silver Fleece who thinks he is the only one fit to lead. I have never dared to think of virtual murder before but the idea becomes more appealing especially since the email harassment from Joachim, the chronicler.

Or I could obliterate these Coblynau data, and therefore kill an aspect of myself that was once so important to me. All the dreams of Coblynau in the city would disappear at my command. I could destroy my/her house and garden, cover up my/her trails down into the mine, erase the products of my/her mind that helped to create the fantastical landscape. Virtual suicide. The death of everything except the body.

But a substitute must be found. I hate living in the body, it is too demanding, too there. One day, I will achieve the ultimate detachment, I will scatter across the Net so far and wide that the filaments of skin and bone will stretch into nanothreads of the purest gossamer, sweet strings waiting to be played, my lyre, myself . . .

It's the sweat I hate and the blood and the yellow cells of fat and gristle and the discordant tunes, the groans, the cries, the whimpers. I refuse to live solely within the confines of this hardware and I refuse to conform to wetware rules no matter what the method of creation, either cloned or formed in vitro or brought into being by a mindless fuck.

**2Marlene.doc** I am beginning to understand Alice's clumsy attempts at mystification. Her problem is one of focus, she is too unworldly. A good sign that she took the money without compunction. But she is like a magpie, she only wants it to buy useless domestic objects from the Warehouse or K-Mart. But on the whole, I am not displeased. She has some spirit, courage even.

As for Joy, the main purpose of the tapes has not yet been fulfilled. I want a portrait of my birth mother through her own mother's eyes. Hester, my grandmother, told me childhood stories of my adoptive mother Beverly . . .

I am forced to stop reading. Beverly takes me by the throat and seizes me. So this is the name of the woman who was presented with the gift of my beloved baby. Without my consent. I see her as beautiful, rich, in possession of a perfect figure untouched by the rigours of childbirth. She is married to a clever man who adores her, she lives on the North Shore in a luxurious house with a designer garden, palm trees, ceramic tubs of trailing flowers, a weeping cherry. Rangitoto Island stands in the gulf like a water-colour painting in subtle shades of blue and green and the harbour tides come and go at the whim of Beverly . . .

I throw the papers down on the grass beside the river. I want to throw Beverly into the water but I restrain myself. I must read these files again and again until I can make sense of them.

I drive home over the winding hills to Raglan.

I cook a simple meal of vegetables. I make a list of food to buy tomorrow at the supermarket and I sweep the kitchen floor and wipe down the windowsills. I resolve to walk along the beach every morning before breakfast, to read more books, to plant tomatoes in my garden.

The rain has stopped and the sun is trying to break through the low clouds. The westerly wind is rising, I can hear the familiar howl at the seaward side of the house.

I am comforted by Marlene's desire. I want, she had said, a portrait of my birth mother. She wants to know me!

I cling to this as I sit in my armchair and begin to read the files from the point where Marlene revealed to me the name of her adoptive mother. This woman has for forty years evoked such strong feelings of jealousy in me that she has become a symbol of everything that I could never be, almost a holy figure, beyond the reach of human influence.

I read on. I am deeply relieved to learn that Marlene was given to a loving couple who obviously adored her. I have always had a huge fear that she was given to an abusive family and that she would accuse me of ruining her life. But I am envious of the wealth that gave the Hunters easy access to my child. I was considered too poor, too young, too unstable. I envy their privilege and eminent suitability for parenthood. If I had been like them, I would never have been forced to give up my baby.

Then I read that Beverly and her husband Richard are both long dead. Killed in a plane crash twenty years ago. Marlene has been free of their influence for the second half of her life. I am more than ready to step into the gap and play the role of mother.

I don't understand some of Pixel's writing, but I will meet her soon and then she can explain. Wayne Marsh said she looks like something out of a vampire movie then admits that he has never laid eyes on her. He is making this up. Is he trying to warn me off making contact? I don't care what he thinks. She is my own flesh and blood and I am determined to love her just as she is.

Twenty-seven Hillside Crescent Devonport, this is where they live. I have already marked it on my map of Auckland and telephoned the directory service for their number. I was told that Ms Marlene Hunter and her daughter Ms Patricia Hunter have a confidential listing. Pixel must be her nick-name. I wonder if Marlene is married. There is no mention of a husband in her files. Maybe she is divorced. Pixel is eighteen so she must have been born after the Hunters were killed.

I could go to Hillside Crescent and park close to number twenty-seven and observe the house. Just to see what it looks like, to check it out against my fantasy. And maybe I will see my daughter Marlene come out of her house unaware that her birth mother is sitting close to her, just feet away. The strength of my emotion may cause her to turn her head at that very moment when her car passes mine and I will gaze once again into her brown eyes.

I promised Wayne Marsh I would not make contact with Marlene but I did not promise anything about visiting the street.

I resolve to drive to Auckland early tomorrow morning. Before sunrise.

# 8

# *Alice*

I am busy serving poor Wilf some hot scones in my lounge when Wendy knocks on the door. I am surprised to see her. She is not due until tomorrow. Or am I getting confused? My arthritis has given me trouble these last few days and I have reluctantly taken some strong anti-inflammatory drugs. Although they have dulled the grinding pain in my joints, I am left with a haze in my head that blurs my sense of time passing. The overcast skies and warm showers of day have merged with the dark humidity of night.

This morning I felt the need to have some company so I went next door to ask Wilf to come and share some food with me. I thought his conversation might help to ground me. The drugs must have affected my memory as well as my sense of time. I had forgotten how boring he could be with his talk of his dead wife's cooking and the merry time he had in Te Awamutu when he had his own herd of dairy cows. Ah those were the days, he said, a man worked hard, handling heavy cans, throwing them onto the cream stand, two milkings a day, feeding out, fencing, grubbing out the ragwort, a man built up an appetite. Going inside the warm house on a freezing winter's night, the wife always had a pot of soup, thick and meaty and brown, three courses, soup, roast hogget, steamed suet pudding covered in yellow custard . . .

My problem is that I've heard this before, word for word, and although I empathise with his grief and loneliness, I sometimes wonder why he never calls his dead wife by her proper name and only ever mentions her in relation to the food that she seemed to prepare so endlessly for him.

I am pleased when Wendy rescues me. She looks surprised to

see Wilf in my lounge. He is eating and talking at the same time, and bits of scone are falling down the front of his shirt. He flaps his loose dentures at Wendy, grinning through a film of melted butter and raspberry jam.

Here at the pensioner flats, we know most of the people who come and go, we know whose grand-daughter visits or whose son. Poor Wilf is obviously curious about my visitor.

I offer no explanation to him. Neither does Wendy. He rises unsteadily to his feet and hobbles to the door on his walking stick, thanking me for the scones, so delicious Alice, takes me back . . .

Wendy is dressed in her usual long black clothes and looks particularly beautiful today. She declines my offer to make her a fresh pot of tea. "I tried to ring you. Is your phone out of order?"

I lift the receiver. No dial tone. I ask Wendy to ring Telecom for me on her cellphone. She does, and then I ask her why she has come to visit me a day earlier than planned.

"We've gone through your tapes," she said. "And we have discovered a problem."

"I have been as honest as I can," I say stiffly. "I have held nothing back."

Wendy looks embarrassed. "I'm not criticising you, far from it. But the editor of the book picked up a contradiction and she asked me to clarify things with you as soon as possible."

I ask her what the problem is.

"About your mother Elva," she answers. "You said she came here to New Zealand and then later you said she died of TB when you were still a child."

"I was merely repeating what was told to me. And I did tell you that I found out later that the letter about her death was a vicious lie."

Wendy places the tape recorder in front of me on the coffee table and runs a check with the external microphone. "Would you explain further into the tape?"

"Is this the tape I was going to do with you tomorrow?"

"No, this is an extra bit."

I am relieved that she is coming again tomorrow. The truth is that I am beginning to rely upon her visits. The recounting of my life story is helping me to make sense of my past. After making the last tape, I felt so clear and strong about Joy. In spite of everything I love my girl so very dearly, I would not care to be without her. She argues with me, and reprimands me, but she visits me often and helps me, which is more than Morry ever does. And I am reconciled with Emily too. Now that I have confronted her death, I visit the green bead every night and I have heard her repeating many things that I had sealed away and pretended to forget. Now I understand that Emily did not take Harry's eye just for me, she did it for herself as well, for his abuse of her.

"It is true that my mother Elva came to New Zealand when she was 49 years old and that I met her again. Miss Catley had lied to me when she told me that my mother had died in a TB sanatorium. But it was not her fault. She merely repeated the information that the director of the orphanage had given her at the time when I went to live with her and Miss Forester at *Emain*. He actually showed her a letter. All lies. Here's how I found out. Remember Jean? She was the young girl of twelve who came out on the ship with me and Emily. She went to a wonderful family in Whangarei. They did not treat her like a servant and she had a good education and eventually became a lecturer at Auckland University. I read an article in a newspaper about her and her field of research. There was a photo of her, a woman historian, unusual for those days. I called out to Jack, come quickly, here is Jean after all these years. And this article said that she had investigated a big scandal where young children had been brought from institutions in England under false pretences to be used as workers on farms and as servants for the rich. Jean revealed that this had happened to her but that she was adopted rather than being used as a servant. She was told that her mother had died but she had discovered that this was not the case. She went back to England and traced her mother and horror of horrors, she found out that her mother had been told that Jean too had died, of diphtheria. Jean wanted to make contact with other adults who had been brought to New Zealand as children through similar trickery. There was a box number to write to and a promise that all information would be treated in the strictest confidence.

"I contacted her immediately and she made inquiries for me and we found out that Elva had also been told that I had died of diphtheria in the same epidemic that had supposedly carried of so many of the children at Moncreiff House. There was more. Elva had married and had two more children and had migrated to New Zealand just after the war. You can imagine my bitterness. For eight years my mother had been in the same country as I was and each of us believed the other to be dead."

Wendy interrupts. "But this is monstrous, how the hell could this have happened?"

"We have never had a satisfactory explanation. And now that we are all old or dead, nobody cares any more."

"I do I do!" she cries.

"The success stories like Jean were paraded through the papers. Some authorities claimed that we children had a better life through coming to this country. The unfortunate children of these working-class families were locked into poverty they said. We have broken this cycle, we should concentrate on the results not the methods."

"Can you tell me about meeting your mother?"

"Jean organised the trip. Elva and her family lived in the South Island. I travelled overland to Christchurch with Joy and Morry. Jack wanted to come too but he could not get time off work. It was a long and difficult trip. Joy was fourteen and Morry was nine. The train trip from Auckland to Wellington took eighteen hours and we had to sit up in uncomfortable seats all night. The children were filthy with cinders from the steam engine when we arrived at Wellington Station. I cleaned them up as best I could and then we walked around the freezing windy streets to keep awake until we could board the inter-island ferry at tea time. It was July, and the winter was in full blast. There was a southerly gale blowing through Cook Strait.

"In those days, the ferries went down the coast to Lyttleton and we had to sleep overnight on the ship. We travelled second class, in a twelve-berth cabin. I had not been on a large ship since I came to New Zealand with Emily and Jean. The motion of the boat, the sound of the wind howling, the sight of the huge waves breaking across the bow brought back unpleasant memories.

"Both Joy and Morry were violently seasick. By the time we berthed at Lyttleton I was a wreck. And to make matters worse, Elva and her husband Bill were not there to meet us. I checked and rechecked the details that Jean had written down for me. Yes this was the right day and the right time. They did not have a telephone in Christchurch so I could not contact them. I waited for hours in the draughty wharf building trying to comfort my sick children. Another ship berthed and one left for Wellington. There were brief crowds and swirls of people, and each time my hopes were raised that Elva and Bill would be amongst the new arrivals in the crowd. Eventually, a wharf employee asked me to leave the building as they wanted to lock up until the next ship arrived the following morning. We walked out into icy rain and followed the railway track that led to the main street. I had a little money with me, so I decided to catch the next bus to Christchurch and then make my way to Sumner where Elva lived.

"I felt as if I had arrived in a foreign country. The buildings were made of stone and the people were bundled up in layers of clothes. The icy rain had changed into slushy snow during the bus trip and the driver had remarked that we would be the last vehicle to get through the hills that afternoon. Morry had cheered up when he saw snow for the first time and asked if he could make a snowman when we got to Grandma's. I had told them that their Grandma Elva was living in the South Island and they were very excited at the thought of having another grandmother beside their beloved Nana Winter.

"I went into a dairy and asked how we could get to Sumner. The woman in the shop pointed out a safety zone in the middle of the street. If we stood there, a tram would arrive very soon and take us exactly where we wanted to go. Elva's street was at the end of the line, we couldn't miss it.

"We climbed aboard the Sumner tram. It was not a novelty for the children like the train and the boat had been. We lived in a state house near Sandringham Road and the trams clanged noisily past the end of our street from early morning until late at night. The only difference was that the Auckland trams were red and these ones were green.

"The snow stopped falling and the wind dropped. We travelled along the coast for a time, through sandhills covered with clumps of tussock and frost-bitten flax, then swung into a cluster of houses and eventually, a street lined with shops. The tram stopped at a concrete bunker and the driver went outside the tram to change over the poles. This must be Sumner, I said to the children, off we get.

"It was almost dark and I could feel the temperature dropping. I found the street and the house, number ten. It was a small unpainted cottage with a verandah and a front door flanked by two windows. The front garden was unkempt and there were no lights on in the front rooms. I was beginning to panic. If there was no one here, where would we go? I knocked, no answer. I put my ear to the door and heard a low murmur of voices so I knocked again, loudly this time.

"The door opened a crack. Go away, a woman said. No beer tonight.

"I would have known that voice anywhere. It was my mother Elva. I cried out, it's me! it's me! and she opened the door wide and we fell into each other's arms. The relief of finding her there was overwhelming.

"She took us through the dark hallway and into the lean-to at the back and turned on the light. We stared at each other in mutual shock. I would never have known you, she cried. I could've walked right past you in the street . . . is there nothing left of you that I remember? Maybe the expression in your eyes, the shape of your head, I don't know . . .

"I was shocked too but for different reasons. I had recognised her voice at the front door but everything else about her had changed beyond belief. Her face was plastered with orange powder that emphasised the deep grooves and wrinkles in her skin. Her eyelids were smeared with green eyeshadow and her hair had been permed and dyed almost to extinction. A few thin red curls clustered around her ears and the sides of her head but she had more bare scalp than hair.

"She lit the gas stove with a flint gun and heated a pot of milk for hot cocoa. Joy was shivering uncontrollably by this stage and could barely speak. Elva fussed over the children, kissing Morry over and over until he sent me agonised looks of embarrassment. I wanted to say, leave him now, he's tired and hungry but I couldn't.

"Elva said she was sorry they didn't come to meet us. A mix-up, the car was out of action, at the garage, the part was meant to arrive on the service car, the mechanic had promised . . .

"Then her husband Bill came into the kitchen and I saw at once that he was very drunk. He was affable enough but I sensed that he did not want us there. He took another bottle of beer from the fridge and went back down the hall. Elva said that her sons were not there, both gone away up north to work. I said but they are children surely. She laughed at me, you forget how time passes, they are both twenty-one, yes twins, not identical but still double trouble. She dropped her voice, don't talk about them in front of Bill, there's been a quarrel, he doesn't like to hear their names mentioned . . .

"Naturally I was very disappointed. I had looked forward to meeting my half-brothers. The children were put to bed on a double mattress on the floor of the front room. I was worried about Joy, she was burning up with fever. Elva gave her a hot lemon drink and an aspirin and at last she went into a deep sleep.

"I could not sleep and neither could Elva. She went to check on her husband to make sure that he was safely in bed and I checked on Joy. To my relief she felt a lot cooler. Elva made us tea and toast. We sat up all night in the kitchen, talking, weeping, laughing. Elva smoked a whole packet of cigarettes, one after the other. She kept patting my hand and saying I can't believe that you are actually sitting here in my kitchen. In the flesh.

"I told her everything about Moncreiff House and Emily and Miss Catley and *Emain* and the Vetorix family and the boarding house at Market Road and my marriage to Jack and my love of books. Everything except the circumstances of Joy's conception and the death of Emily.

"She cried her heart out over the orphanage. If only I had known she said, I swear to god I would have come and taken you away, but you never answered my letters.

"I never heard from you, not once, I said. They must have hidden them away.

"I wrote to you every week right up to that dreadful day when I received the news that you had died in the diphtheria epidemic. They would not allow me to travel up north for the funeral because the whole area was placed in quarantine for two months.

"They told me you had died of TB.

"Oh the liars, she said, the bloody liars. Then she laughed and said may they rot in hell those so-called Christians, but we have beaten them because we are together in spite of their lies. And you have given me two grandchildren. Dear little Morry, he looks just like you but Joy is the image of your father Nigel Warrington. He was six feet tall at the age of fifteen and I wouldn't be surprised if Joy ended up the same. She looks so like him I nearly fainted when I saw her at the door.

"She told me how she met her husband Bill and about their wedding day in 1933 in London. He came from a big working-class family in the East End. He had nine sisters! Elva was loved by them all. The twins were born in 1934 and Bill's family adored them. The aunties made a great fuss of them. But Bill was not the same when he came back from the war. He insisted that they leave England as soon as possible. They had migrated to New Zealand in 1946. She had found it very hard at first. Of course the food was better and the climate a miracle after London. But she was lonely for the streets and pubs, lonely for her friends and for her sisters-in-law. But the boys had loved this country right from the start. The beaches, the people, the bush, the wonderful freedom. She looked so sad when she talked about them. I asked her why they had quarrelled with her husband but she would not tell me.

"I never met them so I never did find out. Here's what happened. We stayed a week with Elva in Sumner and the children fell in love with her. She was a wonderful woman. Strong, kind and clever. Exactly those qualities that I had loved her for as a young child. But she had a fatal flaw and that was drink. Drink and men. Usually together.

"After the first night of tea drinking, she dropped her guard and went back to the bottle. Gin and whiskey were her drinks. Straight. No mixers. And she wasn't a secret drinker like other women alcoholics of that time. Far from it. The second night we were there, people drifted into the house and the party started. They brought bottles in brown paper bags and cases of beer and battered guitars.

"She drank hour after hour. She sang, she danced suggestively with the men, she told dirty stories. Bill didn't seem to notice. He spent most of the time arguing with the others about the hops and yeast and sweeteners he used in the making of his home brew or discussing the merits of horses due to race at the next meeting at Addington. I crept around quietly the next morning thinking that she would be suffering from a terrible hangover. But she was already up, cooking breakfast for the children, cutting Bill's sandwiches for work and clearing away the stinking ash trays and the empty bottles from the night before.

"The next night, exactly the same thing happened. The same men came, the same songs, the stories, the booze. I couldn't understand it. During the day she was a companion and a cook, a clever woman who could turn her hand to anything; at night, this drunken flirt. I went to bed early with the children to avoid the pain I felt at watching her play sexual games with those rough types.

"The night before we were due to leave, I had to go to the toilet in the middle of the night. The bathroom was at the back of the house at the side of the lean-to. It was freezing. Elva was lying on a wooden bench on the back verandah, dead drunk. A man was kneeling beside her, touching her private parts. He had pulled her panties down to her knees. I flew at him, I punched him between the shoulder blades. He turned and seized my arms and lifted them up high above my head. He did not say a word. I screamed out for Bill but nobody came. He held my arms up until the blood drained from my hands. Then suddenly he threw my arms down and walked down the side of the house.

"I managed to drag her inside into the warm kitchen. I placed a rug over her and stoked up the coal range. Her eyes opened briefly and she murmured thank you darling, thank you.

"We were due to leave the next afternoon to catch the night ferry from Lyttleton. I was determined to talk to Elva about her drinking behaviour. In the morning, I sent the children down the road to buy sweets from the dairy. For the trip I told them, you can each have a shilling. I made Elva a cup of tea and told her what I had seen the night before. She denied it at first but then cried and said she was sorry. I don't usually drink that much she said, but last night I tried to drown my sorrows. I'm scared that I won't ever see you or the kids again. You live so far away.

"Don't use me as an excuse, I said. I have seen you drinking every night and playing games with those awful men that come here. How can you?

"I need to sing and drink and have a good time, she said. I have had too much sorrow in my life. Surely I deserve a little fun?

"I put my arms around her and asked her to promise me that she wouldn't get dead drunk around men again. It's not safe, you cannot protect yourself. She said she was sorry that she had caused me worry. She would try to drink less but I knew from the expression in her voice that she had no intention of changing her ways.

"Three months after we left Sumner, she turned up unexpectedly in Sandringham. I opened the back door of my house one morning and there she was, ill and tired and desperate, clutching a small brown bag.

"Bill had told her to come to Auckland. She couldn't go back, not after what had happened. He had been caught selling home brew and had been arrested. She had given information to the police against him. Or so he said. She could not remember going to the police station with him. And he got nine months and the landlord gave them notice and Bill had written to her from prison and said he didn't want her back, she had dragged him down, ruined his life. It was all her fault, the parties, the trouble with the twins, everything.

"I had no choice, I took her in. Jack didn't say much except that I should try to get her to eat more. Mrs Winter said she's your mother and she's got no money and no home, of course she must stay with you. I hoped that Mrs Winter would be friendly with

Elva and help to ease her loneliness. She tried, we all did, but it was too late for Elva. After a few weeks, I realised that she would never stop drinking and that she was determined to drink herself to death. So I stopped hiding her bottles and learned to live with her slurred speech and her raddled face and her forgetfulness. But there were no parties and no men. And after one unpleasant incident I made sure that the doors were locked at night so that she couldn't wander. This was the first time we had ever locked our back door at night. Nobody did in those days. But one of my neighbours, Mrs Mason, asked me to make sure that Elva didn't come to her house again. There had been some trouble between Elva and Mrs Mason's elderly father who lived there. Elva had brought a flask of whiskey into his room and they had been caught 'being silly' together. She wouldn't tell me the details.

"I was horrified to think that the women in my street would find out that my mother was a drunk. I begged Mrs Mason not to tell anyone and promised to guard Elva at night. But of course she did spread it around and there was a coolness between the women and Elva when they saw us walking to the shops. I felt so sad for Elva. Up until then, she had been treated very kindly. Nobody snubbed her outright but there was a lack of warmth and she felt it and cried and said I am bringing you down Alice just like I did to Bill. You should send me away.

"We had lived in the same street ever since Jack and I married in 1940. It was one of the early state houses, two bedrooms, a sun porch, a washhouse at the back door, weatherboards, tile roof. The neighbours were all married couples like us, working men, fulltime mothers with large numbers of children. People stayed year after year in those houses. On the rare occasion that a family moved out everyone knew where they were moving to and why. And when a new family moved in, there was great excitement and discussion about the state of their furniture and what sort of woman she was and how she kept her house and her children.

"To tell you the truth, we women ruled that street, we laid down the standards of behaviour and morality. The men were always out at work or drinking at the pub or going to the races or to football.

So it was the wives who interacted with us. A bad egg in the nest could make our lives hell so a new woman was very important. And we had strict rules. Never speak badly of another woman's husband to her face, never be caught gossiping in your kitchen when your husband came home, always have tea on the table the moment he walked in, always look busy when he was around. The men were made to feel that they were the hub of the household, it was part of the deal.

"This worked well for me until my mother came to live with us. Then I understood what it was like to be on the other side of the fence. The trouble was that Elva was too far gone into her illness to comprehend the rules of the community. She blundered into deep waters time and time again. The incident with Mrs Mason's father happened within a few weeks after she arrived. The women on my outer circle were disapproving but my close friends did not mention it. Except for Mary Crawford, my best friend, who got the giggles and said the old man probably thought he'd died and gone to heaven.

"But then Elva began to say tactless things that she had no right to say. She told Mrs Calvert she'd seen her old man with a young bit of fluff on his arm coming out of the bookie's house near the Sandringham shops. And the time she overheard Mrs Simms complaining in a round-about way about her husband's sexual demands. I think she described him as being too manly, or words to that effect. We never mentioned the word sex in those days. Elva told Mrs Simms she should point at his dick and laugh. Best thing to make a man go flabby, she said, point and laugh.

"I was mortified. I went to each woman and tried to explain that Elva was ill but they said they would not be coming to my house again. I was welcome to come and drink tea with them but I was to leave Elva behind. Mrs Calvert said it was bad enough to see a man falling down drunk every Thursday night like your husband does Mrs Winter if you don't mind me saying so, but a drunken woman is much worse, pitiful in fact.

"She was paying me back for what Elva had said about her husband by showing that she knew that my Jack got drunk on pay nights. I couldn't blame her, that is how the code worked and I had done similar things to other women over the years.

"It took a year for Elva to die. Eventually, her liver swelled and her kidneys broke down. The last two weeks she could keep nothing down except gin and water and she saw imaginary animals and monsters and foreign landscapes. She recited her visions as if she were seeing a film passing in front of her eyes. Mean streets filled with marching soldiers, planes dropping from the sky, the dead faces of children gazing up at her, white and swollen with water, drowned in flooded air raid shelters. Why are you making me watch these black and white movies she cried, where has the colour gone Alice?

"And she would cling to me and scream for her dead boys and I had to keep telling her over and over that they were alive and well and that we were in New Zealand and the war was long over.

"The last few days she became very peaceful and seemed to know where she was. She died so quietly it took me a minute or two to realise that she had stopped breathing. I was sitting beside her bed in the sun porch. It was early in the morning, a cold clear spring day. Jack had gone to work and the children had just left to go to school. I was thankful that I was alone in the house. I sat over her for hours, watching the reflection of the sun moving along the side windows and listening to thrushes and blackbirds squabbling over straw and insects from Jack's newly dug garden.

"I thought of her long fine hair lying down her back, the candle-light shining on her rosy face, the cold water from the washbowl making her gasp and the careful way she dressed every morning in the black and white uniform of servitude. Eggs broken into creamed butter and sugar, long spirals of apple skin, a pool of yellow from the electric light over the scrubbed kitchen table. And I wept for the pain that she had endured through her life. My illegitimate birth, my spurious death, the alienation from her husband and sons at the end of her life. And I was consumed with a terrible rage. All her life she had been flung from one temporary refuge to another. She had never been allowed to find a place of safety. And the letters that she had sent to me at Moncreiff House, those unread words of love that I had almost died for want of hearing. She never received one word back from me but she kept writing, week after week, believing that I too had abandoned her. She was treated like a nothing. A nobody. And she believed it about herself, she thought she deserved to be treated badly. Send me away Alice she had said during her final illness. Get rid of me before I drag you down like the others.

"And I rang Jack from my friend Mary Crawford's house and he came home at once and comforted me and rang her husband in the South Island. Bill did have the grace to cry a little over the phone but he said he didn't have the money to come north for the funeral and that was that. My half-brothers were working their way around the world. I had sent a postcard to the New Zealand Embassy in London and Jonathon had written me a letter of thanks for caring for Elva. Is she really dying? Please let us know if and when it happens. We plan to go to Greece next but use this box number if you need to contact us. I did write to them but I never heard back and to this day I don't know where they are or what happened to them.

"In the end, only Jack and me and the children and Mary were at the funeral. My rage sustained me through that sad day. Into the kaleidoscope I travelled, into the diagonal shapes, each one filled with glass beads like multi-coloured tears. I added the sights and sounds of this funeral into the blue bead of weeping and cold corridors and abandonment, I did see it, I did see . . .

"The next few weeks passed in a tired fog. I had not realised how much energy I had expended in caring for Elva. I was tired right down to my bones. Mary came every day and helped me do the housework and cooking. She was my only friend at that time. She was ten years older than me and a recent widow. Her husband had been crushed beneath a pile of coal at the bottom of a shute. An unavoidable accident they called it at the inquiry. They gave her a widow's pension and reduced her rent by five shillings. She was wonderful to me, I don't know what I would have done without her. I tried to pay her for the housework that she did for me but she wouldn't hear of it.

"The Spring that year was very unusual, no wind, no rain, just day after day of calm warm skies. The blossoms hung like fragrant white stars on the plum trees on Mary's front lawn and the air was vibrant with the sound of bees and the flutter and flash of butterfly wings. It deepened my sadness to observe the activities of spring, the beating of carpet squares, the airing of blankets, the scrubbing of weatherboards. I could not raise the energy to do my usual tasks.

"All through this time of mourning I failed to notice the changes in Joy. I knew that she spent lots of time alone in her room, but I put this down to the sombre atmosphere in the house. One day, Mary came to me and said that the women in the street were spreading malicious gossip about Joy. I thought I'd tell you what they are saying, she said. Before Joy gets wind of it, I owe it to you.

"She told me that Joy was keeping company with one of the local bad boys who hung out in billiard halls and milkbars. Joy had been seen riding pillion on his motorbike wearing black lipstick and patent leather boots.

"I couldn't believe it. Joy didn't wear makeup and the only shoes she owned were her flat lace-ups for Grammar. They must be confusing her with another girl.

"There's more, said Mary. Mrs Mason saw her smoking a cigarette on the street and talking loudly with a group of rough types. After Mrs Mason walked past, she heard Joy call out a bad name behind her back.

"I was horrified. There were girls in my street who had gone boy-mad or had run off with the bodgies and widgies but Joy was a quiet girl who loved her school work and her family life. I had never had a moment's worry with her. I waited until Mary was gone and then I broke a rule and searched Joy's room. I had not gone through her things since she was ten years old. After living in the orphanage and working at the Vetorix household I knew the importance of personal privacy.

"I found the boots hidden at the back of her wardrobe and I found a bag of makeup, eyeshadow, black lipstick and blue nail-polish, bizarre colours for that era. Worse, I found magazines with dirty pictures and an unopened packet of condoms. To say I was shocked is an understatement. My fifteen "year" old daughter, my child, had a secret life that I knew nothing about. Each day I sent her off to Grammar in her pleated gym dress and starched white blouse, hat, blazer, gloves, tie. The perfect schoolgirl, neat, tidy, respectful to her elders. I couldn't cope with this sudden revelation of a double life.

"I pulled the curtains and I sat in the darkening room until she came home from school. She opened the door and saw that I was holding her boots and the box of makeup. Give me my things, she cried. And get out of my room, you have no right to be in here, bitch.

"I nearly hit her. But I swallowed my anger and asked her to explain where she got the money from to buy the boots and the makeup. I didn't dare mention the magazines or the condoms. She wouldn't tell me at first. I had to threaten her with her father. In the end she told me that she had taken them from shops.

"You stole? I can't believe that you are so stupid. Do you know what will happen to you?

"She didn't answer me.

"I felt afraid for her, terrified that her misdeeds would be discovered. I wanted to protect her from the police and the courts. There was much talk of juvenile delinquency in those days. Children were sent to borstal if they were caught stealing.

"I took complete control of her life from that moment on. I went with her to school to make sure she didn't play truant and I was at the gate waiting for her to come out at three o'clock every afternoon. I watched her night and day at home. She was hardly out of my sight. I did not tell Jack about the things I had found in her room. I explained my actions by telling him that she had wagged school and I wanted her to pass the school certificate exam at the end of the year so that she could gain entry into form six. I was determined that she was going to stay at school until she achieved the qualifications that I never had the chance of getting. Jack was satisfied with my story. He was a typical husband of that time in that he left all the decisions concerning the children and the running of the house to me. He did not even know what class Joy was in or any of the names of her teachers. He worked very hard in his job and came home exhausted at the end of the day. I did not have the heart to worry him over things that he could do nothing about.

"I never discussed my worries over Joy with anyone except Mary. She quelled the rumours in the street and reported back to me that the gossip had died down. I asked Joy no further questions about her bad behaviour. I was afraid to hear what she might tell me and I preferred to let things lie. She apologised for calling me a bitch but otherwise sulked about the house, hardly eating, doing no school work or washing and ironing, the picture of adolescent misery. She hardly spoke a word to me, except to mumble under her breath that I had ruined her life.

"Things got back to normal after a month or two or so I thought. I had stopped escorting Joy to and from school and although she was still very subdued she had resumed doing her share of the housework. Then one afternoon in early December, there was a knock on the kitchen door and to my surprise, Mary came into the house with Joy in tow. I could see that Joy had been crying.

"There is something that Joy has to tell you, said Mary. She wanted me to be here as well.

"I thought oh no, she's been caught shoplifting, I can't bear it, then Joy told me that she was six months pregnant. I could not take it in. Tell me what the real problem is, I begged. Stop playing tricks.

"Listen to her Alice, said Mary. She is telling you the truth.

"They sat me down and Mary made a pot of tea and Joy kept saying I'm sorry Mum I'm sorry, and I kept saying, you are still my daughter, I will take care of you, why are you so thin? And she told me how she bound her body every morning in a corset, hiding her swelling stomach, hoping every day that it would go away and that she would wake up one morning to find that the nightmare was over.

"I was determined that the neighbours would not find out. I could imagine Mrs Mason and Mrs Simms turning on me for giving too much attention over the last year to my dying mother and neglecting the supervision of my daughter. We made plans.

Joy would not reveal the name of the baby's father in spite of our pleas. It's all my fault, she said. And anyway, he has left Auckland, he knows nothing about it.

"Do you love him? asked Mary.

"Of course I do, said Joy. I am not that sort of girl. But I will not tell you his name. He could go to prison because of me and I could not bear that to happen.

"We decided that Joy should leave for an extended visit to relatives in the South Island. This would be the story that we would tell everyone, even her little brother. Meanwhile, she would be placed into a home for unmarried mothers until after the baby was born. Then she could resume her schooling as if nothing had happened.

"Wait on, said Joy. How do we explain away the baby?

"It took me a while to understand what she was saying. Then I realised what she meant. She was so naive. It would be impossible for her to bring the baby here and continue her life as if nothing had happened. She would be frozen out by the women and propositioned sexually by the men. I had seen this happen to other girls in this street. Don't even think about it, I told her. You are far too young. We will arrange a suitable adoption.

"Joy said nothing, but I could see that she was very upset.

"This can be decided later, said Mary. The main thing is to book her into a home and sort out things so that she can resume her schooling by correspondence.

"That night, after Jack and I were settled into bed, I told him about Joy. I was shocked at his reaction. He called her a dirty slut, then said something about bad blood. I thought he meant me at first but after I had burst out crying he took me in his arms and said not you love, not you. That bastard who attacked you, he is the bad half of her and you are the good. If she had been my real daughter this would never have happened.

"I had never heard him talk like this before. I thought he had accepted Joy as his own daughter. He had been a good father to her. He was strict but fair. He never laid a hand on her. Sometimes he did lose his temper and yell at her but this was only if he was tired or had a bad hangover.

"He was an inarticulate man, he hardly ever talked about his feelings. Until this night I had no idea that he thought of Joy as the carrier of bad blood. I tried to explain to him that upbringing was more important but he wouldn't hear of it. The trouble is, he said, everyone thinks that she belongs to me and I am unable to tell them the truth. She has brought shame to this family and I want her out.

"If she goes, I said, I go.

"He didn't answer for a long time. Then he said but Alice what on earth has got into you? You must stay, Morry and I need you.

"I took this to mean that Joy could still be part of our family. I knew him well enough to know that as far as he was concerned the conversation was over. He went to sleep soon after, but I tossed and turned all night, plotting and planning.

"So Joy went away to Bethlehem House, and I hated leaving her there with all those poor pregnant girls and the brisk matron. She was allowed one call a week but we did not have a telephone so I walked to the phone box on the corner every Wednesday morning and spoke to her. And on Saturdays it was family visiting time so I went to see her on the tram and I took cakes and magazines and knitting patterns and wool. The first few visits she clung to me and said she wanted to die. I felt so upset. I wanted to take her away with me but there was nowhere that we could go. The home ran a commercial laundry and my poor Joy had to wash and starch sheets for a local hotel. Her hands became covered in abrasions from hot water and bleach and caustic soda. They worked those girls hard. The matron said it was to keep them occupied and to stop them from fretting for their lost freedom. On Sundays, society ladies visited them and took them out for drives in expensive cars and to afternoon tea just to show their friends how tolerant they were. Some of these ladies took the pregnant girls into their own homes and used them as unpaid servants and child minders. I warned the matron that this was not to happen to Joy. At least she had the company of the other girls in that place and I could keep an eye on her.

"Although Bethlehem House was difficult for Joy, she was away from the gossips and the hostile atmosphere at home. I did everything I could to appease Jack's displeasure. I cooked his favourite meals and said nothing when he came home late for tea night after night, full of beer and rage.

"I had lived with him for over fifteen years and he had been good to me. He had saved my life and given a child without a father a name and a home. I thought he had accepted the situation because he never spoke about it. But something about Joy's pregnancy seemed to throw him into a state of unresolved anguish that he was unable to understand.

"Throughout the months when Joy was away, he suffered terribly. I tried, both for his sake and mine, to clear the air but he would walk away, his face dark with anger. I was desperate to resolve the situation before Joy returned home. She would suffer enough with the pain of childbirth and the parting from her baby. I did not want her to bear the brunt of his temper on top of everything else.

"The adoption had already been arranged. I had been asked to go to the home for an interview with a child welfare officer to discuss the situation. They had a difficulty with Joy, a problem, and they said I had to try and talk some sense into her. She was refusing to consider adoption and told them that I had agreed to care for the baby when she went back to school. I knew that Jack would not hear of this arrangement and to be completely honest, I did not want to do it either. I had found looking after children very difficult, especially when they were little. I had this private world that I went into each morning when I was alone in the house. On week days, after the children had gone to school, I did my housework quickly and then I sat alone and read books. My friend Mary knew not to come to the house for a cup of tea and some company until after lunch. On Friday mornings I would go into the city to the public library and I would spend hours choosing my selection for the following week.

"I read everything, especially history. I was obsessed with it. Not the usual sort of book about kings and queens and wars. I preferred to read about ordinary people's lives, what they believed, what they did. And I loved the books about magic. I discovered that *Emain* is an island from Celtic mythology, a place that provides talismans from fruit trees where the blossom and branch merge together into a healing rod. *An amaranthine place is Emain . . . lovely its rathe . . . plentiful apple trees grow from that ground.* Hazel and apple trees flourish on *Emain*. Hazel is the tree of poetic inspiration; the source of all knowledge of the arts and sciences is held within the sacred nut. And the fruit from apple trees protect the poet's soul from harm. Cut an apple in half. Not through the core, around the middle. Look at the pentacle that is revealed to you. The star of Aphrodite, the sacred heart of the Celts. The *Amaranthine* heart. I love that word. It means having the quality of flowers that never fade. Immortal blooms.

"When I was caring for Elva, I could not disappear into my private world of the mythical past. I felt frustrated but I could see an end to it. I said to myself that the books were waiting for me to come back, they were calling me, and I would return. But no sooner had my mother died than I was faced with another family problem and this time it was a baby and the caring and the worry would go on for years and years. I had known women who had taken on the task of caring for their unmarried daughters' children. Sometimes the mother and the daughter would disappear for months and then return with the newborn and pass it off as the mother's child. Or the baby would be acknowledged as the daughter's but the mother would bond to the child and grieve when the daughter married and took the child with her. Or the daughter would leave home and the mother would be left with a child when she was middle-aged and tired and wanting some peace for herself.

"I'm telling you this Wendy because I don't want you to think that I was uncaring or did not love babies. Quite the opposite. I knew from experience that I would fall hopelessly in love with Joy's little one and then would burn with resentment because I could not live the life that I wanted because of this hopeless love. I knew that once I had bathed and dressed and soothed that little body I would fall victim to the solemn gaze and the shining eyes and the curled fingers. I was deeply afraid of bonding to the child of my child and I knew that once I let that baby into the house, I would be lost.

"I had three choices. One, I could defy Jack and stifle my ambivalent feelings about rearing another child and bring both Joy and the baby back into the family. I was certain that Jack would never throw me out but I also knew that there would be tension and misery for months, maybe for years, and that the happy family life we had enjoyed might not ever return. Two, I could leave Jack and take Joy, Morry, and the baby to another town. But I had no job, no money, nowhere to go. In those days it was difficult for a wife to leave her husband. I would have lost custody of Morry and I would not have been permitted to take anything from the house except my clothes. Jack could have taken me to court, and if the judge willed it, I could have been forced by law to return to the marriage. And if that happened, I would have gained nothing.

"But apart from the practical difficulties, I did not want to leave Jack. I was fond of him and I would worry myself sick if I left him. He could not cook or do housework and he would get depressed without me. He would die of loneliness. And I would die of guilt. So I took the third option, the one of adoption. The child welfare officer was very positive about my decision. Our families are vetted most carefully Mrs Winter, the wee one will have every advantage. We insist that Baby has its own room, and the husband must be in a suitable profession and the wife emotionally secure. They must own their own house of course. Stability is most important. No, we can't tell you where Baby Winter will be placed. Confidentiality is most important. And of course it works both ways. We never divulge the name of the birth mother to the adoptive family. Baby is then accepted more readily by the adoptive parents in our experience. You see Mrs Winter the sad fact is that some of our girls are shippies and other unmentionables, and we would not want our families to know this now would we. This is one case where ignorance is bliss ha ha. And if the birth mother doesn't know where the child is, she doesn't worry about it. It disappears into thin air, as if it has never been. The birth mother can wipe the slate clean and make a new life for herself.

"It sounded so convincing. And I believed that adoption was the best chance both for Joy and the baby. So I agreed. I gave Joy no option. No, I will not care for the baby, no you cannot bring it home. We will sign the papers and that will be the end of the matter."

I have been sitting in the same position ever since I began to talk. My arthritic pain is coming back. The pain killers are wearing off. I look at Wendy. She touches my hand gently and suggests that she comes back tomorrow. "This must be hard for you to talk about," she says.

I can see that she is upset about what happened to Joy. I feel the need to find out more about her. Throughout the telling of my stories, I have sensed her approval of me. I realise how little I know about her.

"Are you adopted Wendy?" I ask.

"No, I'm not." She hesitates. "Look Alice, after tomorrow when we finish this bit about Joy and the baby, I'm going to confess something to you and I swear that if you ask me to return the tapes to you, I will do it."

Confess? Wendy is clever and confident and can take control of any situation. Or so I had thought. I ask her to explain.

"Sorry to be so mysterious. But there's something I have to do before I speak with you again."

I wave her goodbye. Another humid day with black clouds moving across the tops of the Waitakere Hills. No rain, just threatening skies. In spite of the pain in my hips and knees and the oppressive heat, I feel much better than I did earlier this morning. It's more than the sight of the folded fifty-dollar notes lying on my table. I love the company of Wendy. She listens to me like my late friend Mary Crawford used to do, without judgement, without censorship. And in spite of her youth, I feel close to her. I want her to keep coming to my house after the oral history project is finished. I want her to be my friend. To tell me things about her life.

I drink a glass of water and take some more anti-inflammatory pills. These are the last ones I will take today. Although the pain is difficult to bear, I want to be clear headed when Wendy returns in the morning. I pull the curtains across my window and lock my back door then lie down on the sofa and fall into an uneasy sleep.

# 9

# *Joy*

I rise early and drive through the sleeping towns of the Waikato; Te Kowhai, Ngaruawahia, Ohinewai. The river runs sleek and dark beside the highway, keeping pace with my speeding car. The sky becomes flushed with pink light as I pass the thermal electricity station that dominates the skyline of Huntly. The huge installation creates a reflected double of itself in the smoothly flowing water. Plumes of white smoke stand perfectly still in the windless dawn.

I swing between elation and terror. I have no guilt about breaking my promise to Wayne. I said I would not make contact with her, I said nothing about entering the space where she lives. How could he possibly have expected me to sit passively in my house in Raglan waiting for her to lift the embargo? After she's heard what Alice has to say about me, she may decide to stay hidden from me for ever. Maybe he already knows that she does not want to meet me, maybe this is why he has given me the address. Surely he knows that I would be unable to resist the temptation.

My mind races with a multiplicity of plots and counterplots until I feel myself slipping under the surface of rational thought. I divert my mind to images of physical realities, surf breaking over the Raglan Bar, cliffs at Mussel Rocks veiled in salt spray, spinifex driven by a brisk westerly along a rainy beach. It does not work. My imagination is literally running away with itself.

I begin the long climb through the Bombay Hills. There is little traffic except for the trucks and semis that dominate the highways at all hours of the night and day. My real fear is that if I see Marlene, I will be unable to control myself. I have absolutely no idea of what I might do. I am afraid that my obsession may overwhelm me to the point of madness. I do not want her first sight of me to be that of a crazy woman, pulling out my hair and pleading for forgiveness.

All too soon, the Harbour Bridge looms. Even at this early hour the traffic coming into the city is bumper to bumper. I leave the highway at the Devonport Turnoff and follow the map that is etched into my mind. I drive directly to number twenty-seven Hillside Crescent.

The house is just as I had visualised it; three-storeyed, luxuriously endowed with smooth white curves and high private windows and discrete iron security gates. In the front, there is a cluster of small palm trees and large ceramic pots planted with trailing herbs and succulents. The back half of the garden is hidden behind an apricot-coloured wall. The only difference between this house and the one that has lived in my imagination for forty years is the view. This house is on the city side of the peninsula and Rangitoto Island is invisible. Marlene's house faces the high glass towers that stand in austere formation along the opposite shoreline.

The street is wide and flanked by phoenix palms and pohutukawa trees. I sit in my car and wait. Now that I have safely accomplished the journey to this house, now that I know that she is here, in this space, breathing out in concert with my breath, sharing the same seconds ticking towards a resolution, I feel a disconcerting sense of anticlimax. Am I behaving foolishly? I want to turn the key and drive away but I am unable to do it.

For an hour, I watch the closed door of the garage like a fox awaiting its prey. Willing the door to open, fearful that if it does, I will have to make a decision on what to do next.

Then it happens. The door glides noiselessly open and a white Honda Accord backs out. It has darkened glass windows and I cannot see clearly within. There are two people, a man and a woman. I am convinced that the woman is Marlene. She is at the wheel and I can see that she is tall like me but I can't see the shape of her features or the colour of her eyes. Within seconds, the car has driven away towards the city.

My body is quaking as if I have been dealt a savage blow to the abdomen. This is the place where I carry the ugly scar that provided a doorway for Marlene to enter the world. Too young, they said, and such a big baby. No alternative but to operate. So they cut my stomach down from the navel into two separate halves. They told me it would fade but it never did. I hate the sight of it. My stomach is puckered with a purple zipper. I hate it because of what it means. It signals to me that I have sacrificed my body to provide a child for another woman. A more deserving woman. And the terrible thing is that when I saw Marlene flash past me, I wanted to tear off my clothes and expose my scar to her. Gaze upon this my daughter, gaze. I have sacrificed the centre of my being for you. I offer my defective body as proof that I wanted you born alive.

The tail lights of her car vanish around the corner at the bottom of Hillside Crescent. I am disappointed that I did not have a clearer view of her but I am relieved that I have survived the first sighting without making a fool of myself. During the drive to Auckland, I had harboured wild fantasies about our first meeting. One of the more fanciful was that she would pull up beside my car and look into my face and instantly recognise me as her birth mother and cry, I have waited so long for this moment!

I turn the ignition key and idle the motor. What now Joy, I say aloud. Deliver this document to Wayne Marsh. My side of the story of Marlene's adoption to feed to the hacker TIM. Drive back to Hamilton and get to his office before he goes to lunch. I don't want to fax it, too risky. He has made me nervous with his talk of hackers.

On the other hand, I could ring Alice and see if she wants me to pop in and see her. She would appreciate an extra visit. I could take the opportunity to drop a hint that there may be an addition to the family soon. Two in fact, Marlene and Pixel. I wonder how she'll take to the idea that she has a great-grand-daughter of eighteen. Morry's girls have two boys each, but they are still toddlers.

I drive to Devonport. I am hungry and I have an urgent need of coffee. I decide to find a breakfast café before I join the rush-hour madness on the motorway. I find a parking area and pay fifty cents at the automatic ticket machine. There is a white Honda Accord parked near the centre of the lot. I pull up beside it and peer through the windows. Is this her car? I did not see her number plate when she drove out of her garage. This one reads RURICH.

I feel excited as I enter the nearest café. Maybe she is eating her breakfast here. I order croissants and a double espresso and seat myself at a window with a view of the beach and the ferry buildings. I look around the café. It is almost full. Oh god there she is, a tall woman sitting with a well-dressed man. I can't help myself, I stare at her.

She is talking languidly to the man, who appears to be very irate about something. She is beautiful. Smooth white skin, rounded nose and chin set in perfect symmetry. Then I overhear the man calling her Sylvie and the bubble bursts. I remember that Marlene's car had tinted windows and the car outside did not. And of course this woman is far too young to have been Marlene. Wrong car, wrong woman.

I drink my coffee and eat my croissants. I find a public telephone in the parking lot and ring Alice. No answer. I can't hear her phone ringing at the other end. Immediately I see her on the floor, dead or dying, the phone ripped from the wall and her flat ransacked.

I ring Telecom to report the fault. Yes they are working on it, someone has already reported it. No, the fault is not at Mrs Winter's residence, there is a problem at the exchange. I feel relieved. I decide not to visit her without warning. It is a long detour to go over to Sandringham. She drives out every day to St Luke's Mall or to the library. She may not be there. I am due to come and see her in a few days and besides, my head is so full of Marlene that I do not want to talk about other things.

In spite of my long-term fantasy of Marlene living with rich parents in a big house on the North Shore, I am afraid of her wealth. I deliberately constructed the notion of a privileged childhood to stop myself from worrying that she had been placed with poor or abusive parents. I clung to the belief that she must be better off with them than she ever could have been with me.

I invented multiple scenarios for her life as an adult. I had her married to a farmer, plump and cheerful and overworked, living with a bunch of unruly kids and a milking herd in Pirongia. I had her a high-flying secretary, divorced, living in a tasteful apartment in Mission Bay. I had her the widow of a working man, sweeping her porch every day in a home unit in Mt Roskill. I had this fantasy of rescue, yes, I will take the children off your hands, yes, I will give you advice on redecorating, yes, I will provide companionship when you are alone.

Now here she is in real time, the owner of successful companies and many properties, with a life style of travel and sophistication that I cannot imagine. What can I talk to her about? The tides that ebb and flow in Raglan Harbour, the state of my house, my failures in marriage and in work? I have nothing to offer her.

And yet I feel a compulsion to tell her the story of her birth and consequent abduction by the welfare officer. I hope that this will awaken a desire in her to meet me, then I will fulfil my need to hear her voice and see her face. If she finds me hollow after she gets to know me, so be it. I will explain to her that I don't want to share her exotic life or take anything material from her. All I ask for is evidence of her bodily existence. I will ask for photographs to serve as proof of the immortality of flesh, just one or two pictures to keep me company after she dismisses me.

I drive over the Harbour Bridge. The traffic is still heavy but moves at a brisk pace. I am pleased now that I decided against going to visit my mother. I want to get my document to Wayne Marsh as soon as possible, I want TIM to lay the bait for Pixel tonight, I want her to run down from the tower at the top of the house at Hillside Crescent, yelling to Marlene, read this! Read this now! You were taken from the womb of a heroine!

I have titled this document, **For Marlene and Pixel Hunter: The True Story of Joy.** And I began with the poem, *i have no name, i am but two days old . . . i happy am, joy is my name . . .*

This is what I wanted to call you. And I did give you this name, behind their backs, right at the end. But let me begin at your beginning. Your father was a bikie and a rebel. I met him during the time when my grandmother Elva was living in our house in Sandringham. Although I was fourteen years old when Elva came to live with us, I was still a naive child. Children were over-protected from the terrors of life in those days. It was easy. No television, no radio, no travel.

Elva was dying, slowly, painfully. I knew that it was drink that was killing her. Yet I saw my mother giving her gin, glass after glass. I couldn't understand this. Was she a murderer? Until Elva got sick, I thought my mother could do anything, she was the healer of the world. For months, I heard my mother weeping, I saw her helpless in the face of grief, and I blamed her for not being strong enough to make my grandmother well again.

This was my first encounter with the certainty of death. But I found it hard to accept that there are painful things in the human condition that even the fiercest will cannot change. Looking back, I know that my rage was wrongly directed. I should not have punished Alice for my loss of faith in the power of the mother.

I fell into a deep depression. No one noticed. They were too preoccupied with the needs of Elva. I started to hang around the local milkbar after school. This was a time when even the slightest sign of rebellion in young people caused a moral panic. I revelled in the sour looks that people gave me on the street when I lit up a cigarette, dressed in my Grammar clothes. And then I met Robert Goff. He wore black leathers and rode a Harley Davidson. He came from a wealthy family but he refused to conform to their wishes and enter the family firm. He was twenty when I met him, already a man.

How can I describe to you the glamour of his presence? The first time I saw him I was sitting with Sharon, a friend from school, in the Oasis Milkbar in Sandringham. We were eating icecream sundaes. He walked into the shop as if he owned it. He had a crewcut, leather collar turned up against the wind, cigarette at the corner of his mouth, hands in pockets. I knew in an instant that I had found what I was looking for.

This may surprise you, but at that time I was not looking for a boyfriend. I wanted to get pregnant. Simple as that. And he looked old enough and beautiful enough to know what sex was about. The only boys I knew were the same age as me and they were physically unappetising and behaved like idiots. Robert was like a visitor from another planet. On the first afternoon he came into the Oasis, a crowd of girls quickly formed around him. I sat mutely, afraid of the strong sexual arousal he evoked in me. I was nearly fifteen years

143

old and I had never had these feelings before.

I ignored him and that may be why he picked me out of the group to be his girlfriend. He came into the milkbar day after day, causing a frenzy amongst the local girls. I could not look at him. I had this ridiculous notion that he knew about the sexual fantasies that I had woven around him since the first moment I saw him. The things that I had imagined us doing together were so vivid that I felt as if they were tattooed in technicolour all over my skin.

Having an illegitimate child in the fifties was possibly the wickedest thing a girl could do. Forced marriages and banishment were common. In spite of this, I wanted to have a baby of my own. I don't know where this strong desire came from. Looking back, it was something that had always been with me. It seemed as inevitable as breathing that I should have a child of my own. And the sooner the better.

I was also determined never to get married. My parents' relationship was a charade. Alice provided Jack with an image of himself that had little to do with the reality of the man. He never lifted a finger in the house, he left everything to her. And although he never hit us, he had a terrible temper and would yell and scream at us for no reason. It was the inconsistency that made me nervous. I could do something for weeks on end, like singing a particular song, and he would pay no attention. Then suddenly, he would go into a rage and tell me never to sing that song again, I was nothing but garbage and he was going to throw me on the rubbish tip. Sometimes he would go into a mammoth sulk and cut me dead for days on end. My mother Alice would not hear a word against him. He works hard she told me. He only gets drunk one night a week. He deserves to have a social life. And perhaps if you learned not to provoke him, you would find him easier to handle.

It seemed to me that the women in our street were experts on the moods of men. They would wait demurely for their husbands to come home from work each night and carefully study their faces to see which way the wind blew. Women's folklore; never ask a favour of a hungry man, feed him first; keep the children quiet at night, he works hard all day and needs his sleep; never let him see you sitting idle, always have something to occupy your hands. If he is happy, ask him for a few extra shillings. If he is drunk, take it from his pockets. Feed his stomach and the thing that hangs on the end of it and he will never leave you.

I learned from a very early age that the moods of men were not to be trifled with. And I absorbed into my bones the manipulative games that married women were forced to play to achieve their ends. How to keep the husband happy. This was a constant topic discussed by the group of tea-drinking women who sat around my mother's kitchen table. And if a man strayed sexually or deserted his family, the fault usually lay with the wife. Maybe she had nagged him or let herself go, maybe she had been lazy or dirty or both. A desertion was not a common event. But when it did happen, the women agonised over it and could not rest until they had hammered out a mutually agreed upon explanation.

I can see now that my mother Alice and the other women were not as down trodden as I perceived them to be when I was a girl. Although they were subject to their husbands' moods and had little economic or social freedom, they had ways of fighting back. They would mimic the men behind their backs, call them little boys and go into gales of laughter over their domestic ineptitudes. If a wife was ill or in the maternity home, she would later relay to the other women the hilarious outcome of trusting men to perform women's work. The way that men hung out washing on a rotary clothesline was greeted with gales of laughter. The sheets were in the middle and the underclothes on the outside! The shirts and blouses were hanging sideways, and he boiled the cardigans! The kids ate meat pies every night with lumpy mashed potato, you should have seen the state of the stove . . .

I was afraid of ending up like the women in my street. I did not want to spend my life making trivial jokes about men or holding out my hand for money every pay night. But I wanted sex and I wanted babies and I had this dream that I could live alone in my own house and have as many boyfriends and as many babies as I wanted. I was hopelessly impractical. I thought I could give birth to babies first and then things like money and houses would magically come to me.

I had not reckoned on falling in love with the man that I chose to be your father. Robert never saw you, he came off his motorbike one winter's night before you were born and lay in a coma for five weeks before he died. If he had lived he would have been in danger of being sent to jail. I was under the age of consent. They were very strict about consent in those days. The police often turned up at Bethlehem House, the unmarried mothers' home that I was sent to. They came to interrogate the underage girls about their sex lives. I refused to speak to them. I never told anyone his name, not even after he died.

A week after I first saw him, he came into the milkbar and bought me a spider; a bottle of soft drink tipped over a lump of vanilla icecream and stirred into a froth. He put a shilling into the juke box, and played *Don't Step on My Blue Suede Shoes*, *Rock Around the Clock* and *In the Mood*. I sipped my spider, unable to speak a word of thanks. He sat beside me in the booth and kept time to the music by tapping his spoon on the side of the table.

Sharon came into the milkbar and did a double-take when she saw Robert sitting next to me. We sat in silence until the trumpet played the last high note of *In the Mood*. Then he turned and looked at me. We got up and left the milkbar together.

The crowd of young girls hanging around outside the door moved aside to let us out. They stared at me as if I were royalty. A rush of feeling that I later identified as sexual triumph drowned out my fear of riding on the motorbike.

I climbed on the back of the Harley and we roared off. I clung to his waist. We went driving as fast as the wind, twisting and turning, heading out west towards the shores of the Manukau Harbour. At first I was terrified of the speed and the way that the bike leaned over when we turned a corner, but soon I became so exhilarated with the sensation of movement and the strength of Robert's body, that all fear left me.

We went as far as Huia. For the last few miles the road was metal and stones flew up and stung my legs through my thick black stockings. We stopped at a place where the bush grew right down to the road. The damp trees and ferns gathered us into that peculiar state of listening where every drop of water falls with crystal clarity and the beat of a pigeon's wing sounds as loud as a kettle drum. We climbed and fought our way through thick vines and manuka brush until we came to a shack. No birds except for a lone fantail who appeared almost at once and hovered just above my head. The stillness of the bush in winter. A sound of running water somewhere above us in the distance. The lichens and mosses soggy with rain beneath our feet. I asked Robert if he lived here. My voice sounded squeaky and immature.

He laughed and said of course not, he hadn't been here for ages. Surprised the shack is still here. Me and some mates of mine built it years ago. Probably too overgrown for the council to find it.

We went inside. The walls were constructed out of ponga logs lashed together with twine and the roof was made of corrugated iron sheets. The floor was dirt, stamped down into a hard dry surface, and there was a sleeping platform of wooden slats and a wooden table with a bench attached.

If I had known that Robert was planning to bring me here today, I would have gone home first and changed my clothes. I cursed my school uniform to hell, with its pleated gym slip and girdle, white collar, tie, lisle stockings, navy bloomers. Being dressed like this was not part of the fantasies I had been inventing around my first sexual encounter with Robert.

As it turned out, nothing happened. We sat and talked and he told me a few things about his childhood and the big house his father owned and how he had a little room at the side to come and go as he pleased. No sisters. Just him and his older brother Rex. His old lady had done a runner, taken off with another man.

Did that hurt you? I asked.

He shrugged. No, she was right to go. My old man's a bastard.

I was thrilled to hear him speak that word. We were never allowed to say anything negative about our parents. Honour thy mother and father. Never tell family secrets outside the house. I said, my father is a bastard too.

Mine is a rich bastard and that makes him more dangerous.

Why don't you leave home?

Because he wants me to. I'm a social embarrassment. I won't study or work in the family business. He wants me to sweep the warehouse floor, to teach me the value of work, to find out the source of all the good food I have eaten, all the expensive clothes I have worn, all the motorbikes I have owned. These are the very words he uses. I don't listen to them any more. He said the same shit to my mother and my brother, over and over. Rex has given in. He tried to rebel but the old man won. Now Rex is working sixteen hours a day and has lost all his values. I am determined to hang on and I plan to take the prick for all I can get.

I fell in love with him then and there. He was totally single minded about his revenge on his father. I had never allowed myself to think of paying back my father for his treatment of me. And at that point I still loved my mother enough to protect her from my anger against my father.

We returned to the Oasis Milkbar on the Harley. He said, see you tomorrow? And I nodded and tried to walk away nonchalantly as if I didn't care one way or the other.

I met him there every day after school and soon we became lovers. He gave me money for new clothes and I bought patent leather boots and a black duffle coat and makeup. Some days I did not arrive at school. I would take my bike clothes in my sports bag and meet Robert in Karangahape Road and we would spend the whole day at Huia or at Karekare. Sometimes we went to the hot springs at Helensville. Always out west. Robert had a theory about money and the colour of sand. He said that rich people believe that beaches should be white because this is all they ever see on tourist brochures and postcards. This is why the rich congregate on the eastern side of the North Island where the beaches are made of white sand. They inflate the price of property, leaving the black sandhills of the west coast for the poor and the dispossessed.

Robert thought them fools. Look at this Joy, the wildness of this place, the shifting wind and sand, the pull of this water. I'm glad they chose the other side. We don't have to put up with the sight of their expensive yachts and motor boats and ugly ranch-style houses. The pretence of a return to the simple life. Slumming it. A house built on white sand, empty, except for the Christmas occupation of just three weeks in the year.

Robert said the Waitemata Harbour was kept clean for the use of rich people and tourists coming in cruise ships. He preferred the Manukau Harbour. It was despised in those days. The harbour was used as a dumping ground for animal parts from Westfield Freezing Works and chemicals from paint factories and timber yards. A place only fit for bikies and fishermen dumb enough to want to eat the oily mullet and other disgusting creatures that lived down deep in the mud.

I have never loved anyone as much as I loved him. And I have never been able to recapture the sense of strength that he gave me. Once I had got over my initial sense of shyness with him, I felt free to say and do anything that I wanted. Can you imagine what this meant? At Grammar I had been forced to imitate the fifties version of *the good girl;* chaste, quiet, studious, covered from head to toe in black and white clothes, gloves, hats, stockings, no bare skin showing except for the face. We were taught that our sexuality was a dangerous commodity to be repressed and denied at all costs. It was never as baldly stated as this of course. The accent was on being ladylike. It was purgatory for working-class girls like me. Everything about us was taken to task. Our accents, our dress, our manners, even the way that we walked. In our grooming classes, we had to walk around with books on our heads. We were taught how to cook using the best silver and china. I could never work out if we were being trained to marry up into the middle classes or to lift the standard of the low life families that our backgrounds doomed us to raise.

I would stand at the cooking bench peeling apples for fancy pies, rubbing butter into flour to make short pastry, revelling in my secret life with Robert. I would sit in sewing class learning how to turn shirt collars and sew fine french seams, my body in one place, my thoughts in another, going over and over the exciting things we had done to each other the day before.

I did not lie to him about my intentions. I told him that I never wanted to marry and that I loved babies and that I didn't want to stay at school. He held my face in his hands and said, me too, I will never marry.

Your conception was an accident but not an altogether unwanted one. Robert used condoms and one failed to work. I got pregnant and we planned to run away together after I had given birth and live in another town and pretend that I was eighteen and that we were married.

It would have worked. I was tall and thin and looked much older than I was. Then he crashed and died and I sat waiting for the inevitable day when I would be found out. I bound my stomach with a set of corsets every morning. I had no idea what would happen to me. And at that stage, I was too numb with unspoken grief to care.

I managed to conceal my condition until I was six months pregnant. Then one morning, after a restless night when you kicked and gurgled and swam within my body like a rapturous fish, I knew that the time had come to reveal your presence. I did not want to bind my stomach into that torturous corset again. I was afraid that your skull would be permanently crushed. That daily binding caused me much guilt and fear. But I worried for nothing. I had a caesarian, so your head did not have to fight a narrow pathway through my body. You emerged unmarked.

I left for school as usual but instead of taking the tram I went down the street and knocked on Mary Crawford's door. Although she was much older than Alice, she was the only friend my mother had in the street. Alice had fallen out with some of her old cronies like Mrs Simms and Mrs Mason. I was glad that they no longer visited our house to take tea with my mother. I hated those women for their sanctimonious and rule-bound attitudes. They controlled their families with a rod of iron. Or thought they did. I knew what their kids got up to behind their backs but of course I was never allowed to say anything. The code of silence between children and parents back in the fifties was like a brick wall.

One day, up at the Sandringham shops, Mrs Mason walked towards me and a group of my friends. I was wearing my patent leather boots and my duffle coat and I was smoking a cigarette. She swept past me and gave me the black stare. I blew out smoke in a high plume and said in a big loud voice, *there goes the old bag of May Street*. If you don't know about the black stare, it was how people looked at you back in those days if you were hanging around the streets with Maori kids.

Being rude to Mrs Mason was hardly the crime of the century but what I did was tantamount to causing the sky to fall to the earth. She reported me to the Head Mistress. I thought I was safe because it happened after school hours and I was out of uniform. In spite of this, I was called into the Head's office and severely castigated. Smoking on the street and running with a bad crowd. This is not the first disturbing report I have had about you. You are on thin ice my girl, be careful, or your position here will be under threat.

I hated her cold manner and her air of superiority and her absolute power over me. I left the office weeping with frustration and anger. I regretted my lack of control in front of her. I did not want her to know that her words had upset me.

I was hardly a problem child. I worked hard at school and I was polite to the teachers. This was the extent of my defiance. Smoking a cigarette once or twice a week, dressing after school in a duffle coat that was considered vaguely bohemian and therefore dangerous, and daring to stand and talk on the pavement outside my local suburban shops with a group of school children that included one quiet girl who was the only Maori in my class at Grammar. I can't even remember her name.

I confessed my pregnancy to Mary. I asked if she would come with me to break the news to Alice. I was scared of my mother's reaction and I thought she would be more restrained in her behaviour towards me if her best friend was with me. Mary reassured me by saying that she was certain that Alice would stick by me. Unlike some others in this neighbourhood that I could mention, she said rather grimly.

You will want to know how my mother received the news that you were about to come into the world Marlene. I told her I was sorry for causing her this worry so soon after her own mother had died. And she said, I don't care what you have done, you are still my daughter, I will take care of you.

I was so relieved I nearly cried. But then she told me what she meant by "taking care of me". I was to be sent to a home for unmarried mothers and you were to be adopted. I agreed to the first proposal but not to the second. Let me say it loud and clear. I never wanted you to be adopted, never.

Here is what happened. Alice put me into Bethlehem House. I can hardly bear to think about that place and those poor girls who shared that time with me. There were all sorts there; foster kids, girls with false identities from rich families, girls like me from working-class backgrounds, raped girls, girls pregnant by their fathers.

We were treated like slaves. We had to do heavy laundry work and cleaning. Some of us were allowed to study for school exams by correspondence but I refused. I did not want to study the New Zealand Wars or the life-cycle of the monarch butterfly or the climatic changes wrought by the last ice age. School studies seemed so remote from me in that place, and so irrelevant. I turned inwards away from the world, I became preoccupied with the being that I was growing within me.

I rested as much as I could after I had finished my work for the day. And I cried myself to sleep every night over the loss of Robert. My numbness burst after I was sent to Bethlehem House. I allowed myself to grieve openly for him in front of the other girls. We shared our stories of punishment and shame. Especially the dreadful moment when we had told our mothers that we were pregnant. Some of the mothers screamed, some became violent and attacked their daughters; all wept. I concealed nothing from my fellow prisoners except for the identity of my dead lover. I was terrified that Robert's powerful father might try to get custody of you to replace his dead son.

I want you to know this about your father. He was clever and good and he really loved me. And he loved the idea of you. You were never an unwanted child. Things would have been very different if he had lived. I would have still had to go to an unmarried mothers' home because of my age but I would have run off with him after you were born and we would have been happy together. All three of us.

Alice was kind enough to me while I was in Bethlehem House. She came every week and brought me nice things to eat and soap and perfume and magazines. She refused to allow me to go to afternoon tea on Sundays with the rich women who thought they were doing us a favour. The other girls hated these outings but they were forced to go. They were accused of being ungrateful if they complained. Some of the girls were taken away to be unpaid servants and childminders for doctors and other professionals. Alice would not allow this either, thank goodness. She remembered her own time as a servant in the thirties and was adamant that this would not happen to me.

Your grandmother can be very difficult at times but she is not unkind. The main point of contention we had was over your adoption. She lied to me. She schemed with the authorities behind my back and I was tricked into giving you away. Never believe her if she tells you that I chose to abandon you. I did not. I admit that I signed the papers for you to be given to Beverly and Richard, but I had no choice. Just because I signed does not mean that I gave informed consent. Far from it.

The night I went into labour I was fearful of the pain, but happy that I was going to see you at last. You were born at St Joan's Hospital, but don't go looking for it. The building has disappeared off the face of the earth. Urban renewal. They shouldn't have done it. I believe that it is wrong to take away the buildings where women have laboured and babies have been born. Too much grief and joy and pain have happened within those walls. It is like trampling on a cemetery and bulldozing the gravestones as if nothing of human importance has ever happened there.

I lay in labour for two days in that ward. I remember every detail of the ornate plaster ceiling, primrose in colour, and the stained walls, and the smell of Dettol and the cigarette smoke that drifted from the nurses' alcove. I remember the green curtains swaying around my bed.

I was only fifteen and I'd never been in pain before. I sweated and pushed and screamed. I lay on an iron bed on a closed-in verandah and there were other young girls groaning in labour in the other beds. This was the special ward for the Wicked Ones. And over each bed a label with our names with the prefix Mrs added for the sake of propriety. Push Mrs Winter push! This is what the charge nurse kept shouting at me. And the pain and the fear and the twilight sleep they kept pushing into my face confused me and I thought my mother was there and that she was pushing with me and I cried out to her to tell them to stop torturing me. Save me Mother, I called, save me! But of course she was sitting at home in Sandringham, they hadn't even told her that I had gone into labour.

The girl in the bed next to me made a lot of noise even though she was only in the first stage of labour. I heard the charge nurse say to her, you didn't mind it going in so you shouldn't mind it coming out. I felt like kicking her. But by this time I was flat on my back with my legs encased in sterile cloths and tied to two metal stirrups. I could not move. I pushed and pushed and this same nurse kept shoving her gloved hand up my vagina and telling me to get a move on, they didn't have all day. Then a doctor came and shoved his hand up me and hurt me and said well it hasn't moved enough, it's off to theatre with you I'm afraid.

I was terrified. They did not explain what was happening to me. I thought you had died and that they were going to cut you out in pieces. I tried to fight them off but it was no use. They knocked me out with an injection and the next thing I knew, I was back in the ward, lying on my back with my abdomen strapped up, in shocking pain, and no sign of a baby.

I screamed until someone came. Thank god it was a new nurse, an older woman, who told me yes that Baby was fine, healthy and big, and that I had had a caesarian. Did I know what that was? I shook my head. She explained everything to me and held my hand and got me something for the pain.

Then Matron came from the home to check up on me. I pleaded with her to fetch my baby from the nursery. Now, I said. At once. So that I can see for myself if I have been told the truth. Alive or dead, I must see it.

No, she said. It is better not to see Baby or know whether it is a boy or girl. Then you will get over it more quickly and will go back to your life as if nothing has happened. Your baby is not dead. Trust me. This is the best way.

To say this to me when my womb was cut and screaming with loss and agony, to say this when for months I had longed to see you, to say this when I had gone through the ordeal of mourning the death of your father without speaking his name, to say this! I went berserk. Hysterical. For days on end. They could not control me. In the end, a psychiatrist was called to my bedside and I heard him say, I strongly recommend that this young woman sights her child immediately. I will not be answerable for her mental health if this does take place at once.

I had won, for the moment. The nurse reluctantly brought you to me, wrapped in a swaddling cloth so that only the top of your head was visible. I pulled anxiously at the cloth and I saw your face at last. And you overwhelmed me with your beauty and your presence and your life. You breathed in and out, your fat eyelids were closed against the light, your fingers clung to the edges of the cloth, and I could see that you were determined to cling strongly to life. In that instant, I did not see you as a newborn child, I saw you as an extension of myself and Alice and Elva and all the other unknown women stretching back before us, roped together in a repetitive sequence of ecstasy and pain and love and dispossession.

All I knew was that I had to have you. But as I confessed to you before, I was hopelessly impractical. I refused to hand you over. And Alice was advised not to force me until after I had recovered from the childbirth. It was thought that I was suffering from deep post-natal depression or maybe even a form of childbirth psychosis. I heard them whispering behind my back. She'll soon tire of caring for Baby the doctor said. Give her six months, then we can act.

Meanwhile, I was transferred to another hospital. I was told that it was a special women's place where I could learn to care for Baby. I was placed in this so-called rest home with dozens of poor old ladies who were too crazy to live at home. There were a few younger ones. One thought she was pregnant but wasn't and she kept going into false labour. She'd had a stillborn baby and it had driven her over the brink. Another woman, Irene, had tried to kill her husband with a carving knife. She was the nicest one there, even though she was a potential murderer. She told me that she had pretended to be off her head so that she could keep out of jail. Better food here Kid, she joked. But at night, I would hear her weeping and calling for her little boy and one day she told me that when she got out, the first thing she'd do is get another knife and finish the job on the prick. In the heart next time Kid. Right in.

They allowed me to look after you, wash you, feed you, but only with a bottle. I told myself stories to explain my presence in that place. I didn't mind being there. And I wove fairy stories so that I would not get too anxious about our future. I fooled myself into believing that I would be able to stay there until my father Jack agreed to my coming home with you. The truth was that as long as I had you with me, I didn't care where I lived.

Alice came to see me whenever she could and put on a cheerful face except when I asked her to take her home with me. I hate you being here, she said. But you are not well enough to leave just yet. We are at the mercy of the doctors. Be patient my darling, everything will be all right.

Meanwhile, I spent all of my waking hours with you. I loved the way you gazed up at me when I gave you a bottle of milk. A nurse told me that this is how babies learn the pattern and shape of their mothers' faces. Your deep brown eyes have burned themselves forever into mine. Surely that six months of intensive gazing has not completely disappeared from our memories. I pray that there will be a shock of mutual recognition when we meet.

I was in a room by myself and they let me have a cot for you next to my bed. It was like our own private little palace. Food came three times a day, and our washing and cleaning were done for us. Doctors came and asked me many questions about my childhood and my relationship with Alice. One doctor told me that girls like me got pregnant because they wanted someone to love them. Apparently the fact that I gave birth to you was Alice's fault. She didn't love me enough. So I had gone out and got pregnant so that I had something to love. I thought this a stupid explanation but I pretended to agree. I nodded yes to everything they said so that they would think me mature and well behaved enough to keep you.

Early one morning, Irene sneaked into my room and told me that she had overheard them saying that a social worker was coming to take Baby Winter away for adoption.

I confronted the male nurse when he brought in my breakfast. He told me not to believe anything Irene said. She's very ill, and this makes her unreliable.

You're wrong, I answered. She only pretends to be crazy.

Look, he snapped. She's never been married. Or had a kid. She made it all up.

But I believed what Irene had told me about the social worker coming to the rest home. So I dressed you in warm clothes and stole a tin of formula and some bottles from the kitchen and I crept out of the side door into the cold July air.

I walked for miles, going south, keeping off the main roads. Near Takanini, a man driving a truck loaded with onions stopped and asked me if I wanted a ride. He seemed a decent sort, so I climbed up and we rattled down the Great South Road. I told him that you were my little sister and that I was taking you down to relations in Rotorua because our mother was too sick to care for us. He said you poor kids, where is your father? Dead, I told him. Came off his motorbike ten months ago.

Ian, the driver, bought me toasted sandwiches and a pot of tea at the tearooms in Te Kauwhata. My Uncle Denby and Aunty Sally lived a few miles from where we had stopped. I couldn't wait to get out of that tearoom and back into the truck. I didn't like being so close to Sally's and Denby's house. They might come into the tearooms and although we did not visit them often, they were sure to recognise me. They would be shocked to see me with a baby. They would never believe the story about the little sister.

I remember every detail of that journey; the swamps and the undrained farmland, the Waikato River lapping the edge of the railway line at Mercer, the brown water flowing up over the running boards when we drove through a flash flood near Taupiri, the pukeko that suddenly darted out at us from a clump of flax at the side of the road, Ian's distress at having to hit it on the head with a wheel brace to put it out of its misery.

I got out of the truck in Hamilton. Ian was getting a little nosey for my liking. He wanted to know the name and address of my relations in Rotorua. So I asked him to stop near the main bus station in Anglesea Street.

By this time it was late afternoon and the rain had begun to fall again. I sat on a seat inside the cafeteria at the bus depot and gave you a bottle of formula. The lady serving behind the counter kept coming over and asking if she could give you a cuddle. She was a Maori woman called Deanna Kake. She told me she had five grown-up kids. In the end, I asked her for help. I didn't know what else to do. I told her that my mother had thrown me out of the house for having a baby and that I had no money and nowhere to go. She invited me to stay at her house and I went home with her on the bus. She lived with her husband and two grandsons in an old villa in Claudelands. Her husband was very ill and just sat in a chair all day on the back verandah. He seemed much older than her. Deanna worked very hard, working fulltime at the cafeteria and caring for her husband and two teenagers. I stayed there for almost five days and sometimes did the washing and helped her cook the dinner at night. Her two grandsons attended the local high school and didn't do much work around the house. Deanna sang to you at night and bathed you and said I wish I had a grand-daughter, can you believe my lot have had nothing but boys? Ten mokos, that's right, and not one girl.

On the fourth night, Deanna said I had to leave. She'd heard a police message on the radio at work. About a fifteen-year-old girl called Joy Winter stealing a baby and running away. The police said that fears were held for their safety because Joy was suffering from a mental illness and needed care. Sounds like a pack of lies, she said, but I have to think of the boys. One of them has been in trouble, and I don't want the police to come to my house.

She wept when I left early next morning. She gave me a ten-pound note and some baby clothes and nappies from her linen chest. I wept too. I had been weaving fantasies about staying with the Kake's and doing housework for my board until I was old enough to get a job and a house of my own. Hopeless and impractical to the end.

I bought food and a second-hand blanket and went into the countryside on a bus. I hid for three days in a barn. From the high window near my bed of hay I saw a herd of jersey cows walking in long slow lines across the road to the milking shed. I saw the yellow light turning slowly to warn the cars and a farm boy on a motor-bike opening and closing the gate. I remember the pungent smell of silage and smoke drifting like fog from burning willow stumps down by the creek and each night the sun falling like a stone behind the highest point in the denuded hills. Each morning, the tentative calls of winter birds and the unmelted frost in bog holes waiting to be trodden into the muddied grass by the patient hooves of the milking herd. Each evening, my anxious eyes scanning your face for signs of illness. But you seemed to thrive in that room above the hay barn. I held you and sang to you and prayed that you would not call unwanted attention to us with your mewing cries.

Then the final morning, cold and crisp, not a whisper of wind. Sound carried clearly for miles as if we were travelling on the surface of water deep within a canyon. I heard them long before I saw them, cars and voices and whistles and the bark of dogs. I knew that it was over.

They sent a man in a brown suit into the barn. I am not the police he called up to me, I'm a child welfare officer. We do not want to harm you. If you care about your baby, please give it to me. Or the police will be called and it might get hurt.

It? Before they snatched you from my arms, I whispered in your ear, *Joy is your name, sweet Joy* . . .

I named you after myself. Then I came slowly down the wooden ladder holding you close to my body. The welfare officer seized you and carried you off. He slung you under one arm like a parcel and you opened your lungs and shrieked. The last thing I saw were your feet encased in dirty woollen bootees kicking up and down in protest.

The hardest thing has been the lack of your physical presence. For forty years I have fantasised about your body. What do you look like? Are your eyes still brown? What are the shapes and colours of your toes and feet and shoulders? Are your toenails painted red?

Is there anything of Robert in you?

I need tangible proof of your existence. Sometimes I look down and delude myself that the birth scar has melted and I scrub at my skin with a stiff brush to try and find it again. As proof that you did come into the world through this surgical doorway and that a baby was actually born to me.

I need to meet with you both very soon. I am excited with the idea that there are now two of you. When I first heard about Pixel I had to adjust to the fact that I have unknowingly been a grand-mother for eighteen years. I regret missing out on yet another child-hood. Do you think it possible that we three can make up for lost time? Can we compress the experience of all of our lives into a verbal documentary of anecdotes and events that we can mutually under-stand? And even if this is possible, how can we achieve this without becoming overwhelmed by bitterness for what was done to us?

I have told you the story of events leading up to my desperate journey into the farmlands of the Waikato but I can never adequately communicate to anyone the brute sensuality of those experiences. Does this shock you? There is an enormous gulf between raw emotion and the causes attributed to it after the event, between real lived experience and the retelling of it. My fear made me feel intensively alive. I was marked indelibly by each curl of your finger, each sun-rise, the clarity of sound in the bush in winter, the sun falling like a stone, the glittering frost on emerald grass, the skin of a cow curi-ously marked with brown hatching, the malty rankness of silage.

I know that you have been listening to Alice recording stories about her life and that it is only a matter of time before she tells you some tales about her wayward daughter. I have told you every-thing that I know about your father. I have told you the facts of your conception and birth and the story of your first six months of life. I have explained my futile attempts to keep you close to me. No doubt Alice will tell it differently. Take everything she tells you with a big pinch of salt. She relives her past in England through the medium of novels and this is why her so-called facts are liberally mixed with fiction.

But remember, I have told you what is true for me, not Alice.

# 10

## *Isobel*

Wendy is in such a state that I make her sit down and drink a cup
of coffee before I ask her what the hell is the matter. I am tired
of her coming home at night like this; uptight, tense, her words
jumbling over each other. Especially tonight, when I have good news
to tell her. Two months ago, I sent a short story away to the editor
of a new book of lesbian short stories. And today, idly checking over
the pile of letters that arrived in the mail, (mostly questionnaires for
Wendy who is conducting a postal survey for a lecturer at Auckland
University on attitudes towards Asian migration), there it was! I
read the letter over and over:

. . . We are delighted to inform you that your story *The Queering
of Logophobia* has been selected out of two hundred submissions to
appear in our forthcoming international anthology of lesbian fiction.
Congratulations! We will be contacting you soon for permission
to make some small editorial changes . . .

I have been racing around all day, alternating between excitement and fear. Wendy had seen the call for submissions for the
anthology and insisted that I send a contribution. I would never
have been able to do it without her encouragement. I can't believe
that it's been accepted. I fight the urge to write to the publishers
and demand that they withdraw my story. I am still vulnerable to
the belief that written words are dangerous and that language can
kill. What if another person like my sister Julia reads my story and
finds her mortality staring at her from the page? I could not bear
to have another death on my conscience.

Wendy thinks I exaggerate this relationship between words and
fate but I am still not convinced. I anxiously re-read the story and

try to comfort myself by saying over and over that this is a fictional description of the bodily states of an invented woman speaking an invented language. It is not meant to be a logical treatise on the nature of human consciousness. If only I could be sure that future readers will share the intention of the writer.

I didn't want to ring Wendy on her cellphone. I wanted to tell her face to face. I left the letter lying on the table so that she would see it the moment she walked in. But she didn't notice. She did not ask me why I was looking so excited or why I had set the table with one of Sally's crocheted tablecloths and the special candlesticks. She was full of work woes. I tried to cheer her up by showing her the excellent response to her questionnaire in today's mail. But all she wanted to talk about was her unease over the ethical problems with Alice and the oral history tapes.

"Tomorrow is my last day, I swear to you Bel."

I am distracted by the timer on the oven. I am cooking a dish with kumaras and tomatoes with a glaze of orange juice and shoyu sauce. There is a critical moment in the cooking of this dish between browning and burning and I have to attend to it now. "The last day for what?"

"I have decided to tell Alice everything that I know."

"Jesus. Is that wise?"

Wendy sips the last of her coffee. "Marlene Hunter is a powerful woman and I know that I'll pay for what I'm going to do. But I have grown to love Alice. She is such a gutsy old woman. And I have misled her. I feel a complete bitch."

I serve the meal and we begin to eat. Wendy plays with her food. I am at screaming point. "You knew weeks ago that there was something wrong with the research. You could have spoken up before this."

"You encouraged me to keep making the tapes," she snaps. "Even though you knew that she was related to you by marriage."

"Be fair! I clearly remember advising you to tell Alice that you and I lived together."

"That would have meant coming out to her and she might have sent me packing. I want to be able to keep seeing her after the tapes are finished."

I am surprised by her saying this. I have lived with Wendy for five years. She has always been completely open about being a lesbian. She claims that closeted lesbians oppress the ones like us who are living an honest life. She must have more invested in her relationship with Alice than I realised. "Surely you know what her attitudes are by now?"

"I hardly ever ask her questions. I try to be as non-directive as possible. That's how oral history works."

We drink red wine. I eat the rest of the kumara and tomato dish. I clear the table. I wait until Wendy has washed up the dishes and I have taken the coffee pot and the plate of cheese and biscuits into the living room. Then I lift the letter from the table and place it in her lap, casually, as if it was nothing of importance. She shrieks with joy. "I knew you could do it Bel!"

We spend some time hugging and kissing and making up. Wendy says she is sorry for not noticing the special dinner. She attempts to reassure me about publishing the story. "I think it's great and so does the editor. Otherwise she wouldn't have chosen it over so many others. It doesn't matter what other people make of it."

This sets me off again. "But what if . . ."

To my surprise, Wendy starts to laugh. She laughs until the tears roll down her face. In spite of myself, I begin to giggle too. "What's so funny?" I manage to say at last.

"We are bloody hopeless, me with my bloody ethics and you with your bloody logophobia."

We hold each other and laugh and kiss and drink more wine. Then we talk, really talk, in a way that we haven't done for weeks. Wendy tells me again how much she loves me and I say, me too, me too.

"Whatever happens with your writing," says Wendy. "We will cope. Even if the guilt about Julia returns."

"Whatever you decide to do about Marlene Hunter, I will support you."

Wendy says soberly, "I told Alice today that I had something to confess. I'm going to tell her everything tomorrow and Bel, I want you to come with me. I want to be completely honest with her. This includes the fact that I share a house with her niece."

I am not convinced that this is a good idea. I point out to Wendy that she has contradicted herself. First she wants to conceal her sexual identity from Alice and then she wants me to come with her to Alice's house tomorrow.

Wendy squirms. "I knew you'd say that. But she is seventy-five years old. Couldn't we say we are flatmates?"

I am shocked. "Definitely not. I come as your partner or not at all."

Wendy is silent for a few minutes. Then she says, "You win. Time to tell the truth. And not just about us." She takes some cassette tapes from her brief case and holds them towards me. "There is stuff in here about your cousin Joy that could destroy her. I freaked out when I heard Alice tell me her story. And now she wants a big confrontation with her daughter. I think she is foolish. What is the point of dragging up ancient family history that will only hurt people and make things bloody worse than they already are? I have been placed in an awkward position. I encouraged Alice to make the tapes and because of this, another person is going to get the shock of her life. I won't divulge to Joy what her mother has said but I can't stop Alice doing it."

"Wait," I said. "I don't follow you."

"Alice wants to tell Joy the truth about her father and she has asked me to be there when she does so. I have agreed to do it but when it happens, I want you to come with me."

I am amazed that Wendy has suggested this. "What about confidentiality? I admit that I would love to listen to the tapes, especially the anecdotes about my parents. But what about this other information?"

"The truth is I am out of my depth," says Wendy. "The relationship between Alice and Joy is already difficult. God knows what will happen after Joy hears the tapes. I don't know what to do. I need your help."

I can see that she is deeply disturbed so I agree to go with her to Alice's house tomorrow morning. But I insist that she tell Alice about the nature of our relationship and then, and only then, ask her permission for me to be there while she makes the last tape.

"I want you to listen to all the tapes," says Wendy. "Right through. Tonight."

"No way."

"Is it such a crime? Alice believes that her story is going to be published in a book. She has already agreed to make her story public. What's the difference?"

"You're splitting hairs. She was going to choose which bits went into the book. This way, you are not giving her any choices."

Wendy cries, "Oh god I'm sick and tired of this whole business. I'm going over to Marlene Hunter's office in the morning to throw the fucking tapes in her face! I've had enough!"

I calm her down. She drinks her coffee and nibbles on a piece of cheese. I tell her she is over-reacting. "And what about Alice? She has given you hours of her time and the story of her life as a gift. If you throw it away she will be humiliated. You may as well tell her that her whole life has been worthless."

Wendy says she hasn't thought of it like that. "I hate to bow to your superior wisdom twice in the same evening but I have to admit that you're right. Again."

I grin at her. "You should listen to your elders and betters more often."

She comes over to the sofa and sits next to me and kisses me and strokes my hair. "So you won't listen to the tapes with me?"

I make a compromise. I will listen to the parts about Alice but not the stuff about my cousin Joy. Wendy sets up the tape recorder and once again, I hear the voice of my aunt, older, slightly shaky, but unmistakably her voice. *I was born Alice Nellie Smallacomb . . . are you going to ask me questions?*

I was about ten years old when I last heard her speak. They used to visit us in Te Kauwhata until that day when I overheard a quarrel between Uncle Jack and my father Denby. I had never seen my father hit a man before. Alice tried to prise the two men apart but Sally restrained her. My mother brushed me off by telling me that it was nothing to worry about. Just bad blood between two stubborn brothers. But in spite of her down playing the event, Jack and Alice never came to our house again. I was very upset at the time. I loved my Aunty Alice and my big cousins Joy and Morry. Maybe I'll find out the real reason for the quarrel from the tapes.

*I was born Alice Nellie Smallacomb. My mother was only fifteen when she gave birth to me, but I know who my father was . . .*

Wendy breaks in excitedly, "Now I understand why she said that!"

I ask her what she means. She hits the pause button. "This is not going to work Bel. Either you listen to the whole thing or nothing."

"Turn it on again. Her voice is bringing back distant memories. Me and Julia riding on the train to visit her house in Sandringham, visits to the beach . . ."

"You don't understand. I can't pick out the bits about Joy."

"But she hasn't even mentioned Joy."

"That's where you're wrong."

I'm already hooked. I had not counted on the effect of hearing Alice speaking across a gap of thirty years. There is something in the timbre of her voice that is evocative of hot summer nights and picnics and staying up late and happy childhood events. Something that I didn't know I had lost is being restored to me.

I sigh and give in. I promise Wendy that I will not divulge anything that I'm about to hear. Not to anyone. Under pain of death.

We sit for hours listening to Alice's voice. I try to interject once or twice but each time Wendy places a finger on my lips. At the end of the final tape, I hear Alice say, *I believed that adoption was the best chance both for Joy and the baby . . . I gave Joy no option . . . We will sign the papers and that will be the end of the matter.* Then Wendy's voice, *I'm going to confess something to you . . . Sorry to be so mysterious. But there's something I have to do before I speak to you again.*

I sit stunned for minutes, trying to take in everything that I have heard. I am overwhelmed by feelings of compassion for both Alice and Joy and I'm enraged over what has happened to them.

"For fuck's sake say something," says Wendy. "You're freaking me out."

I rant and rave for minutes. I get stuck into the fucked world, the fucked people, the fucked treatment of women, fuck, fuck, fuck, I say, how dare they? How bloody dare they treat us like this!

Wendy holds my hand. "Please don't be angry with me Bel."

I try to calm myself. "No wonder you felt as if you were drowning."

"I wish I'd never taken on the job."

"You've done nothing wrong. Quite the opposite. Alice was more than ready to tell her story. And I'm glad that she told it to someone as understanding as you."

"Surely some things are better left unspoken," says Wendy nervously. "Jack is dead, Emily is dead. They all are, except for Alice. Why does she want to reveal the stuff about the rape after all these years?"

"Joy has a right to know."

"In principle yes. But what good will it do her in reality?"

"Alice has already made the decision to tell Joy. End of story."

"Maybe she'll change her mind after we speak to her tomorrow," says Wendy.

"We?"

"You promised Bel."

"I've got no intention of talking her out of anything. I think the truth should come out. And Joy should have a chance to tell her side of things."

"Alice might feel differently after I tell her about Marlene Hunter."

"Have you found out any more about her?"

"All I know is what she has told me. The book *Working-Class Foremothers* is on hold. She told me some crap about the market research people advising her to postpone publication until further notice."

"Maybe she is telling you the truth."

"No way. She's a sleaze. Why did she ask me to get one further tape from Alice if she isn't going to use the material in the book? Don't forget the money involved. Five hundred dollars. What for? I don't understand."

"I'm glad Alice is getting paid. She deserves to have some good fortune in her life."

Wendy smiles. "It makes me feel better to hear you say that."

By now, it's one o'clock in the morning and it's very warm. There is a hint of thunder in the air. Another humid Auckland night. This summer is exceptionally hot and wet. If only the rain would disappear for a few weeks. I feel emotionally exhausted. I tell Wendy I have had enough for one night. I need to put my head down and get some sleep. She throws a cushion at me and says that things could have been worse. What if Elizabeth had come to visit? Thank god for that man she is running around with. It takes the pressure off us.

I throw the cushion back at her. "So you admit that your mother can be hard going? Ha! About time!"

We go arm and arm into our bedroom. Christobel the cat is already stretched out on my pillow. I lift her gently onto the floor. She doesn't stir. Wendy goes to take a cool shower and I lie naked on the bed.

I go over and over Alice's story. My rage has left me. I marvel at her tenacity, her fierce will to power, her submerged mysticism. I'm sure there is more to this side of her than she has allowed us to hear. Sometimes she moves a veil aside and speaks of apple trees and Celtic islands and the gathering of herbs but quickly closes it again and returns to the chronology of her life story.

Her memory beads fascinate me. Gold for warmth and blue for cold. The smell of the orphanage is in the blue bead, unsmiling faces, broken skin, the tears of sad children. Her method of remembrance came from looking within a kaleidoscope, the fragile threads like multi-coloured tears, empty glass beads waiting to be filled with the illustrated texts of future experience.

She has invented a private language, one that can never be misconstrued or distorted because she is simultaneously both author and keeper of the beads. This makes her decision to tell her story to Wendy even more mysterious. Why make public a system that has sustained her sanity over the years?

Wendy comes into the bed, cool and clean and smelling of soap.

I kiss her goodnight. "Love you, Bel," she murmurs, and falls asleep instantly.

The rain clouds have cleared, and the full moon is high and bright in the window frame. I close my eyes. As always, when I am sleepless, I hear the voice of my dead sister, *we are swimming in the dream . . . the sea is milk . . . the words are turning into stone . . .*

Once again I perform the mourning cry on that darkening beach; the pulse of the sea falters, the breakers stand still, the same grey gull falls from the sky.

The moon leaves my window and drifts away over the western hills. Finally, just as the sky begins to lighten and the first tentative birdsong trembles through the dawn, I manage to push the sound of her drowning voice away and I sleep at last.

# 11

## *Joy*

I am awakened by the sound of the phone ringing. I run downstairs and grab the receiver. Too late. Whoever it was hung up in my ear. It must be Alice. Who else would ring me at seven o'clock in the morning? Anxiously I dial her number. She answers immediately. Yes, I am already up and drinking the first pot of tea of the day. No, I did not ring you. Yes, I am perfectly all right, thank you very much. Except for my arthritis. No, the pain is no worse than usual. I have to go now. I'm doing the baking, before the heat sets in. Bye, and thanks for your concern.

She sounds more formal than usual. On her guard. I know my mother. She is planning some mischief. I decide to contact her later and ask her what she's up to. Then the phone rings again and it's Wayne Marsh, slightly ill at ease, apologising for ringing me so early. Was I in the shower when he called before? I must come into the office today. He's closing at lunch time for the Christmas break and he won't be re-opening until January the tenth. He's just this very minute downloaded some more files from TIM. No, he can't tell me what they are, he hasn't had time to read them. He wants me to have them before he goes away on holiday. His office is a madhouse. All his clients want their problems to be resolved before the New Year. So my visit will have to be brief. And incidentally, there is a current account waiting for me, in a sealed envelope on the top of the printouts. To be paid in full ASAP.

I am disappointed that he is closing his office for three weeks. I wish he had told me this when I dropped off my papers to him yesterday afternoon. I'm nearing the end of my long wait to reclaim my daughter and I am getting very impatient. I am not sure if I can bear to wait until Wayne Marsh returns to work before I reveal myself to Marlene and Pixel. I decide to contact Welfare after Christmas. Maybe Marlene will lift the embargo after reading my side of the story.

I say nothing of this to Wayne. I am careful not to let slip that I have been to Marlene's house in Devonport. I tell him I'll be in Hamilton within the hour.

Early summer morning on the road. I'm tired. Not much sleep last night. My neighbour Rangi has a crowd of relations staying at her house and the children played video games on the back porch until the early hours of the morning. The same electronic voices over and over and the sound of gunshots and explosions. Mechanical repetitive noise drives me crazy. I willed the wind to rise in a great whirlpool of disturbed air, I willed the sea to form into roaring green tunnels but the night was almost preternaturally calm. The rising tide barely tapped the sea wall next to my house before it turned and flowed back silently through the open mouth of the harbour. It was so quiet you could almost hear the fish thinking. So much for my abortive weather work. I should get some tips from my mother Alice.

I drive across the one-way bridge. The village is deserted and the harbour is almost drained of seawater. Low tide has reduced the estuary to a trickle. Long-legged birds fossick on fields of wet grey mud. In spite of constant rain battering us from the west, December has been unusually hot, and the pohutukawa trees have produced a dazzling display of crimson blooms. Even at this early hour, the flowers are trembling and singing with the activity of bees.

My car hums along the tarseal. A van loaded with workers passes me on the long straight road near the Te Uku store. I arrive at the foot of the deviation. The schools have already closed for the summer so I am spared the horror of toiling upwards behind a convoy of belching buses. I travel the spiralling road through unfettered hills. The sun is glinting and dancing in the east, the solar light flares out in lasers that inflict momentary blindness. I am charged with adrenalin and nervous excitement. Has Pixel

171

walked into the trap laid by TIM? If some new files have been down-loaded, maybe this means that my "secret" communication has already been successfully hacked by Pixel. Perhaps Marlene has already read the papers that I gave to Wayne yesterday afternoon. I can't believe that it has been this easy.

I put my foot down and the car surges forward. I arrive at Wayne's office on the dot of eight o'clock. He is on the phone when I enter and motions to me to sit in front of his desk. I see a file with my name on the top. I take it and open the envelope that contains my account. Surely there is some mistake? Two thousand dollars! I wait until Wayne has replaced the phone on his desk before I ask what the hell is going on. I paid him a thousand dollars two weeks ago. Why two thousand now? The only thing he has done for me since then is to set up the trail for Pixel to follow. He laughs uneasily and tells me that it's not his fault, most of the money is to pay off the hacker. "These guys are experts and they are very much in demand. They don't come cheap. Look, I'll prove it to you Ms Knight."

He turns the screen around so that I can see it. He calls up a file. "That's weird," he says. "It was there an hour ago."

"What was?"

"The account from TIM for services rendered. Which I passed on to you. Hence the two thousand dollars." He taps at the key-board for several minutes. I can see that he is getting agitated. "This is a complete mystery. I'll call him up on-line and see what's going on." He writes: From: Mar@eye.det.org.nz. Subject: Hello TIM where the devil are you :-( ?

The answer comes after a few seconds.

Date: 17 December. Time: 8.15 am: Return Path < >

From: Mailer-Daemon @adhoc.org.nz. To: Mar@eye.det.org.nz

The message that you have sent to TIM@adhoc.org.nz was undeliverable.

Wayne Marsh lets out a yell. "The bastard has changed his email address!"

I take a chance. "Does this mean I don't have to pay?"

He works furiously at the keyboard for a few minutes. "I'm totally mystified. TIM has vanished off the face of the Internet.

And so have all the files that he has provided for my clients."

"Oh god no."

"Don't panic, I've got printouts."

I open the file cover. "Are they all here?"

"Yes. Copies of the ones I gave you before. And the ones I down-loaded this morning."

"Are you certain that the information I gave you yesterday after-noon got through?"

"I scanned it and passed it on to TIM as soon as you dropped it off. But whether or not he actually fed it to Pixel is anyone's guess. And now I can't get through to him to check it out." He looks worried. "I hope to god it's just a technological glitch. He knows too much to go bad on me."

The telephone rings. Wayne places his hand over the receiver. "Sorry. This is confidential."

"Is it TIM?"

"No such luck. I'd like to get my hands on him. Can you wait outside?"

"I'll leave. Just give me the file."

"Okay, okay, take it. There's nothing much more we can do today. I'm logging-off in a few hours in any case. Leave the account with me. I'll try to find TIM when I return in January."

I escape from the office clutching my precious files. I'm happy that I don't have to go to the bank and take out my last five hundred dollars to give to Wayne Marsh. I would have had to borrow the balance from Alice. I wonder how many fifty-dollar notes she has hidden in her unit? Her last bank statement showed her usual pension payments, nothing extra. And she seems to have halted her spending spree. There must be some money left over from the cash that this woman Wendy McDonald has been giving her. No good asking Morry and Bonita. They have less money than I have. Bonita has asked me to buy the turkey for the Christmas dinner this year. A most unusual request. I have been going to their house for Christmas dinner ever since I divorced my second husband and I have never been asked to provide food before. Bonita said sorry to ask you Joy, but Morry's gardening jobs are drying up. More people in the district are out of work. You know how things are.

I desperately want to read the files before I drive back home. I walk to the spot on the river bank where I sat two days ago but there is an old man sitting on my bench staring fixedly at the swift current. I go further along the pathway. Although it is still early, the sun is already hot on my face. I find a seat high up the bank underneath a shady tree. I open the manilla folder.

**3Pixel.doc** That nerd TIM thought he was being smart. As if I couldn't do this hack in my sleep. I think I was meant to see this stuff. Too <flaming> obvious. It must have been deliberate or maybe he sees me as an amateur. Either way no problem. I don't need TIM any more. He has been put on the disposable list and is virtually being made ready to meet his demise.

So this is the saga of Joy. A cry from the wasteland of the low-tech fifties. Mother Marlene hiding out in a hay barn in her dirty bootees. Real stuff, happening in real time, even a real baby.

Total contrast to the wiles of my egg mother. She couldn't wait to give the products of her fertility away. Place of birth, time and date of birth, father's occupation, mother's maiden name, the untrustworthy certification of coming into being. The signifier of the first cry as proof of life. The narrative of identity called forth in agony: I looked down and there you were. The face of my own child, my father's eyes, my mother's skin, my lover's mouth. Dearly beloved, we are gathered here today, some dead, some alive, brought together in one fragile body. I fell in love with you forever.

The redundant mythology of giving birth. A non-issue for the likes of me and my compatriots. Cast adrift birthless in the land of the unknown warrior. The egg as passive victim, the sperm as spear. The new mythology of conception. Who laid your egg? Who projected your sperm? Who or what brought the two of you together in the bridal suite at the Hotel Petrie?

The great leveller of the clinic. A holy place of hushed voices and white coats. Fertility chants performed over flushed ova and glaciated sperm. Christ was born in a stable. I was conceived along with the cows and sheep and other unmentionables. Does this make me a special woman, the daughter of a new God? At least the claim of virginity is real. They insisted on it. Part of the economic deal.

I understand your impatience Joy. I know you are reading this right now. The seventeenth of December, probably early in the morning. Am I right? See, I am still capable of operating in real time, in spite of dire predictions of what happens to netheads. Let me tell you right away that I haven't shown the file that you sent via TIM to Mother Marlene. Yet. I will this afternoon, I promise. Let me put your mind at rest. She will adore what you have to say. She has waited a long time to find you. Mostly because of me. I take some explaining. She is nervous of your reaction. Be warned. You will hear her described as an aggressive bitch. Not true. I should know, I have lived within her and in her house ever since I was conceived. Well, to be strictly truthful, two years after actually.

I'll tell you more when you meet us. I don't want to frighten you off, Mother Marlene would never forgive me.

A tip before I log-off. Go to Welfare. You might get a pleasant surprise: Pixel :-)

I fold the sheets away. I am elated. I know that my story is safe with Pixel. She knows more than she is saying of course, that much is evident. Especially about the activities of TIM. So much for Wayne Marsh referring to her as an arrogant young woman. I laugh out loud. I can't wait to tell her everything he has said about her.

So Marlene will adore my story. I love Pixel for telling me this. She is so sensitive for a young woman of eighteen. My grand-daughter. I say the word under my breath several times. To savour the word.

I climb up the path back to Victoria Street and walk briskly to the four-storeyed building that houses various departments of Welfare. The Adoption and Fostering Information Section is on the top floor. I take the lift and join the short queue at the desk. I am very nervous. I have never confronted anyone face to face over this. All my dealings with Welfare have been by letter or over the telephone. I am shown into a booth and after a few minutes a young woman enters and unlocks the computer with a tiny key.

She asks for Baby's date and place of birth. She taps at the computer keyboard. "That's strange. When did you make your last inquiry? Mmmm. Who did you speak to?"

I have the details written down in the back of my diary. I show it to her. She frowns. "Just a minute," she says. "I need to consult my superior. Something's not quite right." She leaves the booth. I move around to her side of the desk and look at the screen. But she's masked the file with an animated picture of dolphins leaping backwards and forwards over a sailing ship.

The clerk returns with an older woman dressed in a long floral dress. They both gaze at the screen. "Well," the older woman says at last. "We have no option but to give you the information that you have asked for. The embargo on your daughter's whereabouts was lifted years ago. You were obviously given incorrect information by an employee. I apologise if this has caused you any inconvenience. It is most unusual for something like this to happen."

My face goes hot. I feel like hitting her. Then I remember that Wayne Marsh had checked the embargo just a few weeks ago. And it was still there. The hacker has obviously done more than check the information on my file, he has gone back in and altered some critical details as well. I am filled with admiration for Pixel. She knew exactly what the hacker TIM was up to. I wouldn't have bothered to come in here today unless she had suggested it.

"Well these things happen," I manage to say pleasantly. "No harm done."

I sense the relief on the part of the clerk and her superior. "Thank you Mrs Knight for being so understanding," says the older woman. She leaves the booth in a flurry of skirts and perfume. The clerk gives me the information that I already know; namely, Marlene's address and the fact that she has a daughter aged eighteen. But she also gives me the confidential phone and fax numbers of Marlene's Devonport home. At last I can contact her. Legally.

I do not wait for the lift to arrive. I run down the fire stairs, exultant, triumphant. I decide not to inform Wayne Marsh of this latest development. I am not breaking my word to him. Now that the embargo has been lifted officially, there is no possibility that the information he obtained illegally can be traced back to him.

I clutch the printout that the Welfare clerk gave to me and memorise Marlene's phone number. I rush to the nearest book shop and buy a phone card. The streets are full of mothers and children doing their Christmas shopping. There is a queue at the public phone box. I feel like kicking them out of the way. I try to control my trembling body. I have waited nearly fifty-five years to break this silence between myself and Marlene. Surely I can muster the patience to survive for ten more minutes? I try to pull myself together. I shuffle forward. At last I am in front of the queue. The young girl in the phone box is laughing so hard she can hardly get a word out. "Oh no," she shrieks, "you didn't! You dorkhead," giggle giggle, "he's uglyyy!"

I am nearly going crazy. I tap the glass door and mouth the word urgent! She gives me the fingers. I am wild enough to kill. Can't she read the stress in my eyes? At last she hangs up. Oh no! She is dialling another number. I open the door and tell her to get out, she has kept me waiting five minutes, this is a life or death matter. She leaves meekly enough. Until she is under the shop verandah. Then she gives me the fingers again. I don't care. I'm frantically pressing the numbers that I have memorised. Oh god an answer machine. Her voice. *This is Marlene Hunter speaking. I can't come to the phone at the moment but please leave a detailed message after the beep.* I freeze. I wait until the beep sounds but I cannot speak. I hang up and redial time after time just to hear her voice. *This is Marlene Hunter speaking. I can't come to the phone at the moment . . . This is Marlene Hunter . . . This is Marlene . . .*

My phone card runs out. I slam down the receiver and run back to the shop. This time I buy two cards. I can't believe that the same teenage girl is back in the phone box. But I am more patient this time. I have proof that my daughter is alive. She has spoken her name to me. I have heard her voice, educated, well modulated. I practice what I'm going to say into the machine. *This is your mother speaking.* No, too familiar. *Hi Marlene! You'll never guess who this is!* Too flippant. *This is Joy Knight. Please call me back on . . .* No, too formal.

I give up. I will say the first word that comes into my head. The main thing is not to weep. I want to show her that I'm in control of my emotions. The girl finally leaves the phone box. No obscene gesture this time.

I touch dial the number again. Each number plays a note. The sequence is burnt into my brain. Her voice again, then the beep. I say, my name is Joy, and someone picks up the phone.

"Hi. I thought it might be you, ringing and ringing. Why didn't you speak?"

Not Marlene's voice. Someone young. "Is this Pixel?"

"Yep." I can hear rapid tapping on a computer keyboard.

"I got your message this morning."

"Yep."

"Is . . . is your mother at home?"

"Nope."

I'm starting to lose it. I fall silent. The tapping goes on in my ear. I hear Pixel yell, "Got ya prickface!"

I am upset at her rudeness. I wait a few more moments. The money on the second card is running out. Then she says, "Sorry Joy, you caught me at a difficult moment. Someone has been bugging me and he almost had me. He was just about to attack me when you called. But I got him. Panic over."

"Are you safe?"

She laughs. "He'll never come near me again."

"Have you rung the police?"

"What for? I'm not in any physical danger. I'm indulging in a bit of Net warfare."

"Oh. Sorry."

"Is it okay if I call you Joy?"

"Please do." I fall silent. My last phone card is almost finished. "Can I come up?" I manage to say at last.

"Yep. Anytime. I'll square it off with Mother Marlene."

"You mean she doesn't know that I have your phone number from Welfare?"

"Sort of."

I am too shocked to answer. What on earth is Pixel playing at?

"Jesus wept," shouts Pixel. "When are you two going to get your shit together? Just come up. Tonight. I'm sick of these fucking games!"

I break down and weep in spite of my previous resolve. Pixel makes me promise that I'll be in Devonport this evening. At seven o'clock. She'll tell Marlene everything before I arrive. There's got to be an end to this farce. Marlene is driving her crazy.

The phone card runs out. I drive back to Raglan. My mind is raging. I am angry with Pixel for shouting and swearing at me. Wayne is right about her. She is a difficult young woman. Unpredictable. I suddenly feel very inadequate. I have never reared a child. What do I know? I am deeply ignorant about the young. If only I could meet Marlene for the first time without Pixel being there too.

I lie on my bed and try to force myself to rest but it is impossible. I pace from room to room, turning over magazines, going through old letters, staring at the bare windows of the empty house across the street. I wonder if I should take anything to Auckland. Gifts of food and wine. Would this be appropriate? Perhaps some fruit or flowers. Marlene has so much, anything that I take will be superfluous. But I don't want to go empty handed.

Objects from the past? I wonder if she'll be interested in family photos. All I can do is to ask myself how I would feel if I was in similar circumstances. I would crave visual proof of relationship. I hope she feels the same.

I sort out some photos from my camphor-wood chest. Pictures of Alice and Jack and of me and Morry when we were kids. Mug shots. Me in school photos, trapped in class line-ups with Grammar girls in stiff white collars and navy gym frocks. The house at Sandringham, brand new in 1940, standing on bare soil, my father Jack on the front porch wearing a straw hat. The same house in 1975, in need of a coat of paint, surrounded by hedges and trees. Alice's pensioner flat where she moved after my father died. This shot was taken before I cleared the weeds from the front garden. It looks much better now.

What will I say to Marlene? Here are some black and white images of your long-lost kin and their various habitations? There are some significant gaps. No likeness of your father. He died before I could get hold of a camera. You will have to take my description of him on trust.

I have no photos of Marlene as a baby. All I have is her plastic birth bracelet and a rattle. Hardly a treasure trove of remembrance.

The time crawls. I go down to the sea and walk over the narrow bridge that straddles the Opotoru River. The tide is in full flood. The sun is hot and high overhead. A light onshore breeze. The dominance of green. Children leap from the bridge into the swirling water. Except for the sand and sky everything is green; the sea, the grass fields across the tidal creek, the leaves of the pohutukawa trees drooping down over the bank.

The sun moves towards the west. I lean against the trunk of a phoenix palm. The warm fibre scratches my skin. I close my eyes. I can hear the noise of the waves crawling up the strand, the voices of children and birds, the clinking of plates from a nearby picnic, the chugging of fishing boats coming in slowly over the bar.

High summer. The sensations of this estuary are beginning to enter into my body. Sitting here, with the faint drone of bees and the dappled light glinting through my eyelids, I experience a sense of belonging that has always eluded me in the past. No matter where I've gone or where I've lived, I have always felt like an interloper. No rights of membership. The houses of others. Both my husbands left me. I had no children to link me to either family of in-laws. I have tried to grasp the essence of people who acted *as if* they loved me. Lives half lived, imperfect revelations, glimpses of self that seemed almost genuine. But whenever I tried to confront the partiality of the vision that was being offered to me, all I ever received in return was misunderstanding. You want too much of me was the cry, too much! Love as hard labour, never completely achieved, always in the process of becoming.

Time after time I have walked away from the illusion that love can exist in the part but never in the whole. Alice loves me as long as I agree with her version of the truth of both our lives. Jack loved me as a baby but not after I learned to talk. My husbands loved me until I challenged their behaviour and wanted the same freedoms that they had. The first one ran off with his current lover. The second insisted that I either run off with mine or give him up for good. I refused to make a choice. One night my second husband disappeared leaving huge gambling debts and a mortgage on our house that I was unable to repay. I had to start all over again.

This is my fatal flaw. I have never learned to operate within the realms of human possibility. I could never grasp the solidity of anything. I have always lived on the geographical margins of rooms and houses and landscapes invented by others. I came here to Raglan after my working life ended, simply because the houses were cheap and it was not too far from the remnants of my family. There is a subversive form of beauty on this wild coast. Grief with a view. But I have gained a lot more than this. I am beginning to dig myself in, I am discovering a ground.

Time to go. I return to my house and take a shower. Then I dress myself in a white dress with a loose bodice and a pleated skirt to disguise my thinness. I apply makeup carefully and blot my lipstick so that the colour does not run into the cracks around my mouth. I make sure that I have comb, powder and mirror in my purse so that I can freshen up after driving through the afternoon heat. I decide not to wear perfume. I don't have the real thing. My cheap scent lasts a few hours and then smells stale. Better not to take the risk.

It is a long time since I have taken so much care with my appearance. I wonder if Marlene is dressing with the same care for our first meeting. By now Pixel would have given her my story to read. She might be reading it this very minute. I go into a minor panic attack. What if Pixel hasn't given her the files? What if she hasn't even told her mother that I'm coming? I go to the telephone and dial Marlene's number. As soon as I've hit the last digit I throw the receiver back into its cradle. This is it. I'm not going to give her the chance to say no. I'm going to Auckland and I'm going to get into that house. Whether she's read my story or not.

I arrive in Devonport at five-thirty. Too early. I find the same café where I had breakfast yesterday morning after I saw Marlene driving her car out of her garage. I find it hard to believe that it was only yesterday that I was here.

It is very warm. Devonport is full of cars and shoppers and children in swimming costumes coming into the café for icecreams and cool drinks. Striped umbrellas, sun glittering on the sea, outdoor tables, an air of frenetic activity. I alternate between elation that I am going to meet Marlene in a few hours and incredulity that I've had the courage to come here without asking her permission. I see the gaiety of the crowds as bordering on the hysterical. I drink several glasses of gin and tonic to make the time pass quickly. I know that the hysteria belongs to me.

Seven o'clock. I drive to Hillside Crescent. Cars line the street so I have to drive almost to the next block before I can find a park. I walk awkwardly on the concrete pavement in my high heels. I wanted to make myself look glamorous, but now I regret wearing them. They throw my body forward and accentuate my height.

When I approach number twenty-seven, I am surprised to hear loud music and laughter coming from the house. The iron security gate is wide open. So is the front door. There is obviously a big party in progress. Pixel might have warned me. I stand nervously at the gate wondering what to do. Then a group of young people spill out of a taxi and I walk in with them and join the throng. I help myself to a drink from a tray proffered by a young man in a dinner suit. Expensive champagne. I make my way to a table of food; strawberries dipped in chocolate, canapés, smoked salmon. I have no appetite but take a few nibbles so that I don't get too drunk.

No one speaks to me. I stand with my back against a wall. The music hums and throbs through the floor. There must be over a hundred people here. Most of them look very young. Some are eccentrically dressed. Hair of all colours, brown, black, red, bleached, shaved heads, pony-tails, dreadlocks. I must be the oldest person here. I am certainly one of the most conservatively dressed. They are standing on the stairs, sitting in groups, talking in loud voices over the music. A tall young woman with a pale face and dressed in flowing black clothes comes towards me. I freeze. Is this Pixel? She asks me who I am. "Jjjoy Knight," I stutter.

"Come with me," she says. "Bring your food and drink with you."

"Are you Pixel?" I manage to ask.

"No. She's waiting for you. Upstairs."

I follow her up three flights of stairs. We have to push past people sitting on the stairs. On the third landing, a hand-written notice is pinned to the wall. *Absolutely no one allowed past this point. No exceptions.*

I hesitate. My guide, who has identified herself not by name but as Pixel's personal assistant, beckons me on. There is a short but steep wooden ladder leading up into the roof. I have to remove my shoes to climb up. The assistant hands me my glass and plate. I turn. The room is dark and I can't see anything until my eyes become accustomed to the gloom.

A young woman is working at a computer. All I can see is the luminous screen and dark shiny nailpolish flashing on the keyboard. Her face is shrouded in gloom.

"Pixel?" I ask. A small light comes on. She turns towards me. My first shock is her chalk-white face, the second, a tattoo of a barcode across her forehead.

"Come closer," she says. "Let me look at you."

I stand still, cursing my stockinged feet and the glass and plate that I am clutching. She must have understood my embarrassment because the room is suddenly lighter and she is walking towards me. "Here give me those. And have a seat." She takes the glass and plate from me. I look around for a chair. There are some big cushions on the floor. I sink down, trembling. She sits beside me.

Pixel is very beautiful in spite of her unusual facial decorations. She seems so sure of herself, so poised. Everything that I wasn't at her age.

She seems to read my mind. "You will meet Marlene later. I want you first."

We sit and chat. Mundane things to begin with. Where I live, what I do with myself, what music I like, food, books, that sort of thing. I tell her about Raglan, how I came to be there, how I have grown to love the west coast. I tell her about the work I used to do before my working life was cut short by redundancy. She asks if I have a lover but I don't find her question offensive. She seems genuinely interested in my life. Nothing, I tell her. Nothing and nobody. Since I was forced to leave my job, my personal relationships have diminished to the point of extinction.

After a while, I pluck up courage to ask her some questions. I want to find out as much as I can before I meet Marlene.

She tells me to look around this room. She wants for nothing, her life is full. Everything important to her is already here. "Ask whatever you want. I am determined that there will be no secrets between us." She caresses my arm in a peculiar kneading fashion and tells me that she has always wanted to meet the mother of Mother Marlene. I am very moved. Tears prick the corners of my eyes. I hold both of her hands. Flesh of my flesh, this thin white hand with long fingers, dark shiny nails. Her long sleeves ride up. There are other tattoos on her arms. I catch a glimpse of one that looks like an email address.

"You look very much like I imagined you would." She jumps up from the cushion and goes to one of the computer screens. "Check this out."

I am astonished to see a woman looking very much like myself appear on the screen. It is not quite real, more like an animated version of myself, a cartoon character. But an excellent likeness. The woman on the computer speaks in my voice: *Is this Pixel? . . . is your mother at home? . . . are you safe? . . . have you rung the police? . . . can I come up?*

Pixel laughs. "You speak in questions."

"How did you do that?"

"There you go again! Easy. My virtual reality software can do anything. Almost."

I was just about to ask her to explain when the computer screen changes. I get a big shock. It's Robert's face, no not Robert, a woman who looks exactly like him.

"There she is," says Pixel. "A vision of your daughter. I had the real thing to work with. Not like you. That was informed guesswork."

I am riveted to the screen. Marlene is speaking at some sort of meeting. She sits at the head of a long table. Women and men are seated on each side, all are looking towards her. Even when others are speaking, the camera dwells on her face. She is authoritative and confident. She has Robert's eyes and exactly the same shaped jaw. There seems to be nothing of me except for her height. At one point she smiles. The teeth! The same thick blunt incisors he used to call his tombstones.

I sink down on the cushion overcome with emotion. I had always assumed that Marlene would look like me. This is almost like a form of reincarnation. I tell Pixel.

"I knew it!" she says excitedly. "It proves my theory yet again."

I ask her what she means. But she is working furiously on the computer and mumbles something about fractals and how all kinship patterns have the property of the smallest unit resembling the whole.

I give up. I watch her manipulating images and sound. Various screens around the room come alive with movement and noise. If there is a logic to this show it eludes me. Flashing lights, body parts driving wheels, trees sprouting breasts, drums growing hair, beating, howling noises from humans and animals, houses with walls opening up like obscene flowers, bleeding birds, stigmata of wing and claw . . .

She stops after a while and comes back to the cushion. "Question time!" she says. "That's my little joke. Joy the Questioner, your role of the moment."

I open my mouth to begin. She stops me with a finger on my mouth. "One rule. The object must be present in this room."

I am growing weary of her games. But I decide to humour her for a while longer. I will not leave this house until I have seen Marlene. I have heard her voice and seen her computer image. But I have not yet touched her flesh. I ask Pixel what she means.

"Your question must relate to any visible object in this room."

I finish the last of my champagne. "Okay. Tell me about your computers."

She laughs. "I said your role of the moment, not of the century. It would take me years to explain."

"When did you get hooked?"

"I have always had computers. And it helps that Mother Marlene is wealthy. She has been able to foster my addictions."

"Why do you call her Mother Marlene?"

"Foul! She isn't in the room."

"Her face is. On your computer chip."

Pixel laughs again. "You're sharp, I'll give you that. Okay. She's Mother Marlene because I've got two mothers."

'You're adopted too!"

"No way. She gave birth to me. See that Petrie dish up there?" She points to a large coloured photograph mounted on the wall. "That's where I was conceived. Those are photos of the actual deed."

I peer at the photo. It is a collage of several greatly magnified shots; a sperm entering an egg, a fertilised egg swimming in a Petrie dish, a tiny foetus sheltering within an abdomen. "Is that you?"

"Yep."

"Are you telling me that Marlene had an in vitro pregnancy?"

"Yep. But I'm not related. Not to either of you for that matter. I was the first fertilised egg ever to be placed in a surrogate womb. Mother Marlene did the honours."

I find it hard to believe Pixel's story. Surely this technology was not around eighteen years ago? She reads my mind again. "I know what you're thinking and you are right. They could do the external fertilisation way back then but not the implant into a surrogate. Except for animals. Cows and sheep. And that's where I came into being. In a vet's clinic in the Waikato."

I am still battling with this information. "Why for god's sake, why?"

"For the two oldest reasons. Money and obligation."

"On whose part?"

"Marlene's of course. I wasn't in any position to give my view."

I sit in silence while she tells me the whole sordid story. Marlene was paid two million dollars to be implanted with a fertilised ova when she twenty-two years old. She had to sign a contract promising that she would rear the child as her own son or daughter. "Of course it was totally against the law," continues Pixel. "The vet was paid a huge sum of money to use the same techniques on Marlene as he used on the jersey cows."

"And who donated the egg and the sperm?"

She falls silent. I wait for several minutes before I ask her again. I point to the photo on the wall. "Where did those objects come from?"

She is reluctant. I remind her of her promise to answer my questions. "I was going to tell you today," she says at last. "But after you met Marlene. You must understand her side of the story. Marlene felt that she had no choice. Apart from the money which she needed to start her business, there was the question of family loyalty."

"Family?"

"The Hunters gave her everything. They were generous and loving, wonderful parents. This was her way of saying thank you."

A horrible suspicion enters my mind. "Beverly gave the egg."

"Yes. And her husband Richard the sperm."

I almost go off my head with rage. Beverly has stolen everything from me. First my baby and now my grand-daughter. Pixel is not my blood, she is merely a tenant of the family. A manufactured child from long dead people. They adopted my child specifically for this purpose. To hire her womb to deposit their objects extracted from a life time of failed fertility. I scream this accusation at Pixel. I feel like beating her with my bare hands.

She says mildly, "Not true. You are taking liberties with my story."

I am beyond reason. I pummel the cushion, I sob, I want to die. Marlene is a monster. So is this creature that she allowed to be implanted into her body. "Look at you! You with your tattooed codes and white paint!"

Pixel shrugs. "I am what I want to be." She returns to the computer desk and calmly taps the keyboard. She's far too cool for my liking. How dare she sit there like that without acknowledging my anger? I try to provoke her. "Wayne Marsh warned me about you. He said you'd be a problem and he's right."

She smiles and lifts her long black sleeve. "Look at this Joy. Then tell me who's got problems." I lurch across the room. She's dimmed the lights again and I have to peer closely at her arm to see what she's showing me. It is an email address. TIM @adhoc.org.nz

I falter. "What are you telling me?"

"I'm TIM. Or at least I used to be. I obliterated him electronically this morning."

I feel totally used and deceived. I hate this Pixel creature like poison. "Does Marlene know anything about this?" I ask.

"Of course not. She is a brilliant business woman but she knows nothing about surfing the Net."

Waves of relief break over me. Maybe Marlene is retrievable. Pixel says, "She's coming up to my room soon. I have sent her a signal through her fax. Before she gets here, I want you to know that I hold no malice towards you."

"That's big of you," I snap.

"I am here, I exist, I am a fact of life. Whatever the method that brought me into the world, you must accept me. That's if you want to get on with Marlene. We are very close, like sisters. Which is an accurate description of our relationship. We are together because of Beverly and Richard Hunter. Everything they did, they did for love. They gave Marlene a refuge and provided me with the necessary biological means of coming into life. Is this such a crime?"

I fall silent and retreat to my cushion. I don't know what to do. This bizarre room with its twilight haze and the alcohol I have consumed have paralysed my will. I am overcome by an irrational desire for sleep.

Then Marlene comes up the ladder. I stand and confront her. It is the biggest anticlimax of my life. I feel nothing at the sight of this tall woman with Robert's face. I am too numb to take in much more than the fact that we are exactly the same height. But she is obviously pleased to see me because she kisses me on the cheek, and cries at last, at last!

Then she goes over to Pixel and whispers something in her ear. Pixel nods in reply. "Okay Joy," says Marlene. "Let's get out of here. Come downstairs to my sitting room. You'll find it more comfortable there."

I follow her down. My high heels are sitting at the bottom of the ladder. I pull them onto my feet. A niggling feeling that I've been unfair to Pixel is beginning to take hold of me. Maybe I would have coped with the peculiar details of her conception and birth if Beverly hadn't been the egg donor. Jealousy got the better of me. I try to push the guilt away.

Marlene offers me coffee from a silver coffee pot. I accept. Her sitting room is very different from Pixel's room. Pine furniture, golden in colour; curtains of green silk, cream wool carpet, one large contemporary painting, shelves of leather-bound books and a display of exquisite bowls made of opaque blue glass.

I relax a little. Marlene apologises for having me here on the night of the office party but Pixel had insisted. Pixel adores parties, albeit from a distance, and she hopes that I do too. As for herself, she loathes these events but she's obliged to do something at Christmas for her employees. And they do enjoy it. Or at least they claim to do so. She makes a point of spending one hour, no more no less, with her guests. Then she leaves them to it.

I start to notice familiar things. Her fingers are long like Alice's and although she has Robert's features, she has my body. The same sloping back and thin arms, the same long waist and tiny breasts. If we covered our faces, we could be identical twins. I sip my coffee. I ask her if she has read the computer file that Pixel hacked from the private detective last night.

"I've just this very moment put it down," she answers. "I hope you're not angry with Pixel."

I confess that I had placed the file on Wayne Marsh's computer specifically for that purpose. Had she not read the heading, *for Marlene and Pixel Hunter?*

"Yes of course. But I wasn't sure that we were meant to read this document at this particular time. I know the sorts of things Pixel gets up to. She has little respect for private information."

I wait for her to comment on my story. Instead, she pours more coffee into my empty cup. I thank her. The coffee has sobered me up and I am determined to find out where I stand with Marlene. This could be the first and last time I ever see her. She may decide that I am not the right type of person to acknowledge openly as her birth mother. Especially after my performance with Pixel. I can see that she is very close to Pixel and denies her nothing. I must be careful not to let my jealousy get the better of me again.

Disbelief is setting in. I can't believe that I'm actually sitting in this room with Marlene. I force myself to look into her eyes. The same brown colour, the same expression. Her eyes bore into mine. I gasp, and almost spill my coffee.

She comes over to me and compares our hands. "Almost the same size," she says. I tell her that her fingers come from Alice. See, mine are a little thicker and shorter. The hair? Robert's. And you look just like him. It is uncanny seeing those shapes imprinted on your eyes, your nose, your teeth . . .

"I'm finding it hard," she says. "I mean, to believe that this is actually you."

"Me too," I say. "Me too . . ."

We hold each other and weep. Two tall women crying on each other's shoulders, such a simple act. But I'm scared that if I weep too much, I'll lose control. I gently push her away. I try to lighten the atmosphere by asking for more coffee. "You gave me a very small cup," I say. "And I admit to a full blown addiction to caffeine."

She smiles. "Me too. Could it be genetic do you think?"

"No doubt about it."

The ice is broken between us. We talk for hours and drink copious amounts of coffee. The fax machine mounted on a wall next to Marlene's chair delivers a message from Pixel that makes Marlene smile. She passes it to me. *Still there Mother M? With the Firebird? She sure ain't meek and mild. (Like mother like daughter ha!). Call up if you need me. Love ya . . .*

The party winds down on the floors below us. The chirp of cicadas takes over from the noise of the music and the noise of the departing cars. I can't leave. I am totally enchanted with Marlene. In the course of our conversation she has told me several times that she does not bear a grudge against me for giving her away. Oh she went through the usual stuff when she found out at age twelve that she was adopted. All bound up with teenage angst. You know the sort of thing, what was wrong with me that the one that brought me into the world gave me away? But after reading my story, she has buried any feelings of residual resentment. Once and for all.

# Joy

Marlene asks me to stay the night. In the guest suite. I agree at once. But I still don't want to let her go. I talk and talk. I tell her about my two failed marriages and the devastating way I was dismissed from my job two years ago. She knows of the firm. One of her companies has dealings with them. Did I know that they are in financial trouble? There is talk of unpaid bills and disgruntled employees.

"This is sweet revenge," I tell her. "I did all the hiring and firing for twenty years. Serve them right! If they hadn't sacked me, this would never have happened."

In the end, her eyelids begin to close and I can see that she is fighting to keep awake. "Let's go to bed," I say. "We can talk again in the morning."

She shows me to the guest suite. What luxury! A bedroom with a sweeping view of the Waitemata Harbour. A sitting room complete with television, telephone, fax and computer. A bathroom with white marble tiles on the floor.

She brings me a silk nightshirt and fresh towels and a nightcap of whiskey. She puts her arms around me and kisses me on the lips almost like a lover. Then she closes the door behind her.

The fax machine bleeps. Pixel, sending me a message. *Sleep well Joy, happy dreams, see ya . . .*

I stand at the window sipping my drink. A tug moves slowly up the harbour guiding a larger boat decked out in coloured lights. I open the window so that I can feel the cool breeze against my flushed face. I hear a bird cheep softly, then another, another. The sky lightens. Dawn is breaking. I had no idea that we had talked for so long.

I take off my dress and shoes and open the wardrobe. There are men's clothes hanging here, shirts, suits, ties. I am immediately on my guard. Marlene never mentioned a husband or a lover. She had talked freely about so many other things; the good life with the Hunters; the death of her adoptive parents and the subsequent birth of Pixel, an event that she described as the happiest day of her life; the tapes she had commissioned for the proposed book on oral history; her business interests and the exciting new publishing

191

company she has just founded.

I push the coat hangers to the end of the wardrobe. I am jealous of these clothes. I have no right. Marlene is forty years old. I must accept her as she is now; a successful, wealthy, and independent woman. The sort of woman that I've always wanted to be.

I open my bag. The photographs and the hospital baby bracelet are still inside. I place them on the desk in the sitting room so that I won't forget to give them to Marlene in the morning.

I take a shower and dress myself in the nightshirt. Does it belong to Marlene or does she keep a supply of spare clothes for guests? I want to believe that I'm lying in bed encased in silk that has once caressed her body.

*i happy am . . . i am but two days old . . . sweet joy befall thee . . .*

# 12

## *Alice*

There's two of them walking through the door into my house. Wendy never told me there'd be two of them coming today. But I'm pleased to see her so I say nothing. Her friend sits on the sofa without speaking while Wendy prepares the tape.

I had arisen early this morning in spite of the pain in my joints. I had prepared a bowl of pikelet batter to be chilled and ready to cook for Wendy's morning tea. Now that there are two young women instead of one, I'm glad that I made the effort.

I make a pot of tea and promise to throw some pikelets into the iron frying pan later. Wendy says that would be great, she would love to taste them again. She turns on the tape and says, "Final tape, oral history project, December eighteenth, ten o'clock in the morning. Present, Alice Winter, Wendy McDonald and Isobel Winter."

Isobel. Is this a coincidence? I look closely at the tall young woman sitting on the sofa. "Are you Sally's girl?"

She speaks in a low voice. "Yes Aunt Alice. It is me."

I am thrown into confusion. I haven't seen my niece for years, not since the quarrel between Jack and Denby, Isobel's father. What is she doing here?

"I should have told you sooner," says Wendy. "About my friendship with Isobel."

"The thing is," says Isobel. "Wendy and I have lived together for five years."

"You are friends?" I ask cautiously.

Isobel looks at Wendy. "More than friends, lovers."

I smile to myself. So these young women are out to shock me.

"Is the tape still going?" I ask innocently. Wendy answers yes. She wants everything spoken in this room to be recorded. For the sake of accuracy.

"Tell her the truth," says Isobel. "About Marlene and the book."

"Before I do this," answers Wendy. "I want to know if you mind Isobel coming here today. If you want her to go, it's fine by me."

I pour myself another cup of tea. I am enjoying myself. "So this is the last tape? Do I get another five hundred dollars?"

Wendy takes some notes from her bag. "Of course."

"And will you still come to see me after today?"

Wendy smiles. "Better than that. I want you to visit us at our house."

I can't resist teasing them a little. "That could be difficult."

Isobel and Wendy exchange looks. "We could come and get you in the car."

"I can drive myself. Not at night though. I don't trust my eyesight."

"Let's make a start," says Wendy. "Just tell me if you want Isobel to go."

It is a strange experience to suddenly be confronted with an adult woman where the last remembered sighting has been that of a ten year old child. Tonight I will have to replace the old child stored away in the Te Kauwhata memory bead with this new vision. She has grown into a beautiful woman. Dark hair, long legs, Sally's smile. I've already decided to allow her to stay. "One thing," I say. "Have you listened to my tapes?"

She looks embarrassed. "I'm very sorry, I had no right."

I shrug it off. "No matter. Soon it will be printed and then everyone will know my story. You are welcome to stay and listen to the last episode."

"Alice," says Wendy. "There is not going to be any book."

"It's true," says Isobel. "She's only just found out for certain."

I can't believe it. All this effort for nothing. "But you paid me . . ."

"I swear to you that I took on this research in good faith."

Wendy tells me everything she knows. About Marlene Hunter and her company that was supposed to be publishing the book. The excuse that the market was not ready. Wendy's annoyance when she discovered that Marlene Hunter did not want her to interview the other old women that she had lined up for the recording of oral histories. All of them came out from England in the twenties and thirties as servants or factory workers. She doesn't know why this Marlene Hunter wanted to hear what I had to say and not the others. She doesn't believe the excuse of lack of funds.

I had not realised that I had invested so much in the desire to see my life in print. The pain in my joints flares outwards into my flesh. Is my life worth nothing? I am bitterly disappointed.

Isobel says excitedly, "I've just had a brilliant idea."

"What," says Wendy.

"We could do the rest of the interviews and give the book to another publisher."

"But Marlene Hunter has paid Alice so she owns the information."

"Like hell she does. Alice lived it, she told it, it is hers."

Wendy is getting interested now. "Hey, this could work! We could edit it together. What do you think Alice?"

I want to get on with my story. I am excited with the possibility of another publisher. And I would love to hear the other women speak of their lives.

"One last point," says Wendy. "Isobel and I think that parts of your tape should be deleted."

"Which parts?"

"The stuff about the conception of Joy."

"But she is going to listen to them. You promised that you would be there too."

"There is a big difference between knowing something in private and having it published in a book," says Wendy.

"The right words in the wrong place can be dangerous," says Isobel. "You may as well put a gun to her head."

I am amused by Isobel's advice. How could I have lived for so long without knowing this? I am the ultimate survivor of the word. All those lies that were fed into me at the orphanage. The word of God. Be good and God will love you. Be evil and he will revenge himself upon you. I don't know why they bothered to invent this role for God. They were perfectly capable of humiliating children without his help . . . *she has forgotten who she is or maybe the cat has got her tongue . . . we shall call her Miss Nobody . . . my name, Alice Smallacomb written into the punishment book for stealing food, a leather-bound book with neatly lined pages and copperplate writing . . .*

My greatest challenge was the foul utterance of the rapist. I tried to bury that logomachy along with my burnt clothes in the mud at Judge's Bay. A relatively unsuccessful ritual of banishment in that I never completely rid myself of the power of his words. But now that I am approaching my death, I have this urgent need for complete retrieval. Joy must be my chief witness. It is time to transfer the responsibility over to her. I want my daughter to enter into my past and experience the rooms that I have kept locked against her. I want her to come with me to *Emain* and see for herself the windows with the panes shaped like diamonds. I want her to help me gather sweet woodbine and thyme, swim in seas of pink and purple heather, lie with me on the stones of ruined villages on warm summer nights. I want her to see the old landscapes, be a keeper of the sedge, a wizard of the hedgerows, a manipulator of oak and ash and apple. Walk with me into that bead of remembrance where your origins are stored. Understand that you have a right to enter this amaranthine place in spite of your violent beginning. Learn to forgive me.

"Okay," says Wendy. "Let's go."

"Where did I finish yesterday?"

"You were talking about the decision to have Joy's baby adopted."

"I was persuaded that this was the best course of action. But I wavered when I saw how distressed Joy was. She refused to give the baby up. The doctors told me that she was having a breakdown, and that to drag the child away from her could permanently affect her. She was taken to a rest home and the baby was made into a ward of the state. This was the end of the matter as far as I was concerned. I would not have been allowed to rear the baby even if I had changed my mind.

"She seemed to settle into the rest home and was in a better state of mind than she had ever been while she was in Bethlehem

House. And they allowed her to handle the baby. I thought this rather cruel but the doctors assured me that this was the best therapy. Then a most unexpected thing happened. She ran away with the baby. In the middle of the winter. She ended up in a hay shed in the Waikato. It was a miracle that the baby did not die. I knew then that Joy would never be able to care for the child. She totally lacked any sense of responsibility.

"She was very withdrawn when she returned home. I was worried that she would run around with rough street types again. One of the doctors at the rest home had warned me to guard her in case she went straight out and got pregnant again. He told me that young girls are prone to do this after an adoption. He didn't know if it was an act of revenge against the mother or a search for love. I tried to talk to her about the dangers of sex but she just looked at me as if I was stupid."

Isobel says, "Do you mind if I interrupt you to ask questions?"

"It's up to you Alice," says Wendy. "Now that we know this is not part of a larger study, we can make our own research rules."

"I don't mind," I say. "Ask away."

"Was Joy offered contraception?" asks Isobel.

I smile. "You don't understand the times. There was no such thing for unmarried women no matter what age."

"What did you do?"

"I watched her for a few months. I followed her wherever she went so that I could see if she was meeting any boys. I was especially nervous of boys on motorbikes. Although she would never admit it, I knew that she had been seen hanging around with a bikie and that it was probably him who had got her pregnant. I felt bad about spying on her but I was terrified of her getting pregnant again. It would have been the end for both of us. I needn't have worried. She always walked alone.

"She hardly spoke a word to Jack. She acted as if he wasn't there. It was a difficult time for me. I tried to re-establish the relationship between them but it never returned to normal. One good thing was that Jack resumed his previous pattern of drinking every Thursday night along with some of the other husbands who lived in our street. This was a great relief to me. The nightly drinking of the past nine months had been very trying."

Isobel says, "Did anyone know that Joy had a baby? I can't remember Sally and Denby mentioning it."

"No, they didn't know."

"Did they know about Jack not being Joy's father?"

"I made a stupid mistake, I told your mother about the circumstances of Joy's conception. Let's see, this was just after Joy got married for the first time so she must have been twenty-five. Jack and I were staying at Te Kauwhata for a few days. You would have been about ten or eleven. One night, Sally and I stayed up late and talked for a long time. She knew there were difficulties between Joy and Jack. Joy had refused to allow Jack to give her away at her wedding. It was very embarrassing. Joy had that part of the ceremony deleted. Unheard of in those days. Sally and Denby were at the wedding and of course questions were asked. Sally kept on and on at me to tell her what the problem was between father and daughter. I broke down and told her about the rape. This was the first time I had broken my word to Jack that I would never tell anyone that he was not Joy's father. I made Sally promise that she would not tell Denby. But she did, the very next night. Denby didn't believe her. He went and asked Jack what the hell was going on. There was a quarrel."

"I remember it," says Isobel. "I had never seen my father hit anyone before."

"You and your little sister Julia were in the kitchen eating lunch. You came running into the sitting room, screaming, your mouth full of yellow cake. I tried to make them stop but Jack was very angry. He hit poor Denby until the blood ran all over the carpet. Jack never forgave me for telling Sally. He said I had betrayed him. Made him look weak in front of his younger brother. He never spoke to Denby again. I really missed our visits to Te Kauwhata. Especially Sally. I wrote to her once or twice without telling Jack and gave her news of Morry and Joy."

"Ring her," says Isobel. "I'm sure she would love to hear from you again."

"Are you sure? She might not want to have anything to do with me after all these years."

"Ring her. She still lives in the same house in Te Kauwhata, with her companion Paulette."

I can't help teasing the two of them. "Companion? Like you and Wendy?"

Isobel says seriously, "Aunt Alice, Wendy and I are lovers. Sally and Paulette are just very good friends."

"How do you know?"

Wendy laughs. "She's got you there Bel!"

Isobel says that she'll drive me down to Te Kauwhata to see Sally. I am thrilled about this. I am lucky that I am still able to drive my car to the library and to the shops around Sandringham but I no longer have the strength to drive down the motorway and join the fast moving traffic. Joy sometimes takes me out of Auckland for a trip to Morry's place at Te Kowhai but I can never get enough of travelling in the car. If I had my way, I would keep moving around the country, a new town each night, the moon and I driving each other widdershins around the hills. I did this for a whole year after Jack died. Alone and moving on. For weeks on end I travelled this island, driving, driving. Now, my treacherous body allows me mere glimpses of my former self. This has happened very quickly. It seems just months ago that I could dust lightshades and dig soil and clean my highest window and turn the wheel of my car at speed around the curves of Highway One. No matter how fiercely I command my flesh to obey my desires, it seems to have developed a will of its own. It causes me to rest, to remain still, to hold my hands clasped together in a certain position, as if I am already dead. I find myself staring into mirrors, inspecting my tongue and eyeballs, gazing down at my swollen feet and joints. It is like looking at a stranger. Have I changed form? Or is this merely the final version of Alice Nellie Smallacomb? If it were possible to separate body and soul, I would turn my skin inside out so that my inner weakness is exposed to the light.

Wendy suggests that we go back to my story before the tape runs out. "I want to ask you about Joy. Did she go back to school?"

"No, she never returned. I was so disappointed. I had always wanted her to have access to the books that had been denied to me when I was her age. Instead she went to Smith's Business College and learned typing and Pitman's shorthand. No books, except ones on ledgers and office grooming and business correspondence.

"The women in my street thought it wonderful that Joy was going to work in an office. I could never explain my disappointment to them. Most of their children left school at fifteen and worked in factories or shops. But I wasn't being a snob. I wanted Joy to have adventures and experiences that had always been denied me. I knew that I would end my days with Jack and that there was no hope that he would ever change. He was a good man but he liked structure in his life. He had to know the exact moment when he would be eating dinner and what it would be. He had to know his timetable for weeks ahead. He felt lost without it. If I didn't follow his rules he became upset. I wanted adventure, novelty, but it was impossible to achieve. Jack would never have allowed it and I had no money of my own. My escape was books. Until he died. Then I had the open road. Now it's back to the books again.

"Jack died ten years ago. He was twelve years older than me. The final six months of his life were difficult. He was very ill and weak and needed a lot of care. Morry and Joy were both working and couldn't help me. Bonita my daughter-in-law sometimes came to stay but Jack wouldn't let her touch him. It was a great relief when he died. He had suffered enough.

"Living in that house without him was a huge adjustment. I felt that he was watching me. I would turn suddenly and catch a glimpse of him. The edge of his white shirt, his carefully pressed trousers, his black polished shoes. I would drive to the shopping centre and see him sitting on a bench. Then he would turn and I would see the face of a visitant. The shape of the head, the size of the ears, the colour of the teeth. Phooka, faerie, nixie, he changed his shape to tease me. But I always recognised him. In spite of what he did to cover himself.

"Gradually, these appearances melted away. I missed them. So I travelled the open road, I arrived at a fresh place every few days, to ease my loss. And when I returned to my house in Sandringham, he had disappeared completely. Not even the curls of dust under our bed retained an impression. So I was able to move away. To this pensioner flat. A few streets away from the other house. I have walked these same streets for over fifty years, yet this territory still seems new to me. The first fifteen years of my life in England is my true ground. I understand now that it is not the spending of time that is important, it is the constant rearrangement of experiences within that time. Without my memory beads, much would be lost. There are long stretches of my life in this country that would have blurred and faded away."

"I am interested in how your bead game works," says Isobel. "Do you find it hard to remember your own experience?"

"Quite the opposite. I don't seem to be able to control past events. It's like watching the same piece of film over and over again; every gesture, every line of dialogue, every costume and prop. Worst of all, you already know what the last frame reveals. And there's absolutely nothing you can do to stop the video rolling."

I am excited to hear her say this. "But that's the whole point. If you work the beads, you can do whatever you want."

"Is it because it is a private thing?"

"Exactly. I open the beads according to my will, I control them, they do not control me. Some I enter every night. Some I close permanently. Like the green bead where I buried the story of Emily's death. Until Wendy consented to enter with me."

"But you want this private world to be published. I don't understand."

"Pay no attention Alice," says Wendy.

"Emily taught me to be humble, be grateful, never look them in the eyes. Cross your fingers behind your back, untell the lie. But although this helped me to survive, it began to rebound on me. I became confused. Is this my truth or theirs? Is this what I think or what they think? Is this my memory or their memory? I had to create my own place where I could rely upon myself. But words were not enough for me. I had to invent solid visions. The colours and the shapes of the beads are merely the instruments of my will."

"I'm still mystified," says Isobel. "Why take the risk of turning over your private language to strangers?"

Wendy says gently, "Bel, this is your stuff. Let Alice finish her story."

"To tell you the truth," I say, "I have often asked myself this same question. When I revealed my adaptation of the kaleidoscope to Wendy I was afraid. I asked her to delete that section of the tape. But something changed for me. I decided that I wanted my daughter to know about my life. I don't want the beads to die with me."

"But there's a difference between Joy listening to the tapes and publishing a book," says Isobel. "People who don't know you will distort your meanings."

"I am willing to take that risk."

Isobel seems unconvinced. I am interested in her ideas and I would like to discuss them further with her so when she suggests that I come to their house for tea tomorrow night, I accept with pleasure.

Wendy says, "Let's move on. The tape is almost finished."

"There's not much more to tell. Morry became a train driver and married Bonita and they have three lovely children, two girls and one boy. He is a good son to me, he has never given me any worry. Times are hard for him at the moment. He lost his job and his children have grown up and moved away. In spite of what Joy thinks, he and Bonita are happy together. I don't see much of them now. Sometimes he comes to take me for a drive. But they are very short of money. Joy is my lifeline now. She comes at least once a week and helps me with the garden and the house. She is very good to me.

"Poor Joy. She married twice but had no further children. Her first husband Samuel was a very handsome man. He was rather shy but he loved to argue with people. A verbal fighter, that's what he called himself. The trouble was you never knew which side of his nature would come out, the shy side or the argumentative one. Jack never liked Sam. Especially after he sided with Joy over the wedding business.

"Sam had a bad habit of contradicting Joy in front of other people. She told me later that he almost drove her to madness with this awful habit. You know the sort of thing. Joy would tell me an anecdote about her neighbours and he would say, that's not what you said yesterday. Make your mind up. He challenged her over the most trivial details. Joy never answered him back. She would change the subject or fall silent.

"After two years of marriage he ran off with another woman. This set Jack off again on his old theme of bad blood. And the shame that she had brought to him. A man doesn't leave a woman for nothing, he said. She must have done something wrong for him to up and leave her. But I was glad that Sam had gone. Joy had become increasingly turned in on herself, and I feared that she was having a breakdown. My only regret was that she didn't leave him first. It made her look a fool to be supplanted by another woman.

"A few months after Sam left her, she moved to Hamilton to start a new life. Three years later Sam and his second wife were killed in a car accident. End of story.

"I was pleased when she met Dennis and they decided to marry. Jack liked him too. Joy was determined to make this marriage work. And this time she told me, this time, she would have children. Sam had never wanted them, but Dennis was very keen. But there were no children in spite of the fact that they stayed together for ten years.

"There were financial problems. Once she borrowed five hundred dollars from me and wouldn't tell me why. We have always discussed money openly in our family but she stopped doing this soon after she married Dennis. Although they both had a good salary, Joy was always short of money. One night, she rang me distraught. Dennis had disappeared. He had stolen a large sum of money from his firm to pay off his gambling debts. Joy lost her house, and her good name. She had known that he was gambling but she had no idea that he was in so deep. He was never caught, he simply vanished off the face of the earth. The police believed that he went to Australia under an assumed identity. Although I wanted him to suffer for what he had done to Joy, I was glad that she didn't have to go through the indignity of a court case. There was a huge outcry in the papers at the time. I wanted her to change her name from Knight back to Winter so that no one would associate her with Dennis. No, she said. I have had three names. Winter, Robertson and Knight. I want to stay what I am. I can't take another change.

"She was so strong. She had a wonderful job as office manager for a big engineering firm in Hamilton. She paid off everything that Dennis owed. Just as she was getting to the point of being able to save for overseas travel and to buy a new house, she was made redundant. Since then, her life has been very quiet. I worry about her. She sits out there in her cottage near the sea, alone and brooding. I don't know what has become of all the friends she used to have. I'm glad that I need her more now. It gives her something to do, worrying about me. So I ask her for help. She does all my accounts for me now. I can do it myself but I wanted her to feel useful. That's why it's been hard to conceal this extra money I have been getting from you."

The tape recorder clicks. "That's it," says Wendy. "But I don't want to cut you off in mid-stream. If there's anything you want to add, I have a spare cassette."

"Does this mean the end of our conversation?"

"No way," says Isobel. "There are so many questions I want to ask you."

Wendy laughs. "Watch out for her Alice. Don't give away too many secrets. She is a writer and she may steal your words."

I am thrilled. "How exciting! You should have told me sooner!"

"Wendy is laying it on a bit," says Isobel. "I'm getting my first story published in a book. That's all."

"I am very proud of her," says Wendy.

"So this is why you suggested giving my oral history to another publisher. You are in the business yourself."

"Do you want this recorded?" asks Wendy.

"I have said all I am going to say into that machine."

"That's fine," says Wendy. "I have fulfilled my obligation to Hunter Publications and I have eased my conscience over not telling you the truth sooner about Isobel and the book."

"I forgive you. But don't forget your promise about Joy."

"I have not forgotten. I will be with you when she listens to your tapes."

I pull myself painfully to my feet. Isobel tries to help me but I wave her away. "I can manage. I'm going into the kitchen to get the element good and hot for pikelets."

"Yum, can't wait," says Isobel. "But I don't eat butter. Is that going to be a problem?"

"I've got margarine." I place the iron frying pan on the stove and grease the surface with a butter paper. I hope that Isobel can't see what I'm doing through the archway. I call out to Wendy, "Let's make a time then."

"For the meeting with Joy?"

"Yes."

"I would like to sever my connection with Hunter Publications first. A clean break. I'll take my final pay and then I'll hand over this last tape with this stuff about Marlene Hunter. Then she can listen to what we have to say about her deception."

"But won't this affect future work?" says Isobel. "She could do you a lot of harm."

"I am beyond caring."

"Good for you!" I say. The first batch of pikelets are smoking hot. I turn them with the fish slice. Pale brown smooth surface, perfect.

The phone rings. I am busy putting margarine and butter on the hot pikelets and turning out some strawberry jam into a glass dish. "Answer it someone," I call.

Isobel picks up the receiver. "Alice Winter's residence, Isobel Winter speaking. Can I help you?"

A long silence. Then Isobel puts her hand over the receiver and pokes her head around the archway. "It's Joy. What will I say to her?"

"The truth," I answer. I toss spoonfuls of batter into the iron pan. Sizzle sizzle.

"Yes, Isobel, your cousin . . . how are you Joy? Long time no see . . . I came here to your mother's house with my partner Wendy . . .

that sounds great, I would love to see you, ring me at 09-776-7841 . . . Alice is keen to meet up with Sally again . . . still at Te Kauwhata, same old house . . . thanks, it was a great shock. She's coping okay, better than me in some ways . . . Alice is in the kitchen making pikelets, hold on . . ."

I turn the stove off and put the hot pan in the sink. The pikelets are ready to eat. "Help yourself," I call. "The ones with the margarine are on the left of the plate."

Joy is still patiently waiting on the phone. After a perfunctory greeting and the usual inquiry about my arthritis, she asks me if it's Wendy McDonald who is there with Isobel. I am surprised that she knows about Wendy. She knows about the tapes too. But she isn't angry with me, quite the opposite. She sounds elated. "Something wonderful has happened Mum, you'll never believe, I've found her. My daughter, I've found her."

Then she's crying and I'm crying and Isobel and Wendy stop eating their pikelets in mid bite. "Marlene Hunter," says Joy. "Yes, the one who has been paying Wendy to make your oral history."

"Marlene Hunter?" I repeat stupidly. Wendy is all ears. She is mouthing something at me. I motion her to keep silent. I'm trying to cope with what Joy is telling me. Marlene Hunter wanted to know about me before she made contact. She had planned to do the same with Joy but after hearing me speak she decided that she was ready to meet us. Apparently my tapes did the trick. Joy is at her house right now using her telephone. "Marlene is fantastic, brilliant, you will love her too. You have to come over to Devonport soon, Marlene insists. Wait until you see her house. Today or tomorrow. I'll pick you up in my car. Have a think about it. I'll ring you back later."

I replace the receiver. I can't move or speak. Isobel rushes to my side. "You've gone quite pale. Are you ill?"

I sit very still for a minute. Isobel brings me a box of tissues from my bathroom. I wipe my streaming eyes. Wendy asks gently, "Bad news?"

I shake my head. I repeat every word that Joy said to me.

Wendy is astonished. "This explains why Marlene wanted Alice's story and not the other women. She was doing a private investigation into her birth family's background."

"Why the games?" says Isobel. "I'm bloody angry, this is too devious for me."

"It's clever," says Wendy. "Too clever. There must be more to it than this."

I tell them every word again. And that Joy is thrilled. Over the moon. It seems that Marlene is perfect. "I hope this doesn't mean that Joy won't come here as often."

Isobel says, "I'm sure you will see just as much of her."

"I'm not jealous," I say. "But I'm scared. I don't want Joy to be hurt."

"Is there anything I can do to help?" asks Wendy.

"Sit with me for a while. I am a little dizzy."

Isobel washes the dishes while Wendy talks to me. Do I still want my oral history published now that I know the motive behind Marlene's project? "All the more reason," I say. "Let it all out. No more secrets."

I want to meet this Marlene Hunter. Urgently. I need to know if she holds any resentment towards me over what happened at her birth. I'm glad that she's heard my side of the story. All at once I am overwhelmed with curiosity. To see her, to listen to her talk, to track the colours and sounds of her body.

From Elva to me to Joy to Marlene. There is one bead left unfulfilled in my kaleidoscope. There are still some empty spaces, my half-brothers, womb sharers, holding one hand out of two with me. Her presence will help to fill the vacuum caused by their loss. Tonight, I will prepare the red bead for her, lay out the carpet and the music and the poetry for the blood of my blood.

She should take her rightful place.

# 13

## *Joy*

I wake up startled. The bright sun floods through the open window. A figure stands outlined. Pixel. "Sorry I woke you but it's after eleven. Mother Marlene asked me to give you a message. I've been ringing and ringing but you didn't answer."

Pixel explains that she hardly ever comes down out of her room at the top of the house. Except for emergencies. Or unusual events. And this is one. Having me here in the guest suite. She broke her pattern for me. Impressed?

It takes me at least a minute to understand what she's talking about. Then I remember where I am. Pixel hands me a glass of water. I moisten my mouth before I speak. "Where is Marlene?"

"At a meeting. That's the message. Coffee?"

I nod. She goes to the door and opens it. A young woman dressed in a black and white uniform enters with a tray of breakfast things; coffee, croissants, fresh fruit. She almost bows to me before she places the tray on the bedside. I am unable to look her in the eye. "Thanks very much," I mumble. Pixel ignores her.

I get up to wash before I eat. I peer at my face in the bathroom mirror. Pixel looms up behind me. I notice that the barcode tattoo on her forehead has gone. Instead she has a number printed on the thick white makeup. I ask her what it is.

"My tax file number," she answers. "Not that I've ever paid any tax, but I like to have a number. It keeps the bureaucrats happy." She is dressed in layers of black clothes, either the same set that she wore last night or an identical outfit. "I need to talk to you Joy," she says. "There are things to sort out. For my data base."

I dry my face on a soft white towel. Pixel hands me a tube of moisturiser. I cream my face. We sit together at the table and I eat hungrily. Pixel sips black coffee.

"I hate food," she says. "The necessity for it, over and over again."

I shake my head, my mouth full of raw melon. "Today I have a good appetite."

"Enjoy. Tell me more about Robert Goff. His parents."

I swallow. "What is this data base?"

Pixel smiles. "You read a little about it in my first download to Wayne Marsh. I am making a virtual reality game out of my known ancestors. I have two lines, my nurture line and my biological line. Unlike non-surrogates, my family tree has a double strand. There is the line back from Marlene, the nurture line of caring and feeding and sleepless nights. But none of this would be possible without the alchemy that turns eggs and sperm into flesh. So you see I have to do everything twice."

I sip my coffee. "You are tracing your biological line?"

"Yes. My embryo parents. I know very little about their ancestors. Beverley's mother is called Hester. Marlene has told me some of her stories. But she died when Marlene was eight, so things are a little sketchy. Of Richard I know nothing. He was American, very wealthy, but there are no papers. I think this was deliberate because of the illegal dealings over the surrogacy. He did not want to leave any evidence that would incriminate Mother Marlene."

"What is the nurture line?"

"Marlene and Robert and you and Elva and Jack and Alice and Nigel and the Warringtons."

"You've gone that far back?"

"Yes. It is very important to me, it gave me life. Without my nurture line I would have remained a frozen embryo, successfully conceived, but never born."

I am finding this difficult to comprehend. "But the embryo wasn't really you."

"Who then? Name it."

I'm floundering now. "The possibility of you, a potential . . . I don't know."

"My point precisely," says Pixel. "No words, no meaning. Who is my mother? Who is my father? Who are you? If I am Marlene's sister because her parents gave me their cells, then you must be my mother too. Beverly is both my mother and grandmother. The parents had me implanted into their own adopted child after their death. According to instructions. Am I the result of incest? Of necrophilia? Am I divine? Am I part machine and part human? This has a certain attraction. To quote Saint Donna, if I had a choice, I would rather be a cyborg than a goddess."

I want to apologise for my outburst last night but I don't know where to start. My jealousy of Beverly made me say hurtful things to Pixel. Now I see her as another lost child running through the winter fields of the Waikato with an about-to-be-lost baby in her arms.

"Ambivalent. This is what I am," says Pixel. "I lead a double life that follows on from my double line. I am constantly torn apart. Every emotion flips between the material and the spiritual. My grief for my lost parents exists only at a cellular level. I was an orphan before I was born. They were killed in a plane crash, they fell to earth together. I picture their last moments. Did they hold each other? Did Beverly thank Richard for the gift of sperm? Did she say farewell to me lying in my frozen bed? The death of the body. So clean."

I pour both of us another coffee. "Eat Pixel, eat," I say.

"No, not now." She goes to the desk, opens the top drawer, and takes out a tiny computer, the smallest I've ever seen. "Tell me about Robert Goff's parents."

"I never met them. His mother . . ."

"First name? Maiden name?"

"I wouldn't have a clue. She had run off with someone else by the time I met Robert."

She taps the miniature keyboard. "Father's name?"

"I've forgotten. But the brother is still alive. I see his name in the papers from time to time. Sir Rex Goff these days. Why not contact him?"

Pixel grins. "I've already checked him out. As soon as I read his name in your story. I can't find anything on him. Talk about Mr Clean."

"I wonder how he'll react to finding out he has a niece?"

"I have put his name and the names of his children and his grandchildren into my data base. Marlene's cousins. It spreads out like a fan. The birth mother comes, and she is never alone. Uncles, cousins, aunts, children and children of children. And for me, the inevitable double line, those intersecting maps of blood and nurture."

I drink the last mouthful of coffee. Pixel asks me if I would like some more. "No thanks. But there is something you can do for me."

"Anything."

"You know that I lost my job two years ago?"

"Yep. Mother Marlene told me about it. She knows the firm."

"Could you do something with your computer? I have these fantasies of revenge. Especially against my ex-boss Trevor. But I don't want to get you into trouble."

Pixel smiles. "I'm starting to like you Joy. I'll get the details about Mr Trevor from Hunter Corporation and then we'll have some fun."

The telephone rings. I can hear the noise of traffic. It's Marlene, calling on her cellphone from her car. "Sorry I ran out on you Joy but I had to attend a meeting."

"Pixel has been entertaining me."

"Good. Can you stay a while longer? There's something important that I want to talk over with you. I'm on my way home but I'm stuck in a slow line of traffic. There's been an accident on the bridge."

Something important? Maybe she is going to tell me about the owner of the clothes in the closet. "I'm not going anywhere."

Pixel takes the receiver from my hand. "I need some details about the firm in Hamilton that sacked Joy, have you got an e-mail number? . . . don't panic, trust me . . . okay. Got it, thanks." She replaces the receiver. "Let's go upstairs Joy. And play. Have you had enough to eat?"

I nod. Pixel presses a button. There is a knock on the door. The maid enters and takes my tray away. I feel as if I am in a hotel not a house. Pixel leaves me alone while I shower and dress. There is clean underwear in one of the drawers. I climb back into the same clothes and high heels that I arrived in last night.

Before I leave the guest suite, I ring Alice. A strange voice answers. I am astonished to hear her say that she is my cousin Isobel Winter. She is there with Wendy McDonald the woman hired by Marlene to investigate my background. She tells me that Alice wants to meet up with Isobel's mother Sally at Te Kauwhata again. I am pleased to hear this. I get Isobel's phone number and we agree to meet soon. I don't know whether I should mention the death of her sister Julia. I **have** visited the drowning rocks at Ngarunui Beach and floated flowers and leaves at the breaker line. Twice I have seen other women there, strangers, lighting fires and burning herbs and singing to her. Should I tell Isobel this? I hesitate, then give her my condolences and ask if Sally is coping, and Isobel answers, "Better than me in some ways."

Then Alice comes to the phone. "Something wonderful has happened Mum," I say. "You'll never believe, I've found her. My daughter . . ."

The sound of her tears tells me that she is happy for me. I want her to love Marlene as much as I do. I decide not to mention Pixel yet. I will need to spend some time with Alice to explain the circumstances of Pixel's birth. There is no possibility of keeping it secret. I don't know if Alice will be able to make any sense out of Pixel. At least the barcode was not a permanent tattoo. If I could persuade Pixel to wash all that junk off her face, Alice might find her easier to deal with.

Pixel comes back into the guest suite and we go up to the room on the top of the house. Darkness. The computer screens glow and bleep. Pixel asks me if I use the Internet. I shake my head. I've been reading about it but it remains a technological mystery to me.

"It's my life, my community," she says. "I don't need anything else."

It makes me sad to hear her say this. "What about love?"

"Do you mean bodily love?"

I am confused. She seems to be making a separation between

body and mind. I ask her if this is what she means.

"Of course. And why not. Until now, humans were trapped in flesh, experience had to be physically endured. The only death was the death of the body, by sword and knife and bullet. I have moved beyond this brute existence. There is nothing that I cannot do, I travel the world, I move around imagined cities, I recreate myself at will. The whole world is my body. This is my form of lovemaking."

I fall silent. I can't grasp what she means. I watch her playing with her keyboard. After five minutes she lets out a yell. "Now we have Mr Trevor! Yay!"

I get off the cushion and peer at the screen. Amazing. My name on a file. The last report on me. *The costings done by the consultants show that savings of over twenty thousand dollars a year can be facilitated by using temporary staff and private agencies to fulfil all functions and tasks at present undertaken by Ms Knight. These costings have taken account of her substantial redundancy payment. Therefore, we recommend that Ms Knight's services are dispensed with as soon as possible.*

Signed by Trevor. The bastard. He had pleaded ignorance, but I had suspected all along that he had been behind it. He had lied to me. "I will try to persuade the new directors to reverse their decision. I owe that to you Joy, but my hands are tied. My own job is on the line . . ."

"What has been the hardest part to bear?" asks Pixel gently. "I am about to give Trevor's database a terminal virus and I want to tailor the illness to your feelings."

I think carefully. I make a list for Pixel.

The treachery of Trevor. He and his wife Yvonne came to my house, they ate my food, they held my hand when Dennis disappeared. I cared for their pets when they went away on holidays. We had mutual friends, we were a group. Until the redundancy. I lost my job and my fair weather friends. It has taken me two years to rewrite my naive notions of intimacy and loyalty.

The treachery of games. I became the perfect office manager, the successful woman executive; attractive but not cheap, confident but not aggressive, bright but not too clever. Pixel says this sounds like the perfect wife. I couldn't even play that game right, I answer. Either I wasn't good enough or I misinterpreted the rules.

The treachery of time. My work schedule had invaded me to such an extent that when it was taken from me, I felt disembodied. Time became my enemy, it changed form. The simplest tasks around the house became the object of complicated planning. Although time dragged its feet, there were things that I never seemed to have the time to do. I felt as if I was doing time, but without the possibility of parole.

"I get the picture," says Pixel. "Trevor. Games. Time. There is great scope here."

I retreat to the cushion. For ten minutes Pixel works furiously, consulting manuals, switching from file to file, talking in a low voice to herself. "Gotcha!" she yells. "Listen to this Joy and tell me if you approve. A designer virus, elegant but lethal. I'll call it CAC for cheap, aggressive and clever, those qualities that you felt driven to obliterate in yourself. Trevor is the target, the time game will be his death."

She explains how she has done it but it is too technical for me to follow. "Spare me the jargon," I say. "Just tell me what will happen to him."

"Okay. You will appear on his screen at a time selected by random numbers. This means that he'll never know just when you will appear."

I am scared of this. I don't want Trevor to know that it's me.

Pixel says, "You have misunderstood. A symbol of you, not a realist picture. Cheap, aggressive, clever, a triple image. There will need to be three separate women. Cheap is easy. Tight white satin blouse, big tits, high silver boots, drag queen extraordinaire. Aggressive, mmm, we'll try a woman with a whip, a logomanic dominatrix. Dressed in leathers. She will whip words across the screen."

"I like it!"

"How shall we visualise clever? Just a knowing smile, smug, dismissive, like the cheshire cat? No, she will need to talk. I'll work it out."

"And what will this triple woman do?"

"She will appear in one of her three guises according to what Trevor does. This virus will not obliterate data, it will respond to various modes of language. When he acts like a bureaucrat or uses business jargon or gets unbearably pompous, the drag queen will come into his file. Posture, posture, s/he will strut her stuff. Bring him down to size as it were. And no matter what he does, he will be unable to get rid of her. S/he will appear in various suggestive poses. S/he will sexualise his text, not a subtle form, a crude show-biz type. Sometimes this figure will appear on the screen but not on the printouts, sometimes the reverse will happen.

"Then when he writes emotively, the dominatrix, mistress of the word, will appear. He will write a word, she will whip it away. Adjectives will dissolve before his gaze. He will key-in *a beautiful day,* she will crack her whip and replace it with *a shithouse night;* he will key-in *yours sincerely,* she will put *suck shit fucker.*

I can picture Trevor's face. She has got his measure exactly. I burst into laughter. "And what does the clever one do?"

"Smiles enigmatically. Then cuts his argument to pieces. She will be the master of theoretical speech, the crowned head of the postmodern jargon-jungle. Words become twisted thickets, and if he tries to untangle them, she will retwist them into a noose around his throat."

"Will it hurt him?"

"The violence is virtual. Which is not to say that he won't suffer. At first he won't know what's going on, but soon he will discern a pattern. But the pattern won't always be there. Sometimes he will work for days without Our Lady of Revenge paying him a visit in one of her three guises. Then she'll appear page after page, file after file. Random visits. Much more nerve racking than a one-hundred per cent response."

She asks me if I can use a word processor. She wants to run a test for the CAC virus. I'm rusty as hell but she finds an early version of Word Perfect that I am familiar with. I sit at one screen, she sits at another, and I tap away until I've relearned a few of the basic functions. Pixel dictates a short letter. Each paragraph brings forth a different version of the triple figure. The drag queen appears, s/he looks like a masculine version of Dolly Parton. S/he wags her finger and the words *naughty naughty* flash across the screen, and *hello big boy,* and *come up and see me some time.*

Then I type the words, *it was lovely to see you,* and the dominatrix with the whip appears. She cracks her whip at the word *lovely,* it changes to *spac.*

"Delete," says Pixel. "Try to retype."

I wipe out the sentences and key in the same words. Once again the tiny animated figure whips away the good words and replaces them with bad ones.

"Again," says Pixel.

This time, she does not appear and I am allowed to keep the word *lovely.*

"It's working! He'll never know where or when one of them will strike," exclaims Pixel. "Now. Last paragraph, I want to see Ms Clever."

She asks me to type, *the identification of valid economic units and the selection of true needs and value must be determined by the market without legislative or political intervention . . .* The smile appears, full red lips, perfect white teeth, open throat, you can see the uvula flapping and every roll of the wet pink tongue, and this time, a voice. You can see her mouth forming the words and hear the electronic voice and read the words simultaneously on the bottom of the screen. Each word that she speaks appears in text in iridescent green.

*Come Trevor, truth is in the eye of the beholder and you have not revealed the identity of the subject. Who speaks? What is the relation of the speaker to the text? You are treating me unfairly, you can see the source of my words shaped by my silicon tongue, but you are unwilling to reveal your own . . .*

"We've done it!" cries Pixel. "Are you happy with it Joy?"

I love it. Pixel is a devil, a magician. A buzzer sounds. Pixel says, "Yay, Mother Marlene's back. Caffeine time again." She switches on the coffee machine.

Marlene comes up the ladder and embraces me and apologises once again for having to go to work on today of all days. Pixel says,

"Why drag your flesh back and forth over that bridge? If you'd listen to me and update your technology, you would never have to leave the house. You could conduct a virtual meeting whenever you wanted."

Marlene laughs. "See what I have to put up with Joy?" She sinks down onto the cushion. Pixel hands me a cup of black coffee. Marlene shakes her head. "Whew, no thanks. I've done nothing but drink coffee at that meeting." Pixel opens her mouth as if to speak but Marlene gets in first. "No, don't you dare. I don't want to know that coffee could be virtual too."

I can't stop looking at her. I sit beside her and we hold hands. She says, "When you've finished your coffee Joy, come down to my room."

"Don't take her away from me," says Pixel. "We're having great fun with a virus."

"I don't want to hear about it," says Marlene.

"Why do you get such a kick out of total ignorance?"

"I know, I know, information wants to be free."

I would like to get away from this bickering. Marlene must have sensed my discomfort because she assures me that they are not really arguing. This is normal mother-daughter interaction.

"I know," I say rather sharply. "Alice and I do the same thing all the time."

"I didn't . . . I didn't mean . . ." says Marlene.

I jump to my feet and climb down the ladder. Marlene comes after me. "Did I hurt you? Oh Joy, we must be careful of each other."

I reassure her. We go to her room and sit in her deep armchairs.

"I didn't go to sleep for ages last night," says Marlene. "I kept going over and over everything you said."

"Me too. I didn't sleep until dawn."

"Are you coping with Pixel?"

"Last night was a shock. Her appearance, her computer games, the way that she spoke. Especially when she told me about her birth."

"I was wondering when you would bring that up," says Marlene. "Has she told you everything?"

"I know who her biological parents are."

"Good."

I plunge in. "Why did you bear a child that is not your own?"

Marlene says slowly, "The will left all their money to me if I agreed to give birth to the fertilised ovum."

I am shocked at her mercenary attitude. I try not to show it on my face.

"There is more to it than that of course," she goes on. "I loved them very much and I had already agreed to do it for them before they died. The money was an added incentive. To tell you the truth I never thought it would work. I was stunned when the doctor told me I was pregnant. He never knew the circumstances of Pixel's conception. Nobody does except us. Yet. She is getting ready to tell her story and now that she is at the age of consent she has a right. We're safe now. The vet is dead, and it is doubtful that the police will lay charges against me."

"How old were you?"

"Twenty-two. The pregnancy was dreadful. I kept wondering what the hell I'd let myself in for. My friends were mystified. They had never seen me with a man. In the end I told them I was having a secret affair with a married man, someone very rich and powerful. I was ill a lot of the time and I was punished by everyone around me for daring to get pregnant while I was still single."

"I've been there," I say.

"I know. And it must have been even worse for you. But as soon as I saw Pixel I knew it had been worth it. She looked like a tiny version of Beverly."

"Things would have been very different for us if Robert had not been killed."

Marlene says slowly, "But it worked out fine for me. I had a wonderful life as a child and Beverly and Richard live on through Pixel. They saved me from the horrors of living as a ward of the state and I gave them immortality."

I fall silent. I am gripped by the irony of our situation. I gave the child of my blood away to strangers and Marlene bore and reared a child that has no biological link to her, a stranger. In one sense, she is like an adoptive mother too.

"Money is the key. When I became successful in business, nobody gave a damn that I was a single parent."

"Just how much are you worth?"

Marlene smiles. "A hell of a lot more than you can imagine."

"Sorry. I shouldn't have asked. It's none of my business."

"Yes it is, and if you agree with my plan, it will become even more so."

"Plan?"

"I want you to come and work for Hunter Publications as office manager. Big salary, fringe benefits, and you have the added advantage of being related to the boss. You can tell her where to get off."

My immediate impulse is to accept on the spot. It sounds like a dream job. But since I became unemployed, I have lost confidence in myself. "What would the job entail?" I ask cautiously.

"I'm not doing you a favour, far from it. You are just the sort of person I've been looking for. You would run the office, hire and fire, do the accounts, that sort of thing. Plus editorial input into the books that we publish. You would have to move to Auckland of course. You could live here, or I could buy you a townhouse nearby."

"No," I say. "It's wonderful that you want me to work for you but I love Raglan too much to leave."

Marlene looks rather surprised. "But it's a small town. What is there for you? Look, you don't have to decide now. Think about it for a week or two. It would be nice for you to be closer to me. I want you to meet my friends, come shopping with me, movies, restaurants, travel. I want you in my life."

How can I tell her that this is exactly what I am afraid of? Living on the periphery of the lives of others. Never taking the initiative for myself. My childhood in Sandringham with those dull weatherboard houses and the censorious women who mapped out my life for me over their teacups. My one rebellious act, getting pregnant at fifteen. My marriages, where I learned the truth about myself, that I was not a proper woman, that I could never give myself over completely to the desires of another.

If I agree to Marlene's plan, I will become absorbed into her, this house, her clothes, her food, her conversations. It would only be a matter of time before I did something to make her angry with me. I could not bear to lose her again. I must fight to keep myself apart from her.

"What about your relationship?" I ask her. "If I moved in, what would he think?"

"Who?"

"The man I saw you with in your car." She looks puzzled and then I remember that she doesn't know that two days ago I parked my car outside her house. I am ashamed to admit I spied on her but now that I have let it slip that I saw her with a man, there is no alternative but to confess.

"So you watched my house! Good for you," she laughs. "I did worse, I paid Wendy McDonald to investigate your family history. Anyway, no problem, the man you saw me with is just a friend and business colleague. Paul. Sometimes he stays over in the guest suite. He lives out of town."

There is a knock at the door. The same young woman who brought me my breakfast enters with a tray of coffee and cakes. Marlene introduces her. "This is Maria, my housekeeper's daughter. She helps out at the weekend. Maria, this is Joy Knight, my birth mother."

I almost break down. This is the first time she has said these words aloud. Marlene pours out the coffee and chooses a cake. "Do you mind the birth mother label?" she asks. "I can't think what else to call you."

I tell her it's fine, more than fine, wonderful. We spend the next few minutes talking about names and what is appropriate. She says she can't wait to meet Alice. Soon, I promise her, soon. "I have told Alice that I have found you but she needs to get used to the idea before she meets you."

Marlene and I spend hours talking. The afternoon light moves around the windows. In spite of the coffee, I am very tired. I am sure that I am repeating things that I have already told her last night. "Put your head down if you need to sleep," says Marlene. "This sofa is quite comfortable."

A fax comes from Pixel. Marlene reads it aloud to me. *I have loaded the CAC virus and sent her/them packing, now she/they spin out over the Net, waiting for the right door to open, bon voyage baby, bon voyage . . .*

I doze, and Marlene is massaging my feet, and it's me travelling through the twilight world of laser lights and trees with breasts and wheels with feet and birds shedding multi-coloured feathers, and it's me with the silicon tongue, putting words into green iridescent text that have no right to be written, not by me, sweet Joy, sweet Joy befall thee . . .

# 14

## *Alice*

So much activity, so many new people, events, sights, my body screams for me to stop but I am unable to leave this ship of fools that I have so willingly jumped aboard. Everything is turned upside down, like a ship that travels across the land on wooden wheels, town by town, city by city, causing women to loosen their hair and tear clothing from their breasts. I have experienced this journey in other guises; as a girl wandering through the Peak District with Miss Catley, gathering thyme and woodbine, lighting red candles at the mullioned windows of *Emain;* as a widow playing hopscotch with the moon, driving alone through midnight towns.

Eight weeks have gone by since Joy discovered Marlene and Pixel. Now, a taxi comes for me every day and I ride like a queen across the Harbour Bridge to Devonport. According to the memory beads, I have come full circle. This house reminds me of my first place, the Warrington's house in London. There is a substantive presence of light, a brighter version of the soft yellow candlelight that flickers on my mother's skin when she washes herself every morning in the china bowl. Everything is stronger, brighter, cleaner. The weather is blue and gold instead of grey and gritty. And where the light once struggled to penetrate damp stones, now the sun beats across glistening seawater and white sails.

In each house lives a woman who observes me, one dead and one alive. Pixel is the great-great-great-grand-daughter of Mrs Warrington. Have I added too many greats here? My grandmother Mrs Warrington could not make a public claim on me. To do so would tell the world that her son Nigel had shamed a servant girl. But she was fascinated by the fact that I was her grand-daughter and she couldn't help but watch me. I would turn suddenly and try to catch her out. The swishing of her skirts gave her away. I thought it was a game that women played with little girls.

Now a young woman in a long black dress plays the same game. But I revel in Pixel's attention. It is all part of the great project that we are working on together. She can't believe how quickly I am learning my way around the computers. She explains things clearly, I understand her.

Pixel waits in anticipation for me to arrive every morning. She told me so. We have established a routine. The first thing she does is help me to send e-mail to Joy in Raglan. And I see Joy's answer coming through on the screen.

*Hi Alice, is it sunny up there? Come down here and get a bucketful of rain, it's sweeping in from the ocean.*

I send my greetings to her, slowly at first, finger by finger, but getting faster by the day. *Keep your rain, and your wind. How is the work going? Is the window finished?*

Her answering words unroll swiftly. *The glass is in! My theatre is open; now I can see the harbour and the moving tide and the changes in wind and weather without moving from my desk. There are no curtains across my proscenium arch. The stage is sealed with green-tinted glass, to keep the glare down and to stop the birds from thudding against it.*

Joy works for Hunter Publications. I can't believe the change in her. She visits Auckland once a week but she doesn't do my house-work or my accounts any more. Now she spends time in the office with Marlene and then they both come over to Devonport to have dinner with me and Pixel. Friday night is the one night of the week when we are all together. Sometimes we drive out in Marlene's car to a restaurant and sometimes we eat at the house.

Joy is brisk and happy, full of details about her work and the improvements to her house. She is working with books! Something I always wanted to do but never had the chance. I enjoy listening to her anecdotes about eccentric writers. Sometimes she asks my advice. And last Friday night she gave me a manuscript to read. "Give me your honest opinion Alice," she grinned. "To publish or not to publish."

I opened the cover. It was my story, abridged, some names changed, but almost word for word as spoken. The presentation is rather unusual. There are two columns on every page, one in my voice, one by the editor. "Who?" I asked.

"A gang of three," Joy answered. "Isobel, Wendy and me. But only Wendy's name appears on the text. For obvious reasons. Read on and tell us what you think."

I approve of what they've done. In the editorial column, analysis, comments, historical information. And every so often, Joy's unmistakable and contradictory voice informing the reader that in spite of Alice's compelling words, this is what her (unnamed) daughter experienced. The message seems to be, read both versions, the truth lies somewhere between.

Marlene is reluctant to publish the book. She paid for the tapes so that she could learn about me and Joy. Money well spent she said. But she thinks the book will have limited appeal. Joy and Isobel have persuaded her that it will be successful. I have some reservations about Marlene. She is one of those business women who puts profit ahead of other things. Sometimes I find her rather cold. I can't tell Joy, she is hopelessly infatuated with her. Marlene can do no wrong in her eyes. Sooner or later she will see her for what she is, but until then, I will remain silent. I don't want to be accused of spoiling their relationship.

Today when I arrive at Devonport, I will tell Joy on the e-mail to go ahead and publish. She has taken her name out, and that of Robert Goff's. To protect Marlene. And herself. Now that she is office manager of Hunter Publications, she doesn't want the public to draw a link between her and the old woman who tells her story in *The Silicon Tongue*. I agree with her. Particularly given her reaction to my account of the rape that brought her into life. She has suffered enough.

Pixel chose the title. You speak with a tongue of silk Alice. The past is reconstructed through the visualisation of your voice. When I bring your memory into my virtual world, we are irrevocably joined together; orality translates into video, the silken tongue into silicon.

All this for a book? But Pixel has big plans. She wants to make it one version of many; an electronic publication with illustrations, short excerpts to send over the Internet, copies of the virtual reality game when she completes the design.

Joy wanted to work for Hunter Publications. But she refused to leave her home at Raglan. Not a problem, said Pixel. The technology can give you everything if you ask the right questions. You can work for Mother Marlene and still live on the west coast. There is nothing to be gained by moving to Auckland. You can have access to all the information you need via computers.

Joy misjudged me. She thought I would never accept Pixel as one of the family. She told me in confidence that she is having problems with the way that Pixel was brought into the world. Does she really belong to us? A tenant, she called her. Not of our blood. "Surely the biological link is the vital point? Why else did I go through hell to find Marlene. I wouldn't have bothered if she had not been my own baby."

"Joy," I said. "Everyone thought you were too young to have a baby. Including me. You disagreed with us. Now you are making moral judgements of when and how other women should give birth."

"Pixel asked me if I thought she was the child of incest because she and Marlene have the same parents. Technically she and Marlene could be sisters. Does this make me her mother too?"

"No. Marlene is her mother. She fed Pixel with her own blood for nine months and she suffered pain when she gave birth to her. She is her primary mother, more than Beverly, more than any technology."

Joy liked the word primary. "So the one that gives birth is the most important one? There is sense to that."

I was glad that I was able to help her. I am treading on glass with my daughter. She knows about her origins, she knows that Jack is not her father. I couldn't use the blue bead of fear, the smell and sounds of the orphanage, shaved heads, cold corridors, weeping for lost mothers. Blue is too personal, too full of my own history. I tried the green bead but Joy's story lay uneasily with the memory of Emily.

There is unresolved guilt corrupting that bead. My guilt about Emily's death, and her guilt about getting drunk at the party that led to my rape. Emily asked me not to let Joy into her opened sarcophagus. Bring flowers instead, bring a golden apple. I cannot take another drop of rage or another fantasy of revenge. Particularly, dear Alice, if it is directed towards you. My chalice is already overflowing.

In desperation, I revoked the burnt umber bead where I had once tortured bad books to death. But these fantasies are representations of another era and another race. Joy did not belong. I was forced to do the unthinkable. I created a bead especially for Joy. This is the first new bead for fifty years. I wanted it to have the quality of flowers that never fade, to represent the death of flesh but not of essence. So I named it the amaranthine bead. An end to the drawing of evasive veils across incidents of horror. The truth confronted at last.

When I look into the amaranthine bead this is what I see. A room on the second floor of Marlene's house, a large room set aside for entertaining. Tall glass walls, a polished wooden floor with Turkish rugs, sunlight falling on Pixel's black hair and painted face. She complains of the glare and puts on a pair of sunglasses. Marlene, tense, drinking coffee. Joy, arriving with her briefcase and laptop computer. The maid Maria bringing a tray of fresh drinks and another pot of coffee.

Wendy is sitting next to me on the sofa. She places the tape recorder on the small table in front of her. Isobel is crouching in a chair behind me. I swivel my videocam to include her in my vision. She is stiff-legged, reluctant. She signals to me that she wants to leave the room. You promised, I mouth back at her. She concedes with a nod.

Joy, still in the first flush of her honeymoon with Marlene, unsuspecting. Looking forward to the meeting about the book of my tapes. The only one in the room who hasn't heard them yet. She has seen some transcripts included in computer files from Pixel, but she is totally unprepared for what is to come.

Wendy rolls the tape. *One night, a cold wet Saturday in the middle of winter, I went to the house in Grey's Avenue with Emily.*

Joy says, "Who is Emily?"

"Sshh. Listen," I say.

*I confessed that he had asked me to marry him but I had not yet made up my mind . . . I was still very young and should enjoy my freedom while it lasted . . . Jack is a new boy since he met me, a laughing whistling boy, a pleasure to have around the house . . .*

"I had no idea you went into such personal detail," says Joy, uneasily. "Has everyone here heard this stuff before?"

Marlene nods. Pixel stays very still and quiet behind her sunglasses.

"I think I would rather hear them in private."

Wendy presses the stop button on the tape recorder.

"No," I say firmly. "This is my story and I want the others here with me when you hear it."

She shrugs. "Have it your own way. It's just that I know what's coming and I don't want you to get upset."

"You know?"

"Of course. I can read a calendar. I know that you had to get married."

Marlene pours another cup of coffee and glances at her watch. "Joy has stolen your thunder Alice. Is it necessary to hear the whole tape?" She is cool, calm, composed. I dislike her more than ever.

"Wait," I say. "You don't know the whole story. Play on Wendy."

*When I imagined spending the rest of my life with Jack . . . day in, day out, and me walking around rooms staring at myself in mirrors . . . waiting for him to come home for his tea at six o'clock, I felt a sense of despair . . .*

"I had no idea you ever felt like that!" exclaims Joy.

*But try as I might I couldn't think of any other way to live . . . I'm telling you this because I want you and Joy to know that if nothing had happened to me that night when Emily and I went to Harry's house, I would have probably still have married Jack in spite of my imaginary life of independence . . .*

The tape rolls. Joy interjects from time to time. The others are silent. It comes to the fight in Harry's kitchen. Then to the car ride to Judge's Bay. Then the attack.

*Forgive me, but I must repeat the words that he said... I want to place them outside myself, I want to lift them from my body and seal them into this tape where they will become defused and harmless . . .*

*I clamped my lips together and refused to say what he wanted. This drove him into a frenzy . . . I transported myself somewhere else, I conjured up Emily's voice . . . hold on Alice, hold on . . .*

The tape rolls towards the end. Once again, I am raped and beaten, once again I burn the clothes and plan to throw myself into the sea. Once again I invent words or deeds that could have broken the narrative at any given point. Once again, I fail, and Emily takes out Harry's eye with the heel of her shoe and loses her life.

The amaranthine bead swells and changes colour, first pink, then grey, then the colour of mud. Joy is standing over me, tall and terrifying. Pixel is floating on the ceiling, her long black dress is falling away from her thin shoulders. Heat then cold, sun, snow, there is no logic to the seasons in this bead.

"This changes everything," says Joy. "You tell this terrible story of my beginnings then you confess that you are desperate to make me see that your suffering has a reason, that your inventions are necessary for your survival. What am I to believe? You bequeath to me the words of my father, *teaser bitch, whore, slut* . . . then you claim that this public hearing will defuse them, render them harmless. I did not ask for this burden, I want you to take it back. Tell me a different story."

Pixel comes down to earth. Marlene drinks another cup of coffee and listens to messages on her cellphone. Where are Wendy and Isobel? Have they crept through the skin of the bead? No, Isobel is here. She is trying to comfort Joy. But still the accusations come. We drink too much gin and caffeine, the glass walls circle around us. I am compelled to raise my arms above my head and move slowly with the rocking.

Days pass. The bead fills and matures. Leaves turning gold and brown, a sense of harvests being gathered in smoke from the fires of Lughnasad. Joy is softer with me now. She has listened to the tapes over and over again. "I forgive you Alice. Almost. You should have told me the truth years ago."

I disagree. She had too much resentment towards me for what she believed to be my complicity in the adoption of her child. If I had told her about the rape, I would have handed her another weapon to use against me. She would not have been able to cope with it before she found her daughter. Now that she has become preoccupied with her work and Marlene, her attitude towards me has changed. She sees me as a person in my own right rather than a troublesome old woman who can't handle money or housework.

I must find a place for the amaranthine bead. It is difficult to fit a new bead into old patterns. Each night I try a different position. I have to keep it separate from the blue one. The edges blur and merge. Fear leaks into the amaranthine bead. The other beads are reluctant to make space. The green and gold are set resolutely in the past, they do not welcome events or people from the present. I am trying to break through these chronological barriers. I juggle time and place, sometimes the same experience appears in a different guise, nothing is finite or complete. What we see depends on where we stand. Like bough and blossom welded together on the mythological island of *Emain*. One point of view gives us pink and white flowers and the fragrance of apples, another, the tough brown bark. And yet it is exactly the same object.

Pixel has taught me this; *if you can see what I mean, you can be me . . .*

We spend most of our waking hours together. She tells me all she knows about the potential of computers. I tell her all that I have learned through a lifetime of experience. She wants us to work together to force a reconciliation between machine, body and mind. These are the questions we return to again and again. Can we make memory visual? Can we enter into another person's past life?

Now she takes me into a virtual world, a helmet for each of our heads, metal gloves on our hands. I am afraid. My senses are blinkered, no speech, no sight, no sound. Then suddenly I am flooded with colour and light, there is movement and music, I am flying! Pixel and I join hands, we turn through circles, left, right, left again, while below us, the landscape unrolls. We leave Cape Reinga and the sacred pohutukawa tree, we see the line of white water where the Tasman and the Pacific oceans meet. Birds join us, gannets, mollymawks, a lone albatross. I ride her wide wings, I have her in a harness, and miles below, the sea speeds up faster than sound and carries islands, coral reefs, canoes, coconut palms, tankers, sailing ships, whales, colonial churches and government houses.

Without warning, I am in Pixel's head and I see myself riding the enormous bird, hair streaming wildly, one hand on the harness, the other pointing downwards.

I can hear myself cry, "We are travelling north, lushness, the heat rises."

I answer her/me, "We are crossing the centre of the world."

It cools, and now I am seeing through my own eyes once again. Icy mountains flow past, brown hills, seas, lakes, rivers. Cities flame like exotic flowers, tall buildings glowing with light, luminous columns poking at the sky. The albatross vanishes beneath me. I gasp. Pixel rides past me, sitting cross legged on the wing of a plane. "Hey Alice! Come, ride the jumbo jet."

I lunge towards her and she grasps my hand. We sit on the wing. I can see the passengers looking through windows, frozen with shock. The flight attendant holds out a tray of food and coffee towards us and smiles a lipstick smile, her mouth full of teeth, her cap at a jaunty angle. I touch the window gently and my hand goes right through it. She places a plastic box of food on my palm, I pull it through the glass. The plastic box changes into a yellow peony.

A map of Europe unfolds below us. The borders of the countries are neatly drawn in green hedges and blue rivers. We float to earth. We enter a vast cave where the walls are covered with painted animals, dancing, multi-horned; mammoth, horse, bison. I turn my head, a bison shifts gaze, I blink. I can see Pixel on my left, she smiles. She is caressing a bulge in the rock wall that a stone-age artist turned into the plump flank of a black horse. I see her from the point of view of the horse, I become the horse.

I point, the rock moves, Pixel disappears from view. Someone or something approaches. Is it an animal or a machine? I try to speak but I make the sound of a horse. My mane fills my mouth with hair.

Pixel's voice comes through the ringing silence, "Here comes the guide."

He/she/it speaks. "I am here to fulfil your fantasy." The voice is metallic, synthetic, non-gendered.

Pixel says, "Show us an artist at work."

The guide says, "Follow me ladies." Pixel reappears in front of me and makes a face at the back of the guide. I smile at her. I have become myself again. I am rather sorry to be back, I enjoyed looking out at the world as a horse.

We move along the main vault of the cave to a narrow tunnel that leads to a smaller chamber. There is a small squat woman dressed in skins staring at a wall. It is very dark, the only light is thrown by a flickering oil lamp. There is a smell of rancid fat. The woman is chewing something in her mouth. She places her left hand flat against the smooth rock wall and spits a stream of coloured liquid around the outline of her fingers. She vanishes. But the outline of her hand is there, rough, imperfect, a mixture of red ochre and spit.

We are back in Pixel's room. The helmet and gloves are removed from my body. I am disorientated and upset. I want to go back to the cave. Pixel assures me that we can go back at any time. "I did not invent this virtual journey, I purchased it from the people who created it. I will teach you how to go into it alone. Or you can travel with me. The guide will take us to other parts of the cave, or to other places, both in and out of history. There are hundreds of choices."

I am relieved. Next time I go into the cave, I will make a drawing for myself. I will draw *Emain,* both the cottage and the island of Celtic myth. And Miss Catley, walking on the hills, seeking herbs and moss, talking of celebrations of the seasons, Solstice, Beltaine. And Samhaine, that moment between autumn and winter when the line between reality and fantasy becomes blurred, that time when the people of Eyam light bonfires and spread rumours that the plague has returned.

Pixel thinks that this is a good idea. "You are beginning to understand the potential Alice. So far I have shown you the creations of others but it is not a passive way of seeing. We can change or add to it at will. Or we can make something new. This is what I want to do. Ever since I heard the story of your life on the tapes, I have been trying to reproduce your images and emotions for my virtual reality game."

"What sort of game?"

"The players are the members of our family. The game is a reproduction of every building, every season, every event that you have chosen to speak about on the tapes. A transposition of words into images. We enter at your birth, we leave at your virtual death. This last part can be invented by you."

I am intrigued. "So Joy and Marlene can come to the Warrington's house, to the orphanage, to *Emain*?"

"Of course. We can all come. We can see your mother Elva and her grandmother at the workhouse. We can eat the cold porridge at Moncreiff House, we can have our names written into the punishment book. We can travel to Eyam and read the names of those who died of the plague displayed on boards outside the stone cottages. We can walk the hills with Miss Catley, we can sleep in the cabin on the ship that brought you to New Zealand, all of it. And you can play the guide, you can direct the game any way you want. Any player can experience your life from inside your head. Or become Emily. Or Jack. Whoever. You can fiddle with time and space and identity, you can reinvent the wheel if you so wish."

I have taught Pixel this; *if you experience what I experience, you can be me . . .*

I want Joy to be the first player, I want her to understand the horrors of my childhood. I was there, I had to live through it, moment by moment, day by day. I want her to apologise for her accusation that I have stolen my childhood from the fictional stories of others. If I can compel Joy to play this game, we will become closer, I am certain of it.

Pixel says, "I have already begun. I have taken some of the basic imagery and sets directly from your descriptions on the tapes."

Then she shows me the kaleidoscope on the computer screen, rolling and changing with each turn, primitive, unformed, but unmistakably the same patterns that I saw over seventy years ago. I am dumbfounded, lost for words. Something has been taken from my head and placed into the outside world, colour by colour, shape by shape.

We work on the game for weeks. Joy and Marlene know nothing of what we are doing. Once Joy said on email, half-jokingly, you are over at Devonport so much, you may as well move into the house. Marlene has already offered to build me a self-contained flat in the back garden. She told me that she wants me here for Pixel. According to Marlene, I am the only person who has ever been able to draw her daughter out. Pixel came to Raglan to help set up the office for Joy. She would not go unless I came too. She sat in the back of the car holding my hand. She kept her eyes closed until I told her, let the pictures rush past, they are moving, not you. And she relaxed and looked out of the window at the bush and the bare hills as we drove down into the Te Uku valley until eventually the harbour and the village revealed itself. She let out a gasp of pleasure at the palms and the old wooden pub and the makeshift houses, some like sheds or space ships, others minute copies of the villas of the rich.

After she had finished her work at Joy's cottage, she came down to the water's edge and bathed her feet in the salt water. With me. And although she looked fearfully upward at the sky once or twice, she managed to stay outside for almost half an hour. Marlene thanked me afterwards. She told me that she loves Pixel the way she is but that she has always wished for more balance between the inside and the outside, between make-believe and reality.

I promised to let Marlene know about the flat. I am not ready to leave my pensioner unit yet. It is not the building that I am attached to, it is the streets and the shops and the familiar faces. I am not yet ready to relinquish the site where I have spent most of my adult life.

Today is Thursday. I climb the stairs into Pixel's room. She is sitting in her usual place in front of a computer screen, typing frantically. She is very quiet this morning. She barely greets me. I am used to her formidable powers of concentration so I leave her alone. My first job is to email Joy to let her know that I want her to publish *The Silicon Tongue*. I get into my computer without trouble. After eight weeks, email is the only task that I can do without Pixel's assistance. Yes Joy, yes. Go ahead and change names where required, yes to the editors' comments, yes yes.

Then Pixel calls out, "Alice come quickly, I need you."

I walk slowly to her side. My legs are aching badly today.

"I want to include the memory beads as part of our game," she says. "When a player goes through the next time span, they must go back and alter the contents of the relevant memory bead."

"Why?"

"When you move ahead and look back, the past shifts focus. Enigmatic events become clear, and conversely, things you thought you understood become murky."

I reluctantly agree. I know that the beads have changed across time.

Then she suggests that we provide alternatives at each turning point. For example, we can choose to live at Moncreiff House with or without Emily. The player decides. It will be presented as a t-bar, move left or right. There will be a short preview of what lies ahead at each junction. Remind the player that there is no going back. Once the choice is made, the narrative moves on relentlessly to the next t-bar. You can leave at the age of fourteen to go to Miss Catley's or somewhere else. You can marry Jack or not marry him. Joy will be born regardless. And Marlene. And me.

This is too much. "No," I say firmly. "Important events must not be altered."

"But this will make it more interesting. And there will only ever be two choices, one the real thing, the other the fantasy."

"It won't work," I say triumphantly. "You can't delete anything. Take Emily or Miss Catley away and I would never have come to this country. No New Zealand, no Joy, no Marlene, no you."

She thinks for a minute. "Okay. I give in. But I still think it could be fun to make multiple versions of your life."

I look at the screen. She is working on the blue bead. I can hardly bear to look within. Years of fear and loneliness. And yet this is merely a one-dimensional version of events and I am still linked to the present by the objects and sounds in this room. What will it be like when the virtual reality helmet is on and all external stimuli are obliterated?

Then she flicks over to the mother bead, the gold bead, and I am lost in flashes of liquid metal leaping from room to room, sky to earth, north to south. What is happening? I can see letters forming in the light, I can hear laughter and voices calling from the left, from the right. Who speaks?

The mother bead fades. I ask Pixel to bring her back. She tries. Nothing happens at first. Then a hand, an eye, the flick of a skirt. The picture clears. My joints are burning. I look deeply into the interior of the gold bead.

"What do you think?" asks Pixel. "Am I getting it right?"

There is something missing. I should have told Pixel that colours carry a particular odour. Smoke, gin, powder, these should be built into the mother bead.

"Almost, keep trying."

And this time I did see it, I did see . . . she is tugging at my hair with a small black brush, I can smell her breath, I can feel the soft skin of her fingers on my neck.

A perfect place to begin.

# Acknowledgements

I would like to thank my editors Susan Sayer, Cathie Dunsford, Susan Hawthorne and Jo Turner. Thanks to John Hart for advice on virtual reality. Thanks to Sarah Hamshere for research materials on the Peak District. Thanks to Daniel Rosenblatt for research materials on cyberpunk.

I would like to thank the *Arts Council New Zealand Toi Aotearoa* and the staff at the International Writing Program at the University of Iowa, USA, for providing the opportunity for me to participate in the IWP Program during the Fall Semester, 1994. This provided me with valuable time and a stimulating place to write. I would like to thank my colleagues from the Iowa Writer's Workshop and the International Writing Program for providing a critique of sections of this book at our combined weekly workshop held during my time at the University of Iowa.

I gratefully acknowledge financial assistance in the form of project grants from the Literature Programme of the *Arts Council New Zealand Toi Aotearoa*.

Epigraph from the introduction of *Cyberspace: First Steps*. Edited by Michael Benedikt, IT Press, 1991.

Text on pages 76–7 is taken from *Maori and Settler*, by G. A. Henty, published by Blackie, London, 1911.

"Infant Joy" by William Blake, from *Songs of Innocence*.